AVENGE T

Hitting the ground
wheezed for air as he scrambled to his feet and looked about him—only to realize that the Mexican artillery emplacement was but a few yards away. At that instant one of Santa Anna's fieldpieces roared, spurting flame, and Boone thought he could feel the wind of the cannonball's passage on his face.

Leaping forward, pistol in one hand, the knife Gabe Cochran had given him in the other, Boone cleared the embrasure and shot a cannoneer at point-blank range. An artillery officer came at him with sword raised, and Boone fell back against a wheel of one of the cannon. A Texan hurtled the breastwork and struck the officer with his musket, shattering the stock. The Texan rushed on, yelling at the top of his lungs. Boone picked up the dead officer's sword, and pressed on. The crews of Santa Anna's artillery—those who were still alive—had abandoned their posts.

The Mexican cannon were silenced.

TEXAS BOUND

Jason Manning

SIGNET
Published by the Penguin Group
Penguin Putnam Inc., 375 Hudson Street,
New York, New York 10014, U.S.A.
Penguin Books Ltd, 27 Wrights Lane,
London W8 5TZ, England
Penguin Books Australia Ltd,
Ringwood, Victoria, Australia
Penguin Books Canada Ltd, 10 Alcorn Avenue,
Toronto, Ontario, Canada M4V 3B2
Penguin Books (N.Z.) Ltd, 182–190 Wairau Road,
Auckland 10, New Zealand

Penguin Books Ltd, Registered Offices:
Harmondsworth, Middlesex, England

First published by Signet, an imprint of Dutton Signet,
a member of Penguin Putnam Inc.

First Printing, November, 1997
10 9 8 7 6 5 4 3 2 1

Printed in the United States of America

CHAPTER ONE

The Condemned

When Sam Houston, astride his horse, Saracen, arrived at the village of Washington-on-the-Brazos, it was a raw winter day, the last day of February in the year 1836. The town was a collection of log cabins scattered in no apparent order on a bluff a half mile from the Brazos River. It was not, mused a weary, saddle-worn Houston, a very inspiring site for the creation of a new nation, a sovereign Republic of Texas.

In fact, there was nothing very inspiring about the whole business, and Houston, a man who was usually endowed with indomitable optimism, found his hopes flagging. The future of the republic was not at all bright. Santa Anna, dictator of Mexico, self-styled Napoleon of the West, was marching north with ten thousand seasoned troops—men who had ruthlessly quelled several ill-fated revolts in the southern provinces, men who now slogged northward under the red flag that signified no quarter.

Regardless of the odds, Houston was resolved to stand and fight. He had crossed his personal Rubicon, burned all his bridges, and hitched his destiny to that of Texas. No matter how bleak, the future of Texas was his future. If she flourished, so would he. If she perished, he would fall with her. There was no turning back.

That evening, Houston found lodging in the small but comfortable home of the local doctor. Also boarded there were several other delegates sent by their respective communities to the convention that had been called to formalize the declaration of Texas independence from Mexico. One of these men was Lorenzo de Zavala, a *tejano*, a hero of the Mexican revolt against Spanish rule twelve years ago. Born into a wealthy Yucatan family, Zavala had been provided with an excellent education and had served Mexico with distinction in a number of political and diplomatic posts, only to resign and migrate to Texas upon the coming of power of Generalissimo Antonio Lopez de Santa Anna Perez de Lebron. Zavala staunchly supported the cause of Texas independence, and he explained why to his messmates over cigars and hot coffee laced with corn liquor.

"A people must defend their natural rights," he said solemnly, "even if it is against their own government that they must fight. The American people realized this in 1776, the French twenty years later. Now it is the turn of the Texans."

"Here, here," said Houston, taking a long swig of the liquor-laced coffee. The strong spirits dulled the weariness that lay in his bones like a cancer. It allowed him to view his immediate future with a bit more equanimity. He liked Zavala. Admired the man. The Mexican's patrician bearing belied his abiding egalitarianism. Unlike many Anglos, Houston did not distrust Zavala just because he was Mexican; the fire of freedom blazed in Zavala's heart with just as much intensity as it did in the hearts of Richard Ellis and Robert Potter, who also sat at the trestle table.

"I say we take the fight to Santa Anna," growled Potter. "We flogged the Mexicans like hell at Bexar a few months ago. We can do it again, I am certain."

Houston smirked. Robert Potter was a North Carolina hotspur who, it was rumored, had castrated two men he suspected of having sexual relations with his wife. Potter, however, evidently did not put much stock in the old adage that what was good for the goose was good for the gander; his womanizing had reached gargantuan proportions. Apparently, so had his impulsiveness.

"You must not underestimate Santa Anna," warned Zavala. "Many had done so in the past. Most of them are dead now."

Santa Anna, said Zavala, wore exquisite uniforms—high leather blucher boots with gold hammered into the design, a jewel-encrusted sword made by the best Spanish swordmasters, covered with seven thousand American dollars worth of gold and precious stones, a sash of Persian silk, a shirt of the finest English linen, and trousers of durable French cloth. But, though vain, he was no strutting martinet. He had been a soldier all of his life. He had fought in many campaigns, and served always with distinction. He was a shrewd man, an able strategist, a charismatic leader whose troops adored him.

"Sounds like you love the bastard yourself," said Potter.

"I did, once," confessed Zavala ruefully. "Seven years ago he won a great victory for the Mexican people at Tampico. There he defeated an invading Spanish army dispatched from Cuba by Ferdinand VII to reconquer Mexico. I supported him three years ago when he became president, running on a liberal platform—a federal system of self-governing states, curtailment of the much-abused prerogatives of the Catholic Church, and the abolition of special courts for priests and officers.

"Gradually, then," said Zavala, "Santa Anna began to show his true colors. When he did not get his way, he relinquished the presidency and went to his plantation at Manga de Clavo, where he sulked and schemed until the people begged him to return and save them from his successor, who was, invariably, either corrupt or inept or both. This happened not once, not twice, but eleven times.

"I could see it coming," murmured Zavala gravely. "More and more people began to think that to end this chaos and corruption Mexico needed a benevolent tyrant, a despotism of wisdom and virtue, as if such a thing can ever really exist. And when he judged the time was right, Santa Anna returned and seized power. He threw out the Constitution of 1824. He abandoned the concept of federalism. He restored the special privileges of the Church and the military. By the time the people realized what they had lost, it was too late.

"The province of Zacateca," said Zavala, "had been the first to revolt. Santa Anna made of it an object lesson. Defeating the rebel army, he turned his soldiers loose on the civilians. Thousands of women were raped and murdered. Children were bayoneted. Villages were burned to the ground.

"The same men who did those things are now marching on Texas," added Zavala.

This ominous comment was greeted by a moment of grim silence—a silence broken by the crackle of the fire in the stone hearth and the whisper of the winter wind at the corners of the log cabin.

Houston broke the spell by getting up to pour himself another cup of coffee from the blackened pot sitting on the verge of the fire. The doctor and his wife and two young daughters had turned in, for the hour was late, leaving the four convention delegates to burn the midnight oil in the common room. But were they sleeping? wondered Houston. Had they overheard Zavala? Looking around the darkened room, this spartan but comfortable home, he had a disturbing mental image of the cabin in flames, and the lifeless, violated bodies of the doctor's wife and daughters on the blood-stained floor . . .

"What about it, Sam?"

Houston was shaken from his dark reverie. Richard Ellis was talking to him. "Sorry, Dick. What was that you said?"

"Do you think we can defeat Santa Anna and his army?"

"I don't know."

"My God, man," exclaimed Potter. "This convention will no doubt choose you to command the Texas army. I would like to see more confidence from our commander-in-chief."

"Army?" Houston's blue eyes flashed. "What army are you referring to?"

His sarcasm further dampened the spirits of the other men.

"I apologize, gentlemen," said Houston, remorseful. "I don't mean to sound bitter or defeatist. But please remember what happened last year."

A year ago Sam Houston had been a simple country lawyer in Nacogdoches, trying to keep out of the escalating furor arising between those who advocated armed resistance to Santa Anna and his tyrannical dictates, and others, like Stephen F. Austin, who sought to keep the peace while negotiating some degree of autonomy for the province of Texas.

But 1835 witnessed a tidal wave of American emigrants to Texas, the majority of whom were not so inclined to peaceful reconciliation as Austin. Santa Anna had ordered troops to Anahuac to collect delinquent taxes; "patriots" led by Alabama lawyer William Barret Travis had compelled the soldiers to surrender. In response, a sizeable force of Mexican regulars commanded by Santa Anna's brother-in-law, General Martin Perfecto de Cos, marched on and occupied San Antonio de Bexar.

This "invasion" turned the tide in favor of the Texas "War Party." Even Austin conceded that secession was their only recourse. His blood up, Houston wrote a friend, *"War in defense of our rights, our oaths, and our Constitution is inevitable in Texas!"*

"You weren't with us last year, Potter," Ellis told the man from North Carolina, "so let me explain what happened. There was a meeting in San Felipe last November. Houston was there, serving on the Committee on Indian Relations, due to his friendship with the Cherokees. He was also on the committee to draft the declaration."

"Declaration?" queried Potter. "What declaration was that?"

"The Declaration on the Causes of Texas Taking Up Arms," replied Houston.

"A provisional state government was formed," said Ellis. "Henry Smith was chosen to act as governor, and a general council was selected. The council elected Houston major general of the Texas Army."

"Which existed only on paper," said Houston. "I appointed Colonel James Fannin inspector general and second in command. Fannin, you see, is one of the few West Point graduates in Texas." Houston sighed. "I thought he would behave like a West Pointer and obey the orders of his superior. He and Ben Milam and Edward Burleson were determined to move on Cos at Bexar. I ordered them not to, but they did it anyway."

"Unfortunately," said Ellis, "my friend Houston here was accused of cowardice for not joining the force that besieged San Antonio." Noting the speculative way that Potter was looking at Houston, who now paced the puncheon floor of the room, Ellis added, "Anyone acquainted with Sam Houston knows he hasn't a cowardly bone in his body."

"Of course not," said Potter. "But Burleson and the others won. They forced Cos to surrender. It was a great victory for Texas. Even though the Mexicans outnumbered them three to one, those brave Texas patriots prevailed."

"They were brave, yes," said Houston darkly. "And lucky. But what did they accomplish? They may, in fact, have sealed our doom. General Cos posed no real threat. He was hoping to avert war as much as Stephen Austin. But his surrender has prodded Santa Anna into immediate action. We needed time. Time to create and train an army. But the 'victory' at Bexar cost us that time."

There had been other problems in forming a regular Texas army. Texas commissioners operating in New Orleans had drummed up enough money to charter five vessels as privateers to prey on Mexican shipping; they also recruited hundreds of volunteers. Problem was, those volunteers came to Texas as independent militia companies. The general council—*that damned litter of scoundrels* was Houston's reaction every time the subject of the council came up—had appointed officers to independent commands. Worse, the council had bought into a harebrained scheme to invade Mexico!

Once again Houston had found himself in the position of trying to stop James Fannin and his men from marching on Matamoros. Flush with the San Antonio success, the men would not heed him. Once again Sam Houston was accused of a lack of resolve, not to mention backbone. Fortunately, other factors delayed the proposed offensive on Mexico.

Houston had been thwarted once more by the council when he sent his friend Jim Bowie to the Alamo—that mission turned fortress on the outskirts of San Antonio—with orders to remove all military stores located there and then destroy the place. Bowie had found Travis in possession of the Alamo, and Travis had been recently commissioned a colonel by the council. He was also in possession of orders from the council to hold the Alamo at all costs.

A furious Houston had complained—and the provisional government responded by ordering him north to negotiate a treaty with the Cherokees. Texas could not fight on two fronts, and the Cherokees were making warlike noises. Thoroughly disgusted, Houston had agreed to go. No one knew that he had very nearly decided to stay with his Indian friends, and Texas be hanged. But during his absence the provisional government, torn by factionalism, disintegrated. With Texas in a state of utter political and military disarray, news arrived that Santa Anna was on the march. A convention was called, this time to meet in Washington-on-the-Brazos. *And here we go again,* thought Houston, restlessly pacing the floor.

The sound of a man running outside brought him up short. The door burst open, and a homespun-clad fellow Houston did not recognize breathlessly informed them that news had just arrived from San Antonio. Bad news.

"Santa Anna and ten thousand men had laid siege to the Alamo!"

Potter shot to his feet. "Ten thousand!" He seemed to strangle on the words.

"Less than half that, I'll warrant," said Zavala with confidence.

"I agree," said Houston, knowing he should feel vindicated. Travis had held the Alamo, and now he and his brave men were doomed. Houston had warned any who would listen—and that had been precious few—that if the volunteers remained in small independent commands they would be wiped out one by one. Yet he felt no vindication, for it came at too steep a price—the lives of more than a hundred and fifty Texas patriots.

"We must go to San Antonio at once and save Travis!" exclaimed Potter.

Bemused, Houston stared at the North Carolinian. The man might be a drunk and a fool, but he had courage. But courage without cunning was useless in this crisis.

"Travis cannot be saved," declared Houston. "God willing, he will serve our cause well, and sell his life dearly, by buying us time. Time enough to create a republic, and an army to defend it." He looked at each of them in turn and, with a grave nod, added, "Good night, gentlemen. I have traveled a long way today; I am tired, and there is much to do on the morrow."

He was gripped by an odd calmness now. Perhaps, he mused, it was the calm of the condemned man confronted at last by the gallows that he had dreaded for so long. But, win or lose, the die was cast. There was no turning back—for him or for Texas.

CHAPTER TWO

The Dragoons

Captain Juan Nepucino Galan watched the adobe walls of the Alamo stand stubbornly against a steady bombardment from the Mexican batteries. He used the long glass his father had given him on the day he had received his first commission. Galan was certain his father would have been very proud that his son was afforded the privilege of accompanying His Excellency, Santa Anna, on this campaign to crush the traitorous Texas upstarts. Rodrigo Galan, however, was dead. So his son had not had to feign enthusiasm for the task at hand.

"With twenty cannon, properly placed, that wall could not have withstood an hour of concentrated fire before being reduced to rubble."

Galan lowered the spyglass and glanced at his friend and fellow officer in the Tampico Regiment, Victor Benavides. They had known each other since childhood, and were as close as brothers, though their physical appearance was startlingly dissimilar. Where Galan was tall and impossibly handsome—ask any of Tampico's young senoritas, and they would be breathlessly unanimous in their admiration of his attributes—Benavides was short and stocky and undeniably coarse-featured. But, though he might not be the most beautiful dragoon in the army, Benavides was one of the most intelligent in Galan's opinion. He could also be very outspoken—a virtue, Galan supposed, but not necessarily an asset to an officer in Santa Anna's service.

"Unfortunately," replied Galan wryly, "we only have ten light field pieces, Victor."

"An oversight on His Excellency's part? Surely that can't be. The Napoleon of the West could not make such a mistake."

Galan smiled. It had been his superior, chief of cavalry General Joaquin Ramirez y Sesma, who had first compared Santa Anna to Napoleon Buonaparte, while he, Sesma, portrayed himself as El Presidente's dashing Murat. Victor was no great admirer of either Sesma or Santa Anna. Galan just hoped he would keep his opinions on that score a mystery to everyone else.

Of course, Benavides knew he could be candid on any subject under the sun with his good friend of twenty years. That worked both ways, so Galan felt free to unburden his soul.

"I wish I was back in Tampico, Victor," he sighed, raising the spyglass to his eye in time to see a shell strike an outer wall of the old mission in a cloud of yellow dust and debris—the old adobe absorbed the cannonballs like a giant sponge. "I wish, for the first time in my life, that I was not a soldier."

The revelation astonished Benavides, coming from a man whose only dream and passion had been soldiering. For as long as he could remember, Juan had talked of and worked for nothing else.

"Don't tell me you feel any sympathy for these Texans."

If it were so, Galan could confess it to Victor and not fear repercussions. But it wasn't so; in fact, Galan was a very patriotic man who considered the Texas rebels to be traitors to Mexico. As such they deserved no compassion. For that reason he did not object to the flying of the red flag that signified no quarter would be given the enemies of the republic. He was not moved by the "Constitutional" flag, which waved, bullet-torn, over the Alamo ramparts—the date "1824" on the bars of red, white, and green—because he did not believe the Texan claim that they fought only for the restoration of the principles upon which the republic had been founded.

Galan's martial spirit inclined him to favor the new Mexican flag—the tricolor base of green for the beloved Motherland, red for the blood of her heroes, and white symbolizing the purity of the Catholic Church, and the embroidered eagle in the center, a writhing snake in its beak. Santa Anna likened himself to the eagle on that flag, fighting a heroic battle against the snake of corruption and disloyalty, and Galan—less critical of his country's leader than Benavides—was willing to accept the analogy.

"No, not at all," he replied. "But I miss my Natalia. We had so little time together before the orders came to march."

Benavides nodded sympathetically. Though he

had never had much luck with women, he was a romantic at heart. "Naturally you miss her. She is the most beautiful woman in all of Tampico."

Most beautiful in Tampico? That, mused Galan, did not do Natalia justice. She was the most beautiful woman in all of Mexico. His heart raced as he longed for every beautiful inch of her. He could envision her so clearly in his mind's eye—the long raven black hair with its auburn highlights when the sun touched it, her soft and perfectly sculptured lips like a scarlet blossom, her warm brown eyes filled with such adoration when they looked at him. He sighed again, remembering their wedding night, the cooling, salt-tinged breeze coming in off the bay to move the gossamer curtains that draped the windows of the secluded cottage off the coastal road to Veracruz, the pounding surf a counter-rhythm to the pounding of their hearts as she locked her slender arms and long lissome legs around him, holding him inside of her for one indescribable moment of unbearable ecstasy. And then, when it was over, and they lay spent with arms and legs entwined, she had wept silent tears, for the sea breeze had floated his orders off the table beside the bed, reminding her that in the morning her husband would be going off to war.

"Don't worry, Juan," said Benavides, reading his friend, as always, with an uncanny accuracy. "You will return to her a hero, and soon!"

"Soon?" Galan grimaced. "It seems we have been in this godforsaken province since the beginning of time. For six days we have been here in Bexar, haven't we? It seems like six months. Why, Victor?

There cannot be more than two hundred rebels behind those walls. We could have taken that position days ago, even though the rest of the army had not yet arrived. But now the entire army is in place—and still we wait!"

Benavides shook his head. "It is an irregular fortification without flanking fire, which a good general could have taken with insignificant losses."

Frowning, Galan once again scanned the Alamo with his spyglass. He and Benavides stood about a thousand yards east of the rebel fortress, the river and the town of San Antonio de Bexar at their backs. The Alamo was not a particularly forbidding edifice from a military point of view. It lacked mutually supporting strong points. There were no bastions, no hornworks, no ravelines. The long, low courtyard perimeter wall had been connected to the roofless ruin of the chapel by a rather flimsy-looking picket fence. The position could be taken with ease by an attack on the southeast corner. So why hadn't an attack been ordered?

"Why we have not yet assaulted the place is not really the question," said Benavides. "You remember Vauban, don't you?"

Galan nodded. Victor had helped him master the works of the French engineer whose theories had revolutionized the concept of defensive positions and siege craft. These days it was generally accepted military doctrine that you stormed a fortress only as a last resort. The preferred strategy was a careful siege with powerful artillery that would eventually breach the walls, whereupon the garrison, realizing further resistance was futile, would surrender.

"But those men will not surrender to the red flag," he said.

"The real question," continued Benavides, "is why His Excellency has wasted six days laying siege to this place. A small force would contain the rebels and wait them out; in a few weeks they would run out of food and have to capitulate. This position has no inherent strategic value, Juan. Look about you. Nothing but open prairie. The Alamo controls no pass, obstructs no route. We could be marching east, and the sooner we get around to doing that the sooner this insurrection will be crushed—and the sooner you can go home to your new bride."

"You are absolutely right, Victor. I wish you were commanding this army—even if it did mean I would have to salute you."

Benavides laughed. That was one of the things he liked most about Galan—Juan's sense of humor always appeared in time to rescue one or the other of them from the brink of dark depression. In terms of promotion, Galan had stayed one step ahead of him, and Juan seldom missed an opportunity to kid him about that, always in a good-natured way.

As was often the case, Victor's unassailable logic forced Galan to consider the possibility that he had been looking at the problem from the wrong perspective. His most earnest desire was to see an end to this insurrection so that he could return to his beloved Natalia, who was as the breath of life to him. He had looked upon the Alamo as an obstacle.

But the real obstacle was Santa Anna's failure to pursue sound military doctrine. And, thinking back, the whole expedition had been marred by incompetence, compounded by bad fortune.

The army had begun its long march north two months before. Many officers had argued that transporting the army by sea would spare the men a four-hundred-league ordeal over the *despoblado*, the desert wasteland of Coahuila. But His Excellency had refused to even consider a seaborne invasion of Texas.

Worse, the troops were allowed to carry only one month's rations. Santa Anna wanted to travel light and fast. That limited the average soldier to eight ounces of hardtack or corn cake per day. Water was scarce, and when they reached the Rio Grande, they discovered that no one had brought any water barrels to fill. Wagoners were hard to find, and those that were found were civilian contractors and as such refused to abide by military discipline—many of them had deserted in the first week or two.

The army's logistical woes were exacerbated by the presence of the *soldaderas*—the camp-following wives and mistresses of the soldiers, as well as their numerous offspring, legitimate and otherwise. The women acted as cooks, foragers, and nurses, but they put an additional strain on the army's meager supplies, slowed the march, and distracted the troops. Yet no officer would suggest sending this host of noncombatants home, knowing that half the army would follow.

The *soldaderas* had served the army well enough

when hundreds of soldiers fell to dysentery and *tele*, a fever brought on by drinking putrid water. Santa Anna had failed to provide an adequate medical corps; the few physicians on hand were the dregs of their profession.

His Excellency had ordered a series of depots established along the line of march, but they were poorly defended, and most had been looted by Comanche raiders before the army arrived on the scene. Stragglers were often caught and tortured by the Indians. Galan and his dragoons had very nearly run their horses into the ground in futile patrols—not once had they managed to come to grips with the wily hostiles.

The weather didn't help, either. The winter of 1836 was an especially harsh one. Sudden blizzards covered the desert wastes with snow and ice. In one night eighteen inches of snow had fallen. Those troops recruited from the southern provinces, accustomed to tropical jungle, suffered more than most; some of them perished from exposure.

All along, Galan had thought that the wiser course would have been to send the cavalry to Texas alone. As a rule the cavalry was better trained and better equipped, and a large portion was battle-tested. The same could not be said for the infantry, whose ranks were filled with raw recruits. Many of Galan's fellow officers had nothing but contempt for the common foot-sloggers, deeming them "ignorant peasants" and "cannon fodder." They were the reason Santa Anna had opted for the overland march; he hoped to toughen the replacements en route. But Galan admired the stoic, stalwart resilience of the soldiers. In spite of everything, the army had reached Bexar intact. They had endured incredible privation.

"You realize, of course," said Benavides, dryly, "that our presence here has nothing to do with military doctrine. We're here for revenge, my friend."

"Revenge? What do you mean, Victor?"

"It was here that General Cos was defeated. Since Cos is a member of His Excellency's family by marriage, the recapture of San Antonio de Bexar is a point of honor. And for the sake of his honor Santa Anna will sooner or later hurl his troops against those walls. Many men will die."

"A soldier must be ready to die for his country."

"Spare me, Juan. A good commander's first duty is to plan a course of action that limits his losses. Santa Anna doesn't care how many Mexican soldiers must die in Texas."

"Careful, Victor. Here comes one of Colonel Urizza's aides."

As a matter of course, Galan kept a sharp eye out when his friend voiced criticisms of Santa Anna; even so, he feared that one day Victor would grow careless and be overheard by the wrong person. Then he might very well find himself confronting a firing squad.

The approaching horseman wore a uniform similar to Galan's. His short crimson jacket had a green collar, lapels, cuffs, and turnbacks. His trousers were green with crimson piping and black seat linings. His helmet was black with brass visor and chinstraps, with a horsehair tail. Like all regular cavalry, he was armed with an iron-hilted saber and an *escopeta,* a cut-down Brown Bess musket—a walnut-stocked smoothbore, .75 caliber, manufactured in Great Britain. These weapons were so notoriously inaccurate that Galan considered them a useless encumbrance. Like most cavalrymen in the Mexican Army, he preferred the lance, and his company was drilled to perfection in the use of that weapon.

The adjutant lieutenant checked his horse sharply, and Galan grimaced as muddy snow splattered him and Victor. Not that it mattered; their uniforms obviously belonged to men who had spent the past two months in hard campaigning.

The colonel's aide executed a crisp salute. "Captain Galan, the colonel requests your presence—immediately!"

"What is it, Lieutenant?"

His features animated by excitement, the young officer leaned forward in his saddle.

"Rumor has it that a force of five hundred rebels from Goliad—Colonel Fannin's command—are on the move, intending to relieve the garrison in the Alamo. General Sesma has ordered the Tampico Regiment to patrol the Bexar-Goliad road to the southeast, in hopes of intercepting Fannin."

"Tell the colonel I am coming."

With another salute the lieutenant wheeled his horse and galloped away.

"A rumor," muttered Benavides. "Well, at least it's something, Juan. Perhaps we will see some action at last."

Galan was not enthused by the prospect. There was one thing he did not feel he could share with his good friend. Now that he had something to live for besides the army, the idea of going into action left him cold. He felt guilty because he lacked enthusiasm for the task ahead. The last thing he wanted to do, for Santa Anna or even for Mexico, was to die in this godforsaken Texas, and never see his beautiful wife again.

CHAPTER THREE

The Sacrifice

On the first day of the convention a scare swept through the town of Washington-on-the-Brazos, as a wagoner reported seeing a large body of armed men in the vicinity, and it was assumed that they were Mexican dragoons, or, even worse, the Mexican irregulars attached to Santa Anna's army. These *rancheros*, as they were called, were notorious for their barbarity and lack of discipline, akin to the bloodthirsty Russian Cossacks, who had tormented Napoleon's ill-fated Grande Armee during the epic French retreat from Moscow across the frozen steppes of Mother Russia. Panic was a contagion that sent some of the delegates scurrying. They were well aware that in Santa Anna's bloodstained hands they would be promptly hanged as leaders of an insurrection.

When the truth became known—that the body of men were eighteen volunteers from nearby Brazoria who were on their way to Washington-on-the-Brazos to defend the convention members—Sam Houston scowled at the sheepish faces of those of his fellow delegates who had prepared to scatter like quail, wondering what kind of future Texas had in store for her with such spineless leaders. Demonstrating uncharacteristic discretion, he kept his opinions to himself.

Houston appeared before the convention—a collection, generally speaking, of planters and professional men, the cream of the community—in his travel-stained buckskins. This was calculated for effect; he wished to present himself as a humble citizen performing a citizen's duty to form a new government, not as a military hero.

The delegates met in a small, drafty, clapboard hall that served Washington-on-the-Brazos as church, courthouse, and dance hall. A trestle table and split log benches were the sum total of its furnishings. Deerskins were nailed over the glassless windows, but the bitter cold passed right through the walls and into the bones of the men gathered inside. That first morning, Richard Ellis had been cheered by the clearing sky, and had told Houston that the appearance of the sun after several days of leaden overcast must be a propitious sign, a good omen. Houston sourly observed that there was no warmth in the sun.

There weren't enough places for the fifty-odd delegates to sit, but Houston was quite content to stand, obscured by the others, in a back corner of the hall, where he could inconspicuously nip now and again at a flask of brandy.

The first order of business was the election of officers. Richard Ellis was chosen president of the convention. Committees were appointed. Houston found himself assigned to the committee charged with the authoring of a declaration of independence, an honor he accepted without much enthusiasm. The officers of the late and unlamented provisional government, including the general council, which had made Houston's life a perfect hell, were in attendance, and the convention requested all important documents and reports in their possession be handed over, at which time their functions as provisional governors were officially terminated. A few of the council members balked at such a summary dismissal; they resented the perception shared by most others present that they had dismally failed Texas in her hour of need. This gave ex-President Henry Smith an opportunity to vent his frustration, for he, like Houston, had been thwarted at every turn by the officious and quarrelsome council.

"Look around you," said Smith, with bitter bile, "and you will easily detect the scoundrels. The complaining mouth, the vacant stare, the head hung in shame, the sneaking look, a natural meanness of countenance, a contraction of the muscles of the neck in anticipation of the rope, a restless uneasiness to adjourn as they dread the storm they themselves have raised—and you will see the men who are responsible if this republic is stillborn."

This nasty—though Houston thought justified—piece of elegant slander created an uproar of indignation from the erstwhile council members, and disapproval from many of the delegates, who thought that the words about the contraction of neck muscles and an uneasiness to adjourn struck a little too close to home for all.

The next day, Houston and his committee presented a first draft of the declaration of independence, copied almost verbatim from a document penned by a newcomer to Texas, George Childress of Nashville, Tennessee. Childress had organized pro-Texas meetings in Tennessee, and had called on the young bravehearts of the United States to fight for the freedom of their Texas "cousins" from the yoke of a "cowardly, uncivilized, undisciplined and treacherous" Mexican people. The declaration retained more than a trace of his belligerence.

The Mexican government invited by its colonization laws the Anglo-American population of Texas to colonize its wilderness under the pledged faith of a written constitution that they should continue to enjoy that liberty and republican government to which they had been habituated in the land of their birth, the United States of America. In this expectation they have been cruelly disappointed.

The Mexican government has sacrificed our welfare through a jealous and partial course of legislation carried on by a hostile majority in an unknown tongue at a far distant seat. It has failed to secure on a firm basis the right of a trial by jury. It has suffered the military commandants stationed among us to exercise arbitrary acts of oppression and tyranny. It has dissolved by force of arms the State Congress of Coahuila and Texas. It has demanded the surrender of a number of our citizens. It has made piratical attacks upon our commerce. It denies us the right of worshipping the Almighty according to the dictates of our own conscience. It has demanded us to deliver up our arms. It has incited the merciless savage to massacre the inhabitants of our defenseless frontiers. It has invaded our country with intent to lay waste our territory and drive us from our homes.

The necessity of self preservation, therefore, now decries our eternal political separation.

We, therefore, the delegates of the people of Texas, in solemn convention assembled, appealing to a candid world for the necessities of our condition, do hereby resolve and declare our connection with the Mexican nation has forever ended, and that the people of Texas do now constitute a free, sovereign, and independent republic fully invested with all the rights and attributes which properly belong to independent nations; and, conscious of the rectitude of our intentions, we fearlessly and confidently commit the issue to the decision of the Supreme Arbiter of the destinies of Nations.

Sam Houston was among the first to sign the declaration, and he did so with bold strokes, so that his signature, observed a fellow delegate, stood out much as John Hancock's had done on the American Declaration of Independence. Houston was just pleased to be able to write with a steady hand—he had been indulging rather heavily in strong spirits since the convention began, and had decided that if his hand shook, he would blame it on the cold, as during the night a blue norther had come roaring through, sending the temperature plummeting to below freezing.

It did not escape him that the Texas Declaration of Independence was signed on March 2nd—his birthday. This only confirmed in his mind that his own destiny was linked inextricably with the destiny of Texas. He was forty-three years of age and wondered if he would survive to turn forty-four. There was no elation among the convention delegates, only grim resolve, and a keen sense of the crisis facing them. These were the dark hours for Texas, and few of the men present were truly confident of victory.

All the delegates signed the declaration. Eleven of them were Virginians, nine were from North Carolina, five were Kentucky natives, and nine were from Tennessee. The others had come from Georgia, Pennsylvania, New York, Massachusetts, Ireland, Scotland, and England. Three, including Zavala, were natives of Mexico.

A motion was made to arrange for the printing of one thousand copies of the document, to be distributed in handbill form in the United States. Houston strongly endorsed this measure. It was his fervent hope that the declaration would serve as a call to arms, igniting the passions of adventurous, liberty-loving Americans.

David G. Burnet was selected provisional president of the new republic. Once—or if—independence was won, elections would be held, and the citizens would choose their government. Lorenzo de Zavala was chosen to serve as vice president. And then Sam Houston's name was put forward by James Collinsworth.

"Whereas we are now in a state of Revolution, and threatened by a large invading army, the emergency of the present crisis renders it indispensably necessary that we should have an army in the field, and it is also necessary that there should be one supreme head or commander in chief, and due degrees of subordination defined, established and strictly observed.

"Therefore, be it Resolved, that General Samuel Houston be appointed major general to be commander in chief of all the land forces of the Texan Army, both regulars, volunteers and militia, and endowed with all the rights, privileges and powers due a commander in chief, and that he forthwith proceed to take command."

Only Robert Potter voted against this resolution.

On the following day, March 3rd, Houston begged leave to address the convention. He had decided to accept the position of supreme commander, since Collinsworth's resolution had unambiguously dispensed with the misbegotten concept of "independent commands," which had so enamored the defunct general council, and had so plagued Houston in the past.

He was interrupted by the arrival of a letter from Travis at the Alamo. Thanks to the heroics of couriers like the dashing young Carolinian, James Butler Bonham, Travis was still able to communicate with the outside world. The delegates listened with bated breath as Richard Ellis read the message.

Colonel Fannin is said to be on the march with reinforcements, but I fear it is not true, as I have repeatedly sent to him for aid without receiving any. Unless it comes soon, I shall have to fight the enemy on his own terms. However, I feel confident that the determined valor and desperate courage of my men will not fail them in the last struggle, and though they may be sacrificed to the vengeance of a Gothic enemy, the victory will cost the enemy dear, that it will be worse for him than defeat.

Desperate courage. The last struggle. Sacrificed to the vengeance of the enemy. Such phrases left the delegates solemn and silent.

Ellis continued to read.

Let the convention go on and make a declaration of independence, and we will then understand, and the world will understand, what we are fighting for. Under the flag of independence we are ready to peril our lives a hundred times a day against the monster who is fighting under a blood red flag, threatening to murder all prisoners and make Texas a waste desert. If my countrymen do not rally to my relief, I am determined to perish in the defense of this place, and my bones shall reproach my country for her neglect.

Robert Potter was first to speak. "I move that this convention adjourn immediately, arm itself, and march to the relief of the Alamo!"

Fuming, Houston stepped forward. "Mr. Potter's motion is madness. The convention must remain in session, write a constitution, and create a government. I will join the army at once, and if mortal power can avail, I will relieve the brave men of the Alamo."

With these words he left the hall with long, purposeful strides. While Saracen was being saddled, and with the volunteers from Brazoria waiting to ride with him, Houston gathered his few belongings. He donned a buckskin vest and Cherokee coat. He strapped on a sword and Mexican spurs and shoved a pistol under his belt. All the while, portions of Travis's letter echoed in his mind. *My bones shall reproach my country for her neglect.* The man had gall! Had he obeyed Houston's orders to destroy the Alamo mission and withdraw he would not be in his present predicament. As for Potter—now there was a brave fool! Houston had a mental image of the delegates, the founding fathers of the Republic of Texas, galloping through enemy lines to join the Alamo's doomed garrison. What a coup that would be for Santa Anna! Was it the future of Texas or his own eternal glory that motivated Travis?

Still, Houston could not deny that Travis, perhaps in spite of himself, perhaps for all the wrong reasons, was providing Texas an invaluable service. And this he made clear to Ellis and Zavala, who had come to the log cabin they had shared during the convention in order to see the new commander in chief on his way.

"You gentlemen realize that I have no army to speak of. I cannot save Travis and his volunteers."

Ellis nodded grimly. "They are dead men. May God have mercy on their souls."

"Texas will never forget them, " said Houston. "Their sacrifice must not be in vain. They will buy us precious time. You must make a government, and I must make an army."

"Santa Anna has seven thousand men," said Zavala. "Can you defeat him, General?"

"I will," said Houston, turning to his horse. "Because there are thousands of brave men in the United States who will heed our call and risk their lives for our cause. They are men who love liberty more than life."

"But is there *time*?" asked Ellis.

Houston didn't reply. He didn't have an answer. Time was the key. A few weeks, even a handful of days, might spell the difference between victory and death.

CHAPTER FOUR

The Departed

When Dr. Marcellus Clark came out onto the cabin porch, where Gabe Cochran had spent uncounted hours of anguish waiting for his world to end, Gabe took one look at the physician's haggard face and knew it was over. He rose from the rocking chair where he had endured the torment of his death vigil. An animal sound escaped him. The bluetick hound that had been curled at his feet jumped up and looked at him and cocked its head to one side and whined, sensing that something was terribly, terribly wrong.

"She's gone, Gabe." After twenty-five years of practice, Clark knew of no good way to break such news. "I'm sorry. There was very little I could do. But she went quietly."

"Why?" gasped Gabe. "Why couldn't you save her, Doc? Oh God, please, why couldn't you?" His voice was the pathetic, croaking whisper of a man whose spirit is broken.

Clark slowly passed a hand over his face, pressing hard against his eyelids. He took a deep breath of the cold morning air and tried to clear the smell of death from his nasal passages. The bright morning sun seemed to lance through his skull. He'd been in the cabin most of the night, fighting a battle he knew he could not win, doing all in his power to keep the Grim Reaper at bay, and praying for a miracle. In moments such as this one he felt utterly inadequate.

How could he make this poor man understand? This man who had lost his only child just three days ago, and today his wife, to yellow fever. No one in his profession could say with absolute certainty what caused the fever. Some claimed it was the result of a "miasma," a combination of "terrene" factors that included humidity, high temperature, poor ventilation, and filth. Clearly, Sally Cochran had not recently been exposed to high temperatures—the month of February in Alabama was generally damp and cold, and this February had been no different in that respect.

Clark knew that one of his colleagues, Dr. Josiah Nott of nearby Mobile, was conducting studies to support a hypothesis that yellow fever was transmitted by minute insects called animalcules. Nott believed it was absurd to blame yellow fever or cholera on the weather and climatic conditions—a dose of meteorology and a pinch of geography, as he would say with disdain.

Naturally, since physicians disagreed on the causes of yellow fever, there was a great deal of heated debate about how to best treat the illness. Clark considered himself a fairly forward-looking member of his profession. Nowadays medical schools were numerous—even the South had a few good ones. But in his youth there had been none in his native state of Georgia, and he had gone north to the school in Philadelphia and proven himself a very able student. He could have had a prosperous practice in an eastern city, but he had gone home to Georgia and then migrated westward to Alabama, motivated by a desire to serve his kind of people—people like Gabe Cochran, a hardscrabble yeoman farmer.

Being more forward-looking than the average frontier doctor, Clark did not subscribe to the treatment of yellow fever by bloodletting. Since there was no accompanying inflammation, plethora, or active congestions, yellow fever hardly seemed to him a disease requiring "active depletion." He had heard that quinine had been used with some success in past yellow fever epidemics, but Clark personally put his faith in dosages of mercury.

Yet mercury had not saved poor Sally Cochran or her daughter. Sometimes it worked; more often than not a patient afflicted with yellow fever succumbed. Medicine had made tremendous strides in Clark's lifetime, and yet there was still so much that remained a mystery.

So, in the end, since his craft provided no satisfactory answer to Cochran's query, Clark relied on something else in an attempt to explain his failure. "It was God's will, Gabe," he said. "It was just Sally's time."

"No," said Gabe flatly. "There is no God. I won't believe in a God who can be so cruel."

"You don't mean that." A profoundly religious man, Clark was disturbed when he bore witness to a renunciation of the Supreme Arbiter, even though he was sure Cochran *didn't* mean it, and that the Lord would make allowances for the grief-stricken farmer. "You must trust in God's infinite wisdom. There is a purpose, His purpose, in all things. He giveth life, and it is His to take away."

"And what about me?" sobbed Gabe, trembling. "Where does that leave me? What am I supposed to do?"

"Take comfort in knowing that Sally and Margaret reside now and forever at the feet of God, free for all eternity from pain and want. Know that when your time is done you will be reunited with your loved ones. You have not seen them for the last time, Gabe—unless you really believe that there is no God."

Gabe stared blankly at him for a moment. Then, drawing a long and ragged breath, he turned and shuffled off the porch. "I'd best get to diggin' the grave."

Clark watched him go, a shovel racked on his shoulder, trudging toward the old maple tree yonder, beneath which, a few days ago, he had buried his six-year-old daughter, Margaret. The hound followed its master, tail drooping and head hung low.

"Pompei."

"Yessuh, Marster." The young black boy who had been standing beside Clark's buggy came forward.

"You know Boone Tasker?"

"The schoolteacher? Yassum, I know him."

"You know where he lives, then."

"Yassum, I knows."

"Take the buggy and go tell him what has happened here. Tell him his friend Gabe Cochran needs him, right away."

As Pompei whipped up the cane tackey in the buggy's traces, Clark settled his weary bones in the rocking chair recently vacated by Cochran. He gazed bleakly across the fallow field where Gabe grew his corn—and a little tobacco for some extra cash money—and he pondered the imponderable. He had seen much death, and still he could not grow accustomed to it. The passing of the young was especially difficult to deal with. He had brought Margaret Cochran into the world—and he had presided over her departure from it. He had heard her first breath, and her last. He could only hope he had eased her pain as the end grew near. She'd been the spitting image of her mother—auburn curls and flashing blue eyes and the sweetest little smile . . .

Clark rubbed his eyes again, pressing hard. To endure the misery of life one had to believe in God. One *had* to have faith. Clark didn't think Gabe Cochran's faith was strong enough. Gabe had gone to church on Sunday, and never missed, as far as Clark knew. But that didn't necessarily mean a man's faith was strong enough. Clark didn't think that, come spring, Gabe would be planting a new crop in that field yonder.

Beyond the field a line of timber marked the course of a creek, and above the treetops soared a trio of turkey vultures. Seeing them, Gabe Cochran knew that another creature had died this morning, somewhere down in those trees. Everything died. Death was the great equalizer—no one would escape it. Gabe supposed that fact ought to give him some small comfort in this his moment of deepest despair, but it did not reconcile him, any more than Dr. Clark's preaching had done.

He stood for a long time staring, glassy-eyed, at the fresh grave of his daughter, Maggie. A few days ago he had decided that, as long as they had each other to lean on, he and his wife could overcome the tragedy of their child's death. But now Sally was gone, too, and life no longer held any meaning or value for Gabe Cochran.

Listlessly, he began to dig the new grave. He tried not to think about what he was doing, or why. Instead, vignettes of memory, completely out of sequence, filled his mind. He remembered the first day he'd taken a plow to that field yonder, and looking up from his weary labors to see Sally coming out of the cabin and walking toward him, carrying a ladle and a bucket of water drawn from the well, and marveling at his good fortune, because she looked like an angel, so pretty, barefoot, in a plain gingham dress, the sun touching her auburn hair, and he remembered how every time he saw her he felt a fresh resolve to make a go of this farm carved with sweating brow and aching back out of the wilderness of southern Alabama.

He remembered, too, sitting on the floor by the cabin's fireplace one winter's night, his arms wrapped around his wife, and she pregnant with child, her head resting on his shoulder, and the faint fragrance of flowers and lye soap in her hair, and his feeling the movement of their unborn child in the womb as he lay his big, work-roughened hand on Sally's swollen belly, and all the blessings God had bestowed on him, humbling him so profoundly that the nearly wept.

And he recalled the day of their departure from North Carolina. He and Sally had just been wed—he'd asked her to be his bride and leave her family to accompany him to Alabama, where fertile land could be theirs for the taking, and where a new, promising start belonged to every person who had the grit to make the move—and how her mother had cried inconsolably to see her Sally go, and her father had come close to breaking down himself, because migration was commonly compared to death; when someone spoke of a "dear, departed" relative they might be referring to someone who had gone to the grave or gone to the frontier.

Gabe had been so proud of Sally, the way she bore up so bravely when the time came to cut the ties that bound her to her family. Alabama might as well have been the moon, and Sally had known she would probably never see her parents again, and again Gabe had been humbled by the knowledge that she loved him so much that she was willing to leave her kinfolk, and the only home she had ever known, to venture into the great unknown with him.

Sally's father had solicited a solemn promise from Gabe that he would not let anything happen to his daughter . . .

Crawling out of the half-finished grave, blinded by scalding tears, Gabe dry-heaved on hands and knees, then got to his feet, sobbing and shuddering, and staggered blindly away from the old maple tree, running for the distant trees. Several times he stumbled and fell over the barren furrows of the field laying fallow. Doc Clark called after him from the cabin porch, but Gabe didn't even hear him. All he could hear was Sally's sweet voice and Maggie's giggling laughter, and all he wanted to do was die . . .

Boone Tasker finally found him, hours later, as the day began to darken into bitter winter night, nearly a mile from the cabin, on the far side of the creek and deep in the woods where the two of them had sometimes gone hunting together. Gabe was sitting on an old log, hunched over, shivering violently, and Boone took off his blanket coat and draped it around his friend's shoulders and sat down next to him and for a while said nothing—didn't know what to say, exactly. What good were words at a time like this? So he watched the gray twilight gather beneath the trees and listened to the cold stillness.

Words had seldom failed Boone Tasker. The words he read in his beloved books nourished an insatiable desire for knowledge. And words were his stock in trade, for he was a schoolmaster. He liked to talk; there was nothing he liked better than good conversation.

And yet his closest friend, Gabe Cochran, was a taciturn, inarticulate man. On the face of it they did not seem to have much at all in common. Maggie had been the bond between them at first. Like most of Boone's students, Maggie was devoted to her teacher. Grateful for the way Boone inspired their daughter to learn her three R's, the Cochrans had invited the bachelor schoolteacher to supper. Though they were not at all alike, Boone and Gabe hit it off. Boone was slender and fair-haired and not well acquainted with rifle or plow, while Gabe was a dark, brawny man who knew nothing but hunting and farming and had never even opened a book—books were of precious little value to a man who could not read. Boone put his faith in ideas, Gabe in hard work. One was everything the other wasn't. Maybe, Boone had said, that was why they had made such a stout friendship. Gabe had taught him how to shoot, and Boone had introduced Gabe to the world of books by teaching him how to read.

It was Gabe who finally broke the silence. "I ain't going back there, he muttered, without looking up."

"I'll bury her for you," said Boone, "if you're sure you don't want to do it yourself."

"I ain't going back there."

"Ever? What about the farm?"

Gabe shook his head. "I hate it. Hate it all. Even hate that old maple tree. 'Specially the maple tree, you know?"

Boone nodded. He knew what Gabe was thinking. The maple would be closer to Sally and Maggie than Gabe could ever again be; its roots would embrace their mortal remains, and its sweeping branches would shade them in the bright heat of summer, and in the fall its purpled leaves would fall gently to decorate their graves.

"Where will you go, Gabe? What will you do?"

Gabe just shook his head.

"I think I know what Sally would want you to do."

"Life is over for me."

"No, it just feels that way. Look, Gabe, I think I'm going to Texas. Why don't you come along?"

"Texas?" That made Gabe lift his head and look at his friend. "What about Sarah Ambler?"

Mention of Sarah's name seemed to twist Boone's insides into an excruciatingly painful knot, but he managed an indifferent shrug and ne'er-do-well smile.

"That's just not in the cards. So I'm going over the hill, as they say. Texas is a place where a man can make something of himself. Aren't any limits to what a man can do in Texas if he's got the ambition—and the nerve. Sure, they're having a little scrape down there now, but if a man can survive that he'll have a leg up on life."

"Yeah," said Gabe. "A man could sure get killed in Texas."

Boone gave him a funny look. "Getting killed is not part of my plan."

"Sure. Sure. But what about your pupils?"

"I hate to leave them. But I have to get away." Boone flinched at a mental image of Sarah Ambler.

Sarah was the most beautiful and desirable woman in the country—this was an opinion Boone Tasker shared with every other local bachelor. He'd known in his heart that he was a fool for falling in love with her. But he was a hopeless romantic. And an optimist, to boot. How else to explain his even entertaining the notion that Sarah, the daughter of one of the wealthiest merchant planters in southern

Alabama, could ever be the bride of a lowly, penniless schoolteacher—and a Northerner, too!

Not that she didn't love him. That had been obvious—obvious enough to have troubled not only her father but also the host of beaus who vied for her affections. Randolph Ambler soon rued the day he had employed Boone to tutor Sarah's ten-year-old brother. Randolph, Jr., was of course too good to attend the drafty one-room schoolhouse in town where Boone taught the sons—and occasionally a daughter—of the local middle class. Having been born and raised on the Illinois frontier, Boone didn't have much use for the airs that folks like the Amblers put on, but he couldn't deny that the situation worked to his advantage. Otherwise he would never have met Sarah. They didn't exactly move in the same social circle.

Most of Sarah's other beaus were sons of neighboring planters—dashing young Southern cavaliers, all. Boone considered his competitors featherbrained, strutting peacocks, and he liked to think Sarah was attracted to him because he was a plain-speaking, hard-working, intelligent young man, genuine and dependable and thoughtful of others. Of course, bearing in mind the capacity for violence of the Southern gentleman, Boone had wondered if one of Sarah's home-grown admirers might not decide to dispense with the Yankee interloper. A constant threat, but one Boone had been willing to risk for one of Sarah's smiles.

And yet Randolph Ambler had proven himself to be Boone's greatest enemy. It wasn't really up to Sarah whom she married, and her father wasn't about to settle for Boone as a son-in-law. So Randolph had terminated Boone's employment, and when that didn't serve to keep the schoolteacher at bay, he made arrangements to send Sarah to finishing school in Virginia. In desperation Boone had begged Sarah to elope with him, but she couldn't, being a proper young Southern maiden; she wouldn't dream of disobeying her father—she was going to Virginia, and when the tearful good-byes were over, Boone had made up his mind to go to Texas.

"I carved GTT on the schoolhouse door," Boone told Gabe. "I can't stay here, so I'm 'Gone to Texas.' You can't bear to stay here, either, so we might as well join forces. Captain Jack Shackelford is asking for volunteers to come to Mobile and join his company. He's calling his command the Alabama Red Rovers. His own son has volunteered. If we hurry, we can get to Mobile and enlist before Shackelford sails for Texas. So what do you say, Gabe?"

Gabe Cochran thought it over. All Boone's talk about Texas being a place where energetic and ambitious men could make a name for themselves fell, in his case, on deaf ears. A better future—or any kind of future, for that matter—was something about which he cared little. But that didn't mean Texas wasn't an attractive idea. A revolution was going on over in Texas; a Mexican army was on the march. Everybody in the United States knew what was going on over there. Unlike most, Gabe hadn't been too interested in the Texas troubles. But now he was keenly interested.

Texas sounded to him like a place where a man could get himself killed in a hurry.

The preachers said you met your dear, departed loved ones "on the other side." Gabe Cochran wasn't going to waste any time getting across that Jordan River.

"Yeah, Boone," he said. "Let's go to Texas."

CHAPTER FIVE

The Promise

Mingo Green had spent five years on Magnolia, the Hammond plantation. He knew every inch of the place, and he was well versed in the plantation routine. So he was confident that he could slip away unnoticed under cover of night.

Not that there wasn't plenty of risk involved. Slave patrols were a constant menace. Many poor whites were willing to participate in such patrols because a planter's reward for a runaway slave was a financial windfall for the "sand hillers," as the poor whites were called. Mingo fully intended to be back at Magnolia before daylight, but that he wasn't really trying to run away would make no difference to the slave catchers, and Marse Hammond would be obliged to pay them something for their trouble; it was in every planter's best interest to encourage the slave patrols and reward them for their diligence.

Mingo was well aware of what would befall him if he were caught. It had happened before. That time, the slave catchers—there had been three of them—had beaten him pretty severely, since he'd given them a good run and tried to resist capture.

They would
their hands, th
what he was worth,
trol could not come u
dred dollars between the
and in his prime, and as a fi
a great deal to the owner of Ma

No, if he didn't run or fight, t
wouldn't harm him. But Marse Ha
would. This would be Mingo's second o
got caught, and Marse Hammond woul
break him of the habit for good, while makin
example of him in case any of the other sixty-od
slaves at Magnolia had a notion about running. Most of all, Hammond would be furious at Mingo for being so ungrateful as to disobey a man who clothed and housed and fed him, and who paid for his medical care when he was sick. That was the way Marse Hammond, and most other planters, thought. They just couldn't understand why a well-treated slave would want to run away. It never occurred to them that freedom and self-respect could be of any value to such depraved souls as the Negroes they kept in bondage. Why, only men with honor cared about freedom, and everybody knew that slaves had no honor.

Mingo figured Marse Hammond would be right hard on him this time if he got caught. Last time, Mr. Slade, the overseer, had given him two dozen stripes with the "cowskin." This whip was three feet of untanned ox hide, and it laid the flesh open quite nicely, thank you. Many slave holders preferred lashes of plaited leather with soft buckskin

in.
led
his
nis-
ave
, of

ded.
nond
never
why
unt of
d had

ld cal-
culate the app... a clear,
cold winter sky as he crouched at the co... r of the
double-pen slave cabin, the last in a row of ten,
which he shared with five other male field hands.
Across the way were ten more cabins, virtually
identical one to the other, with walls of crudely cut,
loose-fitting clapboard, clay chimneys, and shake
roofing. In between the rows of cabins were the
vegetable gardens Marse Hammond allowed his
slaves to cultivate. At one end of the rows stood the
overseer's dogtrot house. Behind the overseer's
house was a windbreak of trees, and beyond that
was the main house.

Mingo had waited while Mr. Slade enjoyed his
evening pipe on the porch of the dogtrot house. Inside, his wife cleaned up after dinner. Even after
Slade went back in and the lamp was extinguished,
plunging the dogtrot into darkness, Mingo waited.

Mr. Slade was a man of strong passions and insatiable appetites, and most nights he made love to his wife. Mrs. Slade was a noisy lover—her cries of ecstasy were a source of amusement for the slaves—and so Mingo knew precisely when the lovemaking was over tonight. Even so, he waited yet another hour, until he was certain all the other field hands in his cabin were asleep. It wasn't so much that he thought they might betray him—he knew they wouldn't if they didn't have to. But this way, if they were questioned, or threatened, or even beaten, they could answer truthfully that they had no idea when Mingo had departed.

And so it was nearly midnight when, finally, Mingo made his move. All was still in the slave quarters. He worked his way past the gristmill and gave the barn a wide berth. Marse Hammond's hunting dogs usually spent the night in the vicinity of the big house, but now and then one or two of them would prowl the barn area, and Mingo knew they were his greatest enemy at this moment. Marse Hammond had made sure his hounds hated black folk—he'd have one or two of the house servants beat the dogs with switches when they were pups; in this way Marse Hammond ensured that no slave could hope to befriend any of the dogs, or even walk past one of them without eliciting a hostile, and noisy, reaction.

Once away from the outbuildings, Mingo skirted the fields at a loping run, keeping to the edge of the trees, coming eventually to a creek. He stayed with the creek for a half mile, then cut through the woods, making his way across the slough, praying that he didn't disturb a gator or a cottonmouth. The slough was full of ghosts, too, everybody knew that, but Mingo's desire to be with Sadie overcame his superstitious dread of this foul, stinking, dead place.

Nearly two hours after leaving Magnolia's slave quarters, Mingo was crouched in a persimmon thicket within sight of the slave cabins of Ravenmoor, the plantation owned by Colonel Ambler. Seeing nothing to alarm him, he crawled on his belly across open ground, thankful that the early moon had already set.

Mingo was a big man, but he could move quietly, like a cat, and he was plenty bold when it came to Sadie, so he slipped right on into the cabin. The door creaked on its old leather hinges, and he froze, balanced on the balls of his feet, holding his breath. But no one stirred, and a moment later he was kneeling beside Sadie's narrow bunk in the half of the cabin she shared with the three children of Isaac and Lucinda, the folks with whom Sadie had been quartered. They and Isaac's brother, Abraham, slept in the other half of the double-pen cabin.

Mingo was grateful that Isaac and Lucy had been so kind to Sadie these past six months; they had treated her as they would their own kin. He didn't trust Abe, though; Isaac's younger brother was a bachelor, and Mingo figured he was bound to be attracted to Sadie. And though he liked Isaac, the feeling wasn't mutual. Isaac never had much good to say about Mingo Green. "You ain't nuthin but trouble, boy," Isaac had told him, "and you ain't gwine make life easy for Sadie if you get caught." That was Isaac's way—he didn't beat around the bush. You always knew where you stood with him.

Sadie gasped with delight as Mingo awakened her, but she made no other sound until they had slipped safely out of the cabin and reached the thicket some fifty yards away. She had a blanket around her shoulders, and this she spread out upon the ground. Then with a small cry of delight she wrapped her arms around his neck and kissed him hard on the lips, and the pressure of her slender body aroused Mingo, and he bore her to the ground. Lifting her thin cotton shift, fumbling with his trousers, he was joined with her in a rapturous embrace, and she whispered in his ear, "I love you, I love you, I love you," over and over again until she could speak no more. They were quiet in their passion, and only a bird that had nested in the thicket was disturbed by the small sounds they made. Then Mingo and Sadie lay together and listened to the bird chirrup for a while, as though gently scolding them, before falling silent.

"They say when a bird sing at night, somebody dies," said Sadie.

"I ain't never felt more alive."

"Me neither. I missed you so much, Mingo. I was wonderin' if you'd ever come back." Propped on an elbow, she looked earnestly down at him. "Mingo, I just cain't bear livin' thisaway. Let's run."

"Run where, girl? There ain't no place you can run they cain't find you and bring you back."

"One of Marse Ambler's field hands run off a year or two back. They didn't never catch him, 'cause he went south and they think he's livin' with the Seminoles now. A lot of runaways live down there, they say."

Mingo shook his head. "Won't do, Sadie. I'm tellin' you, it just won't do."

"But why not?"

"They be fightin' down there, girl. The army done gone down there to do away with all them Seminoles and runaways. No, I won't take you down there. You're liable to get killed."

"But I just cain't live like this no more. Bein' away from you, and never knowin' when I'll see you again. Ain't fair."

Mingo sat up and chuckled. "You're somethin', Sadie. Truly, you are somethin'. A slave whinin' on account of life ain't fair. Now that's enough to make an ol' hoot owl smile."

Gazing at her, Mingo was struck by how young she looked. Sadie was about twenty years old, but she hardly looked a day over sixteen. Her willowy figure and urchin's face had a lot to do with it. But it was also her simple, almost childish way of looking at things. Sadie just didn't see why life had to be so complicated, even for a slave. But of course a slave's life was very complicated, and Mingo knew there were no simple solutions.

"So what we goin' to do, Mingo? We gots to do somethin'!"

Mingo grimaced. "When you a slave there ain't much *to* do."

Sadie hung her head in dejection, and Mingo experienced a surge of anger—anger at Marse Hammond and the evil institution of human bondage and most of all anger at himself. This was the cruelest anger of all because it was mixed with a strong dose of impotence.

Born a slave, Mingo had not given much thought to freedom before meeting Sadie; always before he had been relatively content to accept his situation and make life as easy as he could, content to make his way within a system that made property of a human being. He was never abjectly docile, as some "house niggers" became, but neither had he made trouble. He was never hostile, seldom sullen in his obedience. It wasn't that he accepted the white man as superior over him; he simply accepted his lot and tried to make the best of it without stooping so low that he surrendered what little dignity and self-respect the "peculiar institution" of slavery permitted him.

But then Marse Hammond had bought Sadie, and Mingo had fallen in love at first sight, and his whole life changed. He had courted her diligently, in keeping with the ritual of the slave quarters. To win a mate a man had to know how to talk—slaves imitated their white owners in this regard, with their highfalutin language and witty repartee. "Has you any objections to me sittin' down here 'side you, miss?" Mingo had asked Sadie at the outset, "and revolvin' the wheel of my conversation 'round the axle of your understandin'?" Of course she hadn't minded. Later, Mingo had been so bold as to admit that he had never seen a lady that suited his fancy more than she. "Is you cloth that's been spun, or cloth that's been woven?" he had asked, and Sadie had assured him that she was "spun"—or single. And so the courtship was on.

At molasses stews, watermelon feasts, and corn shuckings, Mingo and Sadie were always together no matter what the social occasion. Mingo flattered her, exaggerated his prowess—sexual and otherwise—in her presence, and in every other way demonstrated his wholehearted ambition to have her. He won her heart completely.

Love was no small thing for a slave. Before Sadie, Mingo had sworn he would never give his heart. He had seen his own family torn apart; white owners were not always respecters of slave marriages when it came time to buy or sell hands. And if a slave married a woman from the same plantation, he placed himself in the awkward and sometimes tragic position of having to watch her insulted, overworked, beaten, and maybe even raped, without his daring to say a word or lift a finger in her defense.

Nevertheless, Mingo could not help himself where Sadie was concerned. And so they had "jumped the broom"—gotten married.

But Marse Hammond did not recognize the sanctity of slave marriage, and he refused to sanction the wedding. It had long been his intention to use Mingo as a "breeder"—to have him sleep with healthy young slave women and get them pregnant—and he informed Mingo, the day after the wedding, that his being married wasn't going to change things in the least. The African slave trade had been outlawed twenty-five years ago, and while a few slaves were smuggled into the South, primarily from the West Indies, there weren't nearly enough to fill the need for slave labor called for by the opening up of Alabama and Mississippi and Arkansas and Missouri to cotton production. A man could make good money breeding slaves for sale, and Marse Hammond fully expected to have his piece of that particular pie.

Mingo had not refused outright to do Marse Hammond's bidding, knowing this would be futile at best, if not downright dangerous. But Sadie hadn't been able to accept the arrangement, even though Mingo tried to make her understand that the other women meant nothing to him. Naturally, the more upset Sadie became, the more it disturbed Mingo, until he reached the point that he was unable to perform sexually. Marse Hammond guessed right away what the trouble was, and he sold Sadie to Marse Ambler. "I will give you a pass to go and see her now and then if you do well by me," Marse Hammond had said. But still Mingo was unable to lie with other women, and when Marse Hammond refused to provide him with a pass, Mingo began to slip away from Magnolia without permission.

"We got to do somethin'," Sadie said at length, her voice small.

"What is it?" asked Mingo, heart racing. He could tell by the way Sadie was acting that something was bad wrong. "What's the matter?" He assumed it had to do with Sadie's situation at Ravenmoor—some kind of bad news that would impact their lives in a bad way.

"We goin' to have a baby, Mingo."

He was stunned, and she watched him closely;

clearly she had been uncertain of the way he would react to the news.

"You ain't mad, are you?" she asked tentatively.

He took her in his arms. "'Course I ain't mad. Don't be silly."

"I don't want our baby to be born slave, Mingo. I want him to be free. I'd . . . I'd rather kill him than he be born slave."

"Don't say that!" gasped Mingo, shocked. "You don't mean it. You can't. Long as a person's alive, he's got hope, Sadie."

"I'm sorry," she whispered and buried her face in his chest, and he could tell by the slight shudders of her slender body that she cried silent tears.

He wasn't sure how long he held her, for he lost track of time, distracted by the realization that he was going to be a father. A glance at the stars jolted him; dawn was not far away—he would be lucky to get back to Magnolia before first light.

He hated to leave Sadie at a time like this, but she took the burden from him, urging him to hurry and go, he would have to run all the way to get back before he was missed, and assuring him that she would be all right. She promised she would not do anything to harm the baby she carried. There were potions a woman could take, and every plantation had a slave—sometimes male, but more often female—who knew just the right ingredients, herbs and other things, that would act to purge the womb. But Sadie swore she wouldn't do any such thing. "Only you got to promise me somethin' in return, Mingo," she said in deadly earnest. "You got to promise you'll think of some way to get us away from here. I want my baby born free."

Mingo promised he would try to think of something, then took his leave.

So consumed was he by an inner turmoil, his mind so crowded with a jumble of thoughts, that he wasn't as careful as he ought to have been, or usually was, and got too near the Mobile road, so that a slave patrol spotted him running through the trees, and without thinking Mingo tried to elude them.

He didn't get far.

CHAPTER SIX

The Cavaliers

When Pierce Hammond turned his Kentucky thoroughbred off the road and up the magnolia-bordered lane to the big house, he was in a foul humor. This stemmed in part from losing a large sum of money, betting on the wrong horse in yesterday's race down at the Bottoms—more money than he had carried to the track. Which meant he would have to approach his father again and ask him to make good, not for the first time, on his son's debts. His father would do it—honor would compel him—but Pierce was in no mood to suffer the insufferable lectures Daniel Hammond would give him.

Worse than this, however, was the realization that word of his apparent cowardice would quickly circulate throughout his father's social circle. He had been insulted, and instead of demanding satisfaction on the field of honor, he had chosen to "pocket" the insult—he had taken it and turned his back and walked away. Pierce knew his father would not tolerate this kind of behavior. There would be hell to pay. But Pierce had decided it would be better to come clean with his father right away—better that Daniel Hammond heard the truth from his own son than from someone else. His failure to make a full disclosure would brand Pierce twice a coward.

So Pierce was not in the best frame of mind as he rode up the lane and saw Mr. Slade, the overseer, applying the cowskin to Mingo Green's back. The field hand was staked out on the ground in front of the big house, facedown in the dirt, stripped naked, and every Magnolia slave, save for some of the house servants, had been summoned to bear witness to the punishment that Slade—with a little too much relish, thought Pierce—was administering.

Pierce had never liked Slade. The man had a cruel streak in him. He drove the slaves hard. That was the way Daniel Hammond liked it—Hammond bragged that he had the best overseer in the state. But this only partly explained Pierce's antipathy toward the overseer. From the very beginning of his employment at Magnolia, Slade had astutely sized up the situation, realizing that where the operation of the plantation was concerned, Pierce had little influence with his father. Pierce had never exhibited much interest in Magnolia, which dismayed his father, and for this reason Daniel Hammond rarely consulted his son on the subject. Neither did he choose to delegate any responsibility to Pierce. As a result, Slade had never felt obliged to show Pierce the proper respect. Of course he was never openly disrespectful; Daniel Hammond would not allow him to go that far over the line. But the overseer's contempt for his employer's ne'er-do-well son was plain enough, and demonstrated in sufficiently subtle ways at every opportunity.

Sharply checking the thoroughbred, Pierce leaped from the saddle and lunged through the press of slaves, who parted to let him pass. Slade hadn't seen him coming up the lane; the overseer was entirely too engrossed in the work of flaying the flesh off Mingo's back. When Slade reared back with the bloody cowskin to strike yet again, Pierce snatched the whip from his grasp.

Slade whirled, a snarl on his lips, fist clenched and raised to strike. Seeing that it was Pierce who had relieved him of the cowskin gave the overseer pause. His hooded eyes turned dark and lurid. Pierce braced himself, ready to use the whip on Slade if the man attacked him. For a perilous moment Slade teetered on the brink of doing just that. Then the tension drained slowly out of him, and the raised fist was lowered as a sneering smile curled lazily across his lips.

"You ought to take more care, *Mister* Hammond, sneakin' up on me thataway."

With a smirk that he hoped would irritate Slade, Pierce tossed the cowskin away. It landed at the feet of several of the Magnolia slaves, and they jumped away, staring at it as though it were a poisonous snake.

"You've whipped him enough, Slade." Pierce intentionally omitted the "mister."

"Not nearly," drawled the overseer. "Your father told me to give him fifty stripes, and then brand him for a runaway."

At that moment Jubal came through the circle of

slaves. The grizzled black who worked in the plantation's blacksmith shop was carrying an iron brand, red-hot at the tip. He gave Pierce an apologetic look. The look said, *Dis kind of work aint to my likin', Marse Pierce. You of all folks should know dat. But what's a man who ain't a man but a slave s'pose to do?*

Seeing the brand infuriated Pierce. It wasn't that he particularly cared about the Magnolia slaves—he seldom gave much thought to them—but cruelty for cruelty's sake repulsed him, and he failed to see the efficacy of punishing Mingo in such a barbarous fashion. Planters like his father claimed one had to make examples of recalcitrant slaves, to teach the others a lesson. Pierce didn't believe that, not for a minute.

"Go back where you came from with that thing, Jubal."

"Yessum." Jubal's face brightened. This was one order he didn't mind obeying with alacrity.

"Hold on there," snapped Slade. "Give me that iron, boy."

Jubal glanced nervously at Pierce, who read the worry in his eyes, and knew what the old black was thinking—the same thing all the other slaves present were thinking. They were hoping Pierce would stand up to Slade, but Marse Hammond's son had never stood his ground before. Especially not on their account.

"You're not going to brand him, Slade," said Pierce. "So don't even try."

"You gonna stop me, *Mister* Hammond?"

The overseer was practicing open insubordination now; he fairly reeked of it in tone of voice, stance, and expression.

"Yes," replied Pierce, knowing Slade was more than a match for him. But he wouldn't—he couldn't—back down this time. A man could back down just so many times . . .

Slade lunged—but not at Pierce. He snatched the brand out of Jubal's gloved hand and gave the gray-headed old blacksmith a hard shove. Jubal fell, and Slade loomed over him, menacing him with the brand.

"Take care, boy," snapped the overseer, "or I'll use this on you."

Pierce hit him then, a flying tackle that blind-sided Slade and drove him to the ground. But Pierce quickly lost his initial advantage. Slade was very strong and very agile, and before Pierce knew what had happened, Slade was on top of him, pounding him with his gloved fists, and Pierce was just glad the overseer had lost his grip on that brand when he fell. Once, twice, three times Slade slammed a fist into Pierce's face. The copper taste of hot blood in his mouth, Pierce tried ineffectually to use his arms to block the blows raining down on him, and then the world began to turn dark . . .

He came to, spluttering, cold water on his face, and looked up at his father standing over him with an empty well bucket in hand and a scowl of disapproval darkening his features.

"Get up and go to the house," barked Hammond. "Have Pearl take a look at your face. She'll have to make up a salve . . ."

Pierce was on his feet, aware that blood was

streaming down his cheek from a gash just below the eye. Spitting more blood out of his mouth, he mumbled, "I won't stand by and let him put a brand on Mingo."

Hammond gave him a long, unfathomable look, then turned slowly to Slade.

"Put him in irons, but don't brand him."

"But, Mr. Hammond—"

"Do what I tell you."

Slade was disappointed, looking like a child whose toy has been taken away. His expression turned sullen as he glanced at Pierce, but he nodded and said, "Yes, sir, Mr. Hammond."

Pierce turned his back and walked to the big house with as much dignity as he could muster.

"You countermanded my orders," said Daniel Hammond gravely as he stood at the sideboard and poured himself a strong dose of sour mash from one of several crystal decanters. "By so doing you undermine my authority. You take no interest whatsoever in the operation of this plantation, and yet you see fit to interfere in this instance." Hammond took a drink and sighed. "I confess I do not understand you, Pierce. I never have. I wish your mother were still alive. Perhaps she could talk some sense into you. Heaven knows I can't seem to get anything through that thick skull of yours."

Pierce had changed his clothes, and Pearl, one of the house servants, had applied a salve to the cut on his face. The salve had stopped the bleeding and dulled the pain. But his left eye was swelling badly, one of his teeth was loose, and he had a terrible headache. All he wanted to do was go to bed and sleep around the clock. The last thing he needed was to stand here in the downstairs parlor and listen to his father's old familiar litany; he was well aware that he had become a source of profound disappointment to his father.

He wished his mother were alive, too. They had been close; she had acted as a buffer, a liaison between him and his father. She had understood him perfectly, perhaps better than he understood himself. Elizabeth Hammond had accepted the fact that her son was not cut from the same cloth as her husband. Pierce did not resemble his father either physically or in his dreams and aspirations.

"Whatever Mingo did," said Pierce wearily, "he didn't deserve to be branded. He is a human being."

"He is a slave. But what difference does that really make? The army still brands deserters. It wasn't too long ago that the courts ordered thieves and debtors and adulteresses branded."

"No, not too long ago," said Pierce dryly. "Just a hundred years. This is the nineteenth century, Father, remember? And we're supposed to be a civilized people. This isn't the Middle Ages, and you're no feudal lord, though I must admit you and others like you do rule in a system that is not dissimilar from the one in force in those benighted times."

Hammond finished off his drink and poured himself another. This was even stiffer than the first. "You have too much book learning, and not nearly enough common sense. That's obvious, since you were foolhardy enough to pick a fight with Slade, of all people. You're no match for a man like that. Was he disrespectful? Well, what do you expect? You must earn respect."

"It had nothing to do with that."

"What, then? His wife? Is she the cause of the bad blood between the two of you?"

"I don't know what you mean, Father."

"Don't you? Women are one of your principal weaknesses, Pierce. Especially the wrong kind of women." Hammond glanced reverently at the portrait of his wife, hanging above the sideboard, a somberly hued rendering in an ornate gilt frame, which nonetheless captured the pale, haunting, fragile beauty of Pierce's mother. The painting had been done by a talented itinerant artist only months prior to her untimely death—a peritonsular abscess had killed her in a matter of days.

"That was not the issue," said Pierce hotly. "Slade is a cruel man. He enjoys hurting people. I refuse to stand by and watch it."

"You're lucky he didn't kill you. You're certainly no fighter."

"I'm glad you are aware of my limitations in that regard, sir," said Pierce stiffly. "Then I trust you will concur that I did the right thing by refusing to meet Charles Drayton on the field of honor."

Startled, Hammond gaped at his son. "What are you talking about?"

"There was a race yesterday, at Hickory Bottoms, between Drayton's gray stallion and Colonel Irwin's mare, Delilah. I wagered five hundred dollars on the colonel's champion, and she was beaten.

I was unable to pay the entire sum upon demand. I told Drayton he would have his money by today, but he wasn't satisfied with those arrangements. He called me a scoundrel, and then a coward when I refused to demand satisfaction for the initial insult. As you are no doubt aware, Father, Drayton is an accomplished duelist. There can be no question but that he would have prevailed over me. I'm sure he had no fear that by killing me he would fail to get the money owed him; he would have expected you to make good my debt for me, and of course you would have deemed yourself obligated to do so, regardless of the fact that he would have been the man who killed your only son."

Hammond was stunned. So stunned, in fact, that Pierce's sarcasm was lost on him. It was bad enough that Pierce wagered money he did not have. Worse still was Drayton's reluctance to accept Pierce's note for the money due; by this act Drayton had implied that Pierce was not a gentleman whose word could be trusted. But worst of all, Pierce had refused to respond to provocation, as Drayton had clearly sullied the Hammond name.

Seeing the effect this narrative had on his father, Pierce spared him the rest of the story; how he had found comfort in the silky arms of the notorious mulatto prostitute at Hickory Bottoms. He had given Drayton a hundred dollars in bank notes to apply to the gambling debt, departing the track penniless; but not to be denied the dusky pleasures of the beautiful whore, he had given her a silver pocket flask his father had presented to him on his birthday some years ago. Pierce knew his father was right—women *were* his weakness, especially improper women and yes, that *did* include Slade's fair-haired, buxom, and insatiable wife. But Pierce saw no good reason to contribute further to his father's distress at the moment.

Visibly shaken, Hammond sank onto the horsehair sofa facing the parlor's hearth, where a cheerful fire produced insufficient warmth to cast winter's chill from the spacious and high-ceilinged room. Pierce experienced a sudden stab of remorse; his misdeeds had proved to be a severe blow to his father—very severe indeed. Daniel Hammond appeared to be a robust man in excellent health, but Pierce had witnessed a slow yet steady deterioration in his father, which he contributed to the strain of making Magnolia a success. Magnolia was Daniel Hammond's reason for being, his one all-consuming passion, and it did seem to be draining the life out of him, drop by drop, year by year. His marriage, his son—these were secondary considerations; only honor was as important to Daniel Hammond as Magnolia.

And yet Pierce suddenly felt regret. He was sorry he had caused his father such pain. Gone, at least for the moment, was his resentment of his father for having put the plantation ahead of his family, not to mention his health, and for adhering to a foolish code of chivalry, the code of the cavalier to whom honor was more precious than life itself. In spite of everything, Pierce realized he still loved and even respected his father, for one could not love someone one didn't respect.

"Father," said Pierce, moving hesitantly toward Hammond. "I'm . . ."

Hammond raised a hand to silence him. "You have dishonored me. Nothing more need be said."

Resentment flared in Pierce again, hotter and stronger than ever before. The violent pendulum swing of emotion left him feeling weak. Without another word he left the big house.

CHAPTER SEVEN

The Decision

Without being conscious of doing so, Pierce Hammond steered his angry course from the big house to the blacksmith shop, a large stone structure with a vented timber roof and carriage doors on the east and west sides—this to allow work on buggy, brougham, or buckboard wagon during days of inclement weather. It was as though his feet had a will of their own, and when he thought about it, Pierce decided this had to do with childhood memories, of a carefree and innocent time when he had come here often, looking for Jobe, Old Jubal's son, his boyhood friend and playmate. It wasn't just Jobe, either; Jubal had treated him as though he were a son. In truth, Jubal had, in some ways, been more a father to him than Daniel Hammond.

In those younger years Pierce had never given much thought to the difference in the color of Jobe's skin and his own, much less to the significance of that difference in terms of the future of their friendship. But as the two boys grew up together, close as brothers, Daniel Hammond had concerned himself with the disturbing absence of what he perceived to be the proper master-slave dynamic in the relationship. When Pierce proved reluctant to correct the situation himself, Hammond had finally taken matters into his own hand and sold Jobe to a slave trader. That was the way Hammond dealt with most of his slave problems.

This he had done while both Pierce and Elizabeth were away, so that, returning to find his friend gone, Pierce was unable to learn the identity of the slave trader, or any information regarding Jobe's final destination. He tried as much for Jubal—who was, of course, devastated—as for himself. The best he could come up with were rumors that Jobe had been sold on the auction block in Mobile and carried off to Texas, and that the trader in question had moved on to Florida. One thing was certain; neither the trader nor Jobe ever returned to Magnolia. The deed was done, a dark and dirty deed in Pierce's opinion, and for a long time thereafter he had been unable even to look at his father, much less speak to him.

Jubal was working at the forge, hammering on a bent wheel rim, and at first he didn't notice Pierce standing in the doorway, and Pierce watched the grizzled slave at his work, thinking how much he would miss Jubal—and then thinking how strange it was to feel that way. His mind was playing tricks on him. He was looking at Jubal as if it would be his last chance because his mind was already made up. Without conscious effort he had come to a decision about his future.

When finally Jubal became aware of Pierce's presence, he laid down his mallet and wiped his big, gnarled, scarred hands on his old leather apron and straightened stiffly, his expression one of shame and apology.

"I didn't want no part of it, but Mastuh Slade he tol' me to . . ."

Pierce shook his head. "No matter, Jubal. Don't worry about that."

"I'm right proud of the way you stood up to him."

"Is that what I did?" Pierce smiled, dispirited. "Well, I won't have to again. I'm leaving Magnolia, Jubal."

"Marse Hammond sendin' you away?"

Pierce could tell that Jubal was deeply moved. He'd lost Jobe, and now he was going to lose Pierce. And in that instant Pierce knew exactly where he was going to go and what he was going to do.

"I'm going to Texas, Jubal. Father isn't sending me—it's my decision. I'm going to Texas and I'm going to try to find out what happened to Jobe."

Jubal's rheumy eyes brightened with hope. Hope, mused Pierce, was not something often seen in the eyes of a slave.

"If you be doin' this just for me . . ."

"No," said Pierce. "If anything, I'm doing it for myself. I only wish I could take you with me, Jubal. But Father would never let you go. You're too valuable to him. You're the best blacksmith in the country, bar none."

"No. No, I cain't go." Then, abruptly, Jubal had an idea. More than an idea—an inspiration. "But I knows someone you *could* take with you. Mingo Green."

"Mingo!" Pierce shook his head. "I don't think so."

"Hear me out now. For Mingo, life's gwine be one long misery from here on, iffen he stays here at Magnolia. You know why he was gettin' that cowskin this mornin'? On account he got caught sneakin' off to see that women of his, Sadie. He done got caught one time too many, Massuh Pierce. Marse Hammond, he won't put up with no mo' of Mingo's shenanigans. He either gwine break that fool Mingo of his bad habits, or sell him down the river. Either way, it don't look good for Mingo, now do it?"

"What makes you think my father would agree to let Mingo come with me?"

Jubal's expression was one of foxlike cunning. "You tell Marse Hammond that what that ol' fool Mingo need is some time away from Sadie. Nuff time for him to get that gal out of his head. You tell him he know how a nigger buck be, and that Mingo he won't even remember that gal's name after a few months of bein' gone."

"I thought absence was suppose to make the heart grow fonder." Pierce shook his head again. "I don't think Mingo will forget her as easy as all that, Jubal. He's been willing to risk his life just to be with her."

"'Course he ain't gwine forget. You knows it and I knows it. But what you think Marse Hammond gwine believe? You and Mingo been a heap of trouble for him of late. He'll let you both go, figurin' iffen you come back at all, you be of different minds, and his problems they be solved. And iffen you two don't come back, his problems *still* be solved."

Pierce gazed thoughtfully at Jubal for a moment. "Mingo won't go to Texas. He'll run off."

"You let me talk to Mingo. You go talk to Marse Hammond and make him see the light."

With less than perfect enthusiasm, Pierce agreed. Jubal came up to him and gave him a hug.

"That Texas, she be one dangerous lady, what I hear, Massuh Pierce. You come back safe and sound now."

Gripped by strong emotion, Pierce mumbled that he would. This was more affection than he would get from his natural father. Already he missed Jubal terribly. Jubal had been his one and only rock, dependable and compassionate, and now he was casting off from that mooring. Afflicted with second thoughts, he made his way slowly back to the big house.

He expected to find his father in the parlor, but Daniel Hammond had removed to the veranda, where he sat in grim disconsolation, gazing out across the sleeping fields of Magnolia plantation, not looking at Pierce, or acknowledging his presence in any way until Pierce began to speak—then Hammond interrupted.

"You have brought dishonor to the family name. I would have rather they had carried your bloodied corpse home to me than this."

Pierce smiled bitterly. So much for second thoughts! With fierce resolve he replied, "Father, I have decided to go to Texas."

Hammond was shocked, but he faltered for only a moment. "Texas is no place for cowards."

"I am going to Texas, and I would take Mingo Green with me. He is of no use to you in irons, and in irons you will have to keep him. A year away from Sadie will cure him."

Hammond continued to gaze at his fields, momentarily silent, and though Pierce searched for some sign of his father's true feelings on the hard stone of his deeply lined face, he could find no clue. Dared he hope that his father might be saddened by the prospect of his son's departure, and regretting at least a few of the harsh words he had so recently spoken?

"Go, then," said Hammond finally. "Go to Texas, and take that troublesome nigger with you."

Early the next morning Pierce left Magnolia. Jubal brought his favorite horse, the bluegrass thoroughbred mare, to the front of the house. Many of the other slaves also came to say good-bye. Mingo was there, too. Pierce could hardly believe he was fit enough to stand on his own two feet, much less travel, after yesterday's whipping. But when Pierce asked him if he was well enough to walk, Mingo nodded with perfect stoicism. Securing a rifle and a small carpetbag to his saddle, Pierce mounted up, waved to the congregation of Magnolia slaves, and rode down the lane between the fields where a thin layer of pristine white frost covered the rich black soil. He didn't bother looking back to see if his father had emerged onto the veranda, or was standing at a window to watch him go.

One person Pierce was happy enough not to see that morning was Slade, and he breathed a sigh of relief on that score when he and Mingo had put Magnolia behind them. But they were just a mile or two down the road when the sound of a horse at the gallop turned Pierce's head. To his dismay, the rider was Slade. With a grimace Pierce checked the thoroughbred and waited for the Magnolia overseer.

As he drew his horse alongside the bluegrass mare, Slade flashed a wolfish grin. "You ain't so purty anymore, *Mister* Hammond. You ought to know better'n to tangle with the likes of me."

"If you care to dismount, we can pick up where we left off," snapped Pierce.

"Oh ho!" exclaimed Slade, feigning alarm. "The pup still has a few teeth left in its head."

"Go back to work, Slade."

"I didn't want you to get away without saying good-bye. And my wife sends her best regards."

Pierce was apprehensive now; he could take no moral high ground where Martha Slade was concerned. She was blond and voluptuous and insatiable in her sexual appetites, and his will had not been strong enough to resist her, even though he had known from the start that Slade would try to kill him if the overseer ever caught them together. That hadn't happened, and Pierce was wondering if Slade was trying now, one last attempt, to goad Pierce into a confession. Slade didn't appear to be armed, and Pierce was—the rifle tied to his saddle and a pistol in his carpetbag—but that wouldn't stop Slade; he would try to kill Pierce with his bare hands, and Pierce knew the man was quite capable of doing just that.

"If you've got something to say, Slade, just come right out with it."

Slade leaned forward aggressively in his saddle. "I know you've lain with my woman. I swear there was a time or two I could smell you on her skin. And I would have killed you long before now, had I any solid proof at all. Without proof, though, they'd have hanged me certain."

"You're a damned fool, Slade."

Slade exhaled sharply. Lips compressed, he straightened up in the saddle and glanced darkly at Mingo.

"You won't keep this one around for long, *Mister* Hammond. He's got that rabbit look in his eye. He'll sneak off before you get halfway to Texas. I'll put my brand on you yet, boy. With any luck, your massuh will let me take a knife to you. Once you're gelded, you won't have no further interest in that sweet little piece of dark meat over at Ravenmoor."

That was all he had to say, and he wheeled his horse sharply and kicked it viciously into a canter, heading back down the road from whence he had come.

They made poor time that day. Mobile was eighty miles away, and Pierce knew he could be there by tomorrow morning if he didn't have Mingo to slow him down. The slave never complained, but one couldn't take the abuse he had suffered yesterday without it taking a toll, and Pierce kept his impatience in check and the energetic mare on a short rein throughout the day. By afternoon Mingo's stride had degenerated into a weary shuffle, and finally Pierce stopped and dismounted and told Mingo to get on the mare. Mingo just stared at him as though he thought Pierce was trying to play a trick on him.

"Hurry up," said Pierce, exasperated. "Get into the saddle. We'll make better time if you ride and I walk. That's an order, damn you."

Mingo stubbornly shook his head, and Pierce realized the refusal did not stem from deference, but rather from pride. The slave would accept no kindness from him.

"Don't be so mule-headed," snapped Pierce. "I'm not Slade. I'm not my father. You've got no reason to hate me. I stopped Slade from branding you a runaway."

"And you think I oughta get down on my hands and knees and lick your boots?" rasped Mingo. "Nossuh, Marse Hammond. You ain't all *that* different from your pa."

"You're a fool," Pierce laughed, mildly shocked that Mingo would take such a tone of voice with him.

"Mr. Slade, he be a fool. And I be a fool. But you be the biggest fool of all if you think I'm goin' to Texas with you."

"You're forgetting you're a slave."

"How can I forget that?"

"You should have paid more attention to what Jubal told you. I know he explained what would happen to you if you tried to go back. And I know you heard what Slade said this morning. He'll castrate you."

"I ain't goin' to Texas," said Mingo, sullen.

Perturbed, Pierce glanced down the road in the direction of Magnolia, of a mind to take Mingo right back and be done with him. But he didn't want to go back. He didn't want to waste the time, or see his father again; most of all he didn't want to disappoint old Jubal. But this was an annoyance. This was what he got for trying to help someone who didn't want his help.

Disgusted, he mounted up and gestured curtly at Mingo.

"Walk on ahead of me," he said. "And know that if you try to run, I will shoot you in the leg. It'll be for your own good, of course."

"Oh, thank you, Massuh," said Mingo. Head held high, he proceeded down the road, and for the first time Pierce saw the back of his shirt. Some of the long cuts made by Slade's cowskin had opened up, and the shirt was drenched with blood.

CHAPTER EIGHT

The Dream

On the road to Mobile, Gabe Cochran was reticent. Boone Tasker calculated that his traveling companion scarcely said ten words during the course of the first day of their journey.

While Gabe rode the old plow mare—the only thing associated with the homestead that he had brought along with him—Boone was mounted on a cheap "henskin" saddle strapped to a six-year-old roan who was hardly less phlegmatic than the farmer's ancient, swayback sorrel. During his stint as schoolteacher, Boone had rarely been paid for his services in hard money; what little he had received had been assiduously put back in a fund earmarked for the ring he had hoped to place on the appropriate finger of Miss Sarah Ambler's left hand. It seemed only fitting that now he should have spent that money on the roan—the means by which he intended to put Sarah and that whole unhappy episode behind him.

There was another member of their party. Gabe's bluetick hound, with whom Boone was acquainted from the several hunting excursions he and the hard-luck farmer had shared, followed along behind the two riders. It looked to Boone as though the white-muzzled hound had even less life left in his flea-bitten hide than the plow mare—if that was possible. Boone expected at any moment to see the dog flop down in the middle of the road and watch them ride on with sorrowful brown eyes, and he decided that, if it became necessary, he would carry the dog across the front of his saddle rather than abandon the creature. Gabe paid the hound no attention, as usual, and Boone thought that was a pretty poor way to reciprocate such dumb devotion. But the hound proved resilient, and stuck with them, its black-and-pink speckled tongue lolling and drooling saliva, and its big paws plopping loudly against the road's hardpack.

Boone was anxious to reach Mobile. As he had explained to Gabe, if they wanted a free sea passage to Texas, they needed to enlist in Jack Shackelford's Alabama Red Rovers. Boone had seen an advertisement Captain Jack had run in the *Mobile Register*, urging all those interested in striking a blow for freedom—and earning Texas land in the bargain—to hasten to Mobile and sign up. Shackelford intended to sail by the tenth of the month, at the very latest. There was no time to waste.

As for Shackelford himself, Boone knew little, and Gabe even less. The man was a physician by trade, and he had seen some action against the troublesome Seminoles in recent years. He was acquainted with Sam Houston, and claimed to be engaged in regular correspondence with the famous commander in chief of the Texas army.

In spite of Boone's impatience, an entire day had

been required for both he and Gabe to wrap up their affairs and depart. Gabe's wife had passed away on Tuesday morning; Thursday night found them thirty miles shy of their destination. Resolved to get an early start, they camped just off the road, building a fire so that they could have some hot coffee to go with their smoked venison and parched corn. The night was bitter cold, and the meager warmth of the fire was an absolute necessity, even though the road to Mobile was notorious for being the haunt of a dangerous gang of cutthroat thieves.

"Not that I'm really worried about getting waylaid by those highwaymen," Boone told Gabe as they huddled, blanket-wrapped, around the crackling fire. "Somehow I just know we'll reach Texas. That's where my destiny is waiting for me. I can feel it in my bones."

Gabe merely grunted, only half listening, staring morosely into the dancing flames.

"Oh, I know I probably told you before, at one time or another, that Sarah was my future. But if something doesn't work out after you've done the best you can do, well you just have to move on to something else."

Gabe gave no indication he had heard a word.

"I guess," sighed Boone, trying not to get depressed, "I'm the eternal optimist."

At that moment the bluetick hound raised its big ugly head and let out a deep bark. Boone was so startled that he very nearly pitched forward into the fire as he tried to get to his feet and grab his rifle at the same time—only to discover that, having been seated cross-legged for over an hour, he'd lost all feeling in his right leg. The hound was on its feet now and continued its mournful baying—a noise so loud it jangled every nerve in Boone's body. Hopping around on one leg, Boone tried to check the priming of his smoothbore musket, wondering if it was true that you didn't hear the report of the gun that fired the bullet that killed you—and fully expecting to find out in the next second or two.

"Hello the camp!"

Gabe had melted into the darkness, beyond the reach of the firelight. Now, quite calmly, he said, "Ease up, Boone. I know that voice."

Boone looked up as two men emerged from the night, coming from the road. One was mounted on the most handsome horse Boone had ever seen. The rider was a gentleman if the cut of his longcoat, made of fine pilotcloth, was any indication. The other man, on foot, was black. He had a wary, half-wild look in his eyes as he watched the baying hound with some trepidation.

"It's Pierce Hammond," said Gabe, stepping back into the firelight. "Shut up, dog."

The hound quit barking, wagging its tail at the sound of its master's voice.

"Have we met, sir?" asked Hammond amiably.

"I've seen you a time or two," said Gabe. "At the cockfights, mostly."

Pierce turned his attention to Boone. "And have we met as well?"

Boone shook his head. "I don't think so."

Gabe glanced curiously at Boone. The school-

teacher's tone was decidedly cool. If Boone hadn't met Hammond, why the veiled hostility? Gabe decided it had to be because Pierce Hammond was of the planter class, made from the same mold as Boone's rivals for the affection of Sarah Ambler. Or maybe there was more to it than that.

"Mind if I join your camp?" asked Pierce.

"You're welcome," said Gabe. "There might be a little coffee left."

Pierce dismounted. "Warm yourself by the fire, Mingo."

"I ain't cold."

"Go sit by the fire," said Pierce sternly.

Mingo complied. It was then that Boone saw the blood that stained the back of the slave's shirt.

"Good God," he gasped. "What have you done to this poor man?"

"I've done nothing," said Pierce tersely, reacting to Boone's antagonism with an iciness of his own, "except perhaps save his life."

Boone was clearly skeptical. "There's a novel concept—one of your class caring enough about a slave's life to save it."

"I take it, sir, by your accent that you are from the North."

"I am from Illinois," said Boone proudly.

"Yes. Now I know who you are. You're the schoolteacher."

"Not any longer."

"We're bound for Mobile," said Gabe. "We're aiming to join up with Jack Shackelford and his Red Rovers and go to Texas."

"Texas is my destination, too," said Pierce.

Glancing at Mingo, who sat near the fire, staring off into the night, he added, "*Our* destination."

"You're welcome to travel with us," said Gabe.

Pierce glanced wryly at Boone just as Boone fired a sharp look at Gabe. "Am I?"

Boone grimaced. "It's a free country—if you're a white man, that is."

"Just my luck, to fall in with an abolitionist."

Pierce meant it as a joke, but Boone didn't take it that way. "I believe that this man is a human being," said Boone, pointing to Mingo, "and not chattel property. I believe human bondage is wrong, an affront to God, and that the institution of slavery is morally reprehensible and a stain on the honor of our republic."

"Very nicely said. As to honor, it is a word I've heard too much lately."

"I do not consider myself an abolitionist," continued Boone. "I don't approve of men like William Lloyd Garrison, who have no respect for the Constitution, and who claim they are willing to destroy the Union rather than live in a nation where slavery is tolerated. Such a view is too extreme for me."

"I'm glad to hear it. As for me, I'm no secessionist. So perhaps we can both occupy a middle ground and agree that the Union is precious and must be preserved. But I wonder why you, a Northerner, chose to live and work in the South if you have no liking for Southern ways."

"There are many opportunities for schoolteachers in the South," said Boone. "I thought I would take advantage of the situation. I realize now I made a mistake."

"Then why Texas? Why not go back to Illinois? I presume you have family there."

"I have a brother. Will is his name. But my parents are dead. There isn't much to draw me back to Illinois. I'm going to try my luck in Texas."

Pierce nodded. "And you?" he asked Gabe. "You have a farm and family, don't you?"

"His wife and daughter passed away," said Boone. "They think it was yellow fever."

Pierce saw the grief on Gabe's face and was mortified. "I beg your forgiveness, sir, and offer my most sincere condolences."

Too stricken to speak, Gabe just nodded.

"Well," said Pierce, in a hurry to change the subject, "here we are, then. The three of us, bound for Texas."

"I count four of us," said Boone.

"For the time being. But Mingo swears he won't go to Texas. He will try to run away, perhaps this very night. I would ask both of you gentlemen to help me prevent that."

"Don't count on me," said Boone with a harsh laugh. "I won't lift a finger to stop a man from seeking his own freedom."

"You don't know the whole story, friend," said Pierce tolerantly. "If he runs away, he will surely forfeit his life. His only hope is to stay with me." And he explained the situation—how Mingo had been caught leaving the plantation without permission to see his woman, a Ravenmoor slave; how he had been punished by the sadistic Slade; and what fate lay in store for him if he tried to return. "So you see," concluded Pierce, "that we must protect Mingo from himself."

Boone wasn't convinced. He wanted no part of this. But Gabe nodded, in full accord. "I'll help you keep an eye on him, Mr. Hammond."

"Please, call me Pierce."

Later that night, when Pierce and Mingo were asleep, Boone stirred in his blankets and sat up to find Gabe keeping watch.

"Can't sleep?" asked Gabe.

Disgusted, Boone shook his head. Warming his frozen hands at the fire, he glanced at Pierce. "That figures. The gentleman sleeps, and you do his dirty work for him."

"I can't sleep anyhow. And I believe his story, even if you don't. What have you got against him?"

"It isn't him, personally. Just what he represents. And why do you act so subservient, Gabe?"

"What does that mean? That high-falutin' word."

"You act like he's some kind of lord. *Mr.* Hammond! For God's sake, he's no better than you or I. You're his equal, Gabe. That's what this country is all about."

Gabe frowned. "You reckon you're as good as him and his kind, do you."

"I most certainly do."

"Then how come Miss Sarah Ambler's pa sent her away rather than have her marry the likes of you?"

"That's just the point. They *think* they're better, but they're not."

"I dunno," said Gabe, glancing at the sleeping Pierce. "He don't seem like such a bad sort. And what will it matter what he is, or what I am, once we get to Texas? Like as not, we'll all finish up on the wrong end of a Mexican bayonet."

After a long silence Boone said, "You go on and try to sleep, Gabe. I'll keep watch."

Gabe shook his head. "Can't. Every time I drift off I have this same dream. I see black banners against a red sky, and I hear a booming sound, like thunder, except it goes on and on, and above all that I hear a sweet voice singing, and I know it's Maggie—she always liked to sing, you know . . ."

Choking on his grief, Gabe hung his head.

"You'll see her again, Gabe," said Boone, feeling helplessly inadequate to the task of consoling his friend. "I firmly believe we will meet our loved ones again in heaven."

"Yeah," said Gabe raggedly, swiping at his eyes with a big, work-callused hand. "Sure. I'll see her again. Won't be long, either. No, it won't be long, little darlin', and Daddy will be with you again . . ."

CHAPTER NINE

The Rovers

They reached Mobile early in the afternoon of the following day.

Mobile had grown by leaps and bounds since 1813, when it had first been occupied by Americans following the cession of Western Florida by the Spanish. Under Spanish rule it had been a somnolent and somewhat seedy little seacoast village of less than three hundred inhabitants. Ten years later, that population had increased to three thousand, and now more than four thousand people called Mobile home. *Niles' Register*, one of the country's foremost newspapers, vouchsafed that Mobile was fast becoming "a place of great importance," and predicted that soon it would be one of the biggest and busiest of Southern towns.

There was one, and only one, reason for this. Cotton.

Cotton was King in the "Southwest." Twenty-five years earlier, the "Black Belt" of southern Alabama had produced a paltry twenty-five thousand bales of cotton; in 1836 it would produce a quarter of a million. And most of this cotton moved through Mobile. The export of cotton was Mobile's chief trade. It's citizens were preoccupied with the Liverpool cotton report, for they knew that the rise or fall of cotton prices in England meant life or death for Mobile. As one clergyman told his flock, cotton was "the circulating blood that gives life to this city."

Virtually every commercial activity served the cotton trade, in one way or another. Factors sold the cotton and merchants obtained goods for inland planters and their families. Local bankers provided financial exchange and credit for enterprises directly related to the cultivation, sale, and shipping of cotton. Local hotels and theaters attracted upcountry planters. A fleet of steamboats carried cotton from the plantations to Mobile via the Alabama, Tombigbee, and Warrior rivers. And Mobile's vigorous slave trade provided a steady flow of labor for the cotton plantations.

Several packet lines had offices in Mobile, carrying the cotton to Liverpool, and returning by way of New York with domestic and foreign manufactured goods. Mobile Bay, sheltered from the Gulf's capricious weather by a string of islands, and protected from pirate activity by three forts—Powell, Gaines, and Morgan—was usually filled with lighters, tug steamers, bayboats, sloops, and schooners.

The town itself was located on the western bank of the Mobile River, just above the point of that stream's confluence with the bay. The affluent had their homes in the central section of the city, between Congress and Monroe Streets, and from Royal Street west to Lawrence. Royal joined Water and Franklin Streets in running south to the Lower Docks area on the northern tip of the bay; here were the warehouses and cotton presses and the residences of the city's working class. Here, too, were the less reputable business concerns—the brothels, gin houses, and gambling dens.

Arriving in the city, Boone Tasker and his traveling companions had little difficulty learning the whereabouts of Jack Shackelford and his Red Rovers. Boone, for one, was tremendously relieved to find that the volunteer company had not yet departed for Texas. Shackelford had hired out a meeting hall located between the Public Square and the riverfront. Fortune smiled on Boone; Dr. Shackelford was the first man they met at the front steps of the meeting hall.

The leader of the Red Rovers was a tall, spare man, straight as a lightning rod, with the stern face of the ascetic. His mouth was set in grim lines, thin-lipped and wide; his eyes burned with the fire of the brimstone Bible-thumper. When Boone told him they had come to enlist, Shackelford looked at them one by one with such intensity, such a piercing gaze, that Boone was convinced he could see into the deepest recesses of their souls. Here was a man who could judge the timbre of other men without erring.

"You've cut it fine, gentlemen," said Shackelford, his voice rasping like an iron file on a horseshoe. "Mighty fine, indeed. I have just come from a conference with the skipper of the coastal steamer, *Mathilda*. We board her in the morning and set sail for Texas."

"Does that mean you will take us on, sir?" asked Boone.

Shackelford glanced at the half dozen or so young men who loitered in the vicinity of the meeting hall steps. Two were reading together the day's edition of the *Mobile Register*. A couple more were smoking their pipes and watching the world go by. Another was sharpening an Arkansas toothpick that looked plenty sharp already. From within the meeting hall issued the racket of many more volunteers. Every one of the men Boone could see wore some article of red clothing, a shirt or a pair of trousers or a red ribbon around the crown of his hat or a red sash around his waste. This, then, was the badge of the Red Rover.

"I suppose I could sign on three more," said Shackelford. He eyed Pierce again. "This Negro is your manservant?"

"Yes, sir. My name is Pierce Hammond. My father owns Magnolia plantation, about eighty miles up the Tombigbee."

"I know Daniel Hammond. And you, sir?" He swung his gaze to Boone. "Where are you from?"

"I was born in Illinois, sir."

"Well, we won't hold that against you." Shackelford was only half joking. He looked next at Gabe. "You have the cut of a farmer, my friend. If you want a homestead in Texas, you will have to fight for it."

"I'm all done with farming, Captain. It's the fight I'm after."

Shackelford nodded curtly. "That's what I like to hear. Very well. Come with me, gentlemen."

A few minutes later they were officially enlisted in the Alabama Red Rovers.

The meeting hall had been transformed into a barracks where a hundred or more men had been living for days in cramped and cluttered confines. A single iron potbelly stove, though stoked continually day and night, could not entirely keep the chill at bay, but Pierce decided that was just as well; the stench of unwashed bodies would only have been worse when combined with the sultry heat of the Gulf Coast.

Some of the Red Rovers gathered around the table, located in a front corner of the meeting hall, where Captain Jack, as his men called him, brandished a green leather-bound ledger and had Boone, Pierce, and Gabe sign their names—or, in Gabe's case, make his mark. Looking at the faces of these men, Pierce wondered about their backgrounds. Many, it appeared, were cut from the same cloth as Gabe Cochran—poor dirt farmers willing to risk their lives on the chance of winning a new start in the land of fable, Texas. A few, though, were dressed like Pierce, in good broadcloth and linen. Gentlemen, mused Pierce, of the black sheep variety, no doubt.

"You'll get no wages," Shackelford told them, "unless the Republic of Texas sees fit to pay you, and I doubt if the republic has a handful of shinplasters in its coffers. But, if you survive, and Texas wins the independence she deserves, I have it on good authority—a promise made by General Sam Houston himself, and Houston is a man whose word is his bond—that each of you will receive at least one full section of prime land, if not more. Texas may be short on cash money, but she's got plenty of land, and I'm talking about good, fertile land, gentlemen, where a man can put his roots down deep. Free land, so you'll be beholden to no banker or merchant. That means a lot."

He peered at them a moment, studying their faces, gauging their reactions to his words. Boone realized that neither he nor his traveling companions were too impressed by Sam Houston's offer, and it probably showed. The last thing Gabe Cochran wanted was another farm, and Pierce Hammond wasn't the kind to make his living from the soil. And Boone knew his own hands were not made to fit a plow's handles.

"Tonight," said Captain Jack, "you are free to do what you will. This may be your last chance for a decent meal and a stiff drink or a hot bath. If you've got the money to spend, Mobile offers all the amenities a soldier on leave could ask for. Take advantage of them if you wish, and if you can afford to. But at dawn we leave this place and proceed to the Lower Docks to board the *Mathilda*, and I will wait for no one."

As Boone and Gabe moved among the other Red Rovers, exchanging introductions, Pierce pulled Mingo aside.

"I have a few places to go," he said, "and you can either stay here or come with me. I'm going to be entirely too busy to keep an eye on you all night, so you can try to run off if you're still of a mind to. But remember that you are smack in the middle of Mobile, and you won't get far without papers, of which you have none. You know what will happen if they catch you here. They'll slap you in irons and run an advertisement. But I won't pay a reward to get you back, so you'll end up on the auction block. You'll not see your woman again, I promise you."

"Reckon I ain't got no choice, then, do I?" asked Mingo, surly.

"None whatsoever. So are you staying here, or coming with me?"

"Comin' with you, massuh."

Pierce nodded. He wasn't at all sure he had convinced Mingo of the uselessness of flight—the man still had that look in his eye and that tone in his voice that spelled trouble.

But Pierce would waste no more time trying to save Mingo from himself. He was going to take Jack Shackelford's suggestion to heart. It had hit him with full force that he was going off to war—and, worse still, war in Texas. Half-civilized, frontier Texas, where a man could not expect to find those "amenities" of which Shackelford had spoken, and which Pierce Hammond enjoyed so much. Eat, drink, and be merry, for tomorrow you may die. Wasn't that the soldier's motto?

He wasn't at all sure he was going to like soldiering. But it was a little late now for second thoughts. And he'd be damned if he went back to Magnolia. No, for better or worse he was wedded to Texas. And it would probably be for worse. At least he could have one last fling. He knew Mobile quite well—knew where to find that good meal, that stiff drink, that hot bath. Knew, as well, where to find a high-stakes card game, a cockfight, and a courtesan. It was the latter he was particularly interested in finding, and he had a woman in mind. He wondered if a place like Texas would have any women at all. Probably none worth a second glance.

His first stop was the Bank of Mobile.

There was an association between the bank and the Hammond name going back nearly twenty years. Chartered in 1819, the Bank of Mobile's opening—indeed, its very existence—was threatened by the machinations of a clever embezzler who made off with most of the cash accumulated as capital. Thanks to a loan from Daniel Hammond, the institution was still able to open its doors. A few years ago, the bank had made a public offering of stock; Daniel Hammond bought nearly 10 percent of the $200,000 of stock at a special discount, which he alone, apart from the bank president's brother, enjoyed.

During his stint in the Alabama legislature—every planter worth his salt dabbled in politics—Daniel Hammond had done the bank another favor by leading the fight against the establishment of a branch of the Bank of the United States in Alabama. The BUS was considered a threat to every state bank in existence, the Bank of Mobile chief among them. The BUS resolution failed to pass by a single vote—and that vote had been Daniel Hammond's.

Pierce expected to be treated like royalty as soon as he walked through the doors, and he wasn't disappointed. In the privacy of the bank president's posh office, he very casually and confidently lied through his teeth, claiming that he had lost a note written by his father that authorized him to withdraw all the funds he needed from the Hammond account. The bank president did not hesitate to present him with a bank draft.

As he took up the quill and dipped it in the president's inkwell and prepared to fill in the draft's dollar amount, Pierce had a sudden attack of conscience. He was of a mind to take every penny from his father's account. Not that he actually knew how much that would come to, but he was confident that there had to be a minimum of $25,000 there for the taking. But at the last moment he wrote the draft for $250. He derived a certain satisfaction from knowing that his father would eventually realize that he could have taken it all, and yet had refrained from doing so. That would surprise the old man! Pierce thought of it as making a statement, a declaration of personal independence. As though he were saying that a paltry $250 was all he wanted from his father, and the rest be hanged. *You can keep your money and you can keep Magnolia, too, for all I care. I'll make my own way with this modest sum and I'll need nothing more from you, thank you very much.*

Of course Pierce knew he was just fooling himself. He wasn't going to use the $250 to make a new start; these funds were for one last fling, one final night on the town, and he had no intention of keeping even a few dollars back. What good was money anyway in a war-torn wilderness like Texas?

Leaving the bank, Pierce was a little surprised to find Mingo waiting outside with his horse. This was the first time since their departure from Magnolia that he had left the slave alone, and he'd expected Mingo to run, and damn the risks. But

Mingo had shown better sense. Not that Pierce really cared. He'd done what he could, and not for Mingo's sake, but for old Jubal's.

His next stop was Smooth's Hotel, which could boast of a better than average restaurant. While he was dining, a professional gambler by the name of Duncan, with whom he was acquainted, approached his table, and Pierce accepted the cardsharp's invitation to a high-stakes game of cards in a room upstairs. A few hours later, Pierce had lost nearly all of his money and had enjoyed every minute of it. A few too many gin slings and shots of sour mash had left him somewhat muddled mentally, but not to the degree that he lost every cent.

"You won't get it all, Duncan," he declared. "I'm going to spread it around. I have a particular young lady in mind."

"Unlucky at cards," said Duncan, chuckling, "lucky at love."

"Love has nothing to do with it," replied Pierce with a sly wink and left the room, swaying slightly.

Outside the hotel, Pierce was surprised by the dark. He'd lost track of time, and checked his key-winder—a splendid gold timepiece his father had given him—by the light from the storm lanterns that flanked the front door of Smooth's. It was late and chilly—the cold crept into his bones and sobered him a bit. He shuddered involuntarily. Seeing this as he rose from where he had been sitting on the ground near the foot of the hotel veranda's steps, holding the reins of Pierce's Kentucky thoroughbred, Mingo said, "You get so you don't pay no mind to the cold after you done been sittin' out in it for hours."

Pierce smirked. "I see you've learned better than to run off. Now if you could just learn to show some respect for your betters."

"Yassuh, Marse Hammond." There was no mistaking the sneer in Mingo's voice.

Pierce took the reins, nearly fell as he tried to fit booted foot into stirrup and mount up, then finally settled more or less firmly in the saddle—no thanks to Mingo, who just stood by without making any move to assist him—and, with a slight tap of the heels, got the blooded mare into a walk and proceeded down the street. Mingo followed along behind.

It soon became apparent to Mingo that they were entering the seamier side of Mobile, the area near the Lower Docks. Here were the dens of iniquity, where the cardsharps, whores, and cutthroats plied their trade, the stomping grounds favored by the sailors of a dozen nationalities on shore leave. Pierce Hammond drew a lot of attention; seldom did a blueblood venture into this quarter. Mingo was wary—if a gentleman's life was worth little here, the life of the gentleman's slave was worth even less. Pierce, however, seemed blissfully unaware of the peril. Mingo decided he was too drunk to know any better.

But Pierce knew what he was about. He had a definite destination in mind, and soon he checked the thoroughbred in front of a weathered clapboard house of "shotgun" design, the first in a row of dingy habitations half hidden in the deep black shadows cast by tall oaks festooned with Spanish moss. At the end of the street stood a high wall overgrown with ivy, with a tall iron gate hanging crookedly on its rusting hinges, encompassing an old cemetery. Mingo's skin crawled. He didn't like buryin' grounds.

"Wait until I get inside," Pierce told him, "then take the mare back to the meeting hall. You think you can find your way? Good. I'll expect you back here at dawn. Understand?"

Mingo nodded. He watched Pierce climb the rickety porch and knock insistently on the front door of the shotgun house. The door opened. Mingo couldn't see who opened it, because Pierce blocked his view, but he heard a woman's salacious laughter, and then Pierce was inside, and the door was closed, and Mingo was alone in the uneasy darkness.

"Damn fool," muttered Mingo. He looked at the thoroughbred and contemplated Pierce Hammond's instructions, then thought about Sadie and his unborn child. A wild and reckless urge had been simmering inside him ever since leaving Magnolia, and now it surged against his heart and overcame his common sense, and he began seriously to contemplate his chances. They were slim—very slim. But if he got on that boat to Texas in the morning, he would have no chance at all. If he went to Texas, he was sure he would never see his Sadie again.

"I know what you t'inkin'."

The voice, heavy with the lyrical accent of a man from the sugar islands, startled Mingo, and he whirled, the hair at the nape of his neck standing on end.

A man as black as the shadows that gathered thickly on this old street of sin and death was gliding toward him from the direction of the shotgun house. Oddly, he made no sound as he moved, no more sound than a spirit would make. He was tall and skeleton-thin, and clad in a long, tattered black coat and wore a stovepipe hat, the crown bent, on his head. His hair hung down to his shoulders. His eyes burned like hot coals, as though illuminated from within by their own lurid, hellish lights. A sickly sweet odor emanated from him, an odor Mingo could not identify, and Mingo thought for one irrational instant that this creature was a zombie, arisen from its grave in that cemetery yonder to prowl the Mobile streets in the midnight gloom.

"You t'inkin'," said the man, his voice smooth and sibilant, "you gwine take de massuh's hoss and run for freedom."

Mingo was shocked. Could this scarecrow apparition actually read his mind?

"Who are you?" he asked, his voice raspy and tight with dread.

"Dey call me Big Tom. I be with Desiree, de lady yo' massuh has a strong hankerin' for. But I know what you want. You wants to be free. But ain't no man truly free while he live. Every man be de slave to sumpin. Even yo' massuh is a slave to his passion for Desiree. No man free till he die. You t'ink you got a powerful reason to live. You gots sumpin worth livin' for, but you gots to ask yo'self if it's sumpin worth *dyin'* for."

Mingo instinctively backed away. This was no spirit, no zombie. Just a man—a crazy, wicked, dangerous man, a man who chuckled softly, a sound like the work-callused palms of a pair of hands being rubbed together, as he saw the fear in Mingo.

"Go on," whispered Big Tom gleefully. "Go on and take dat hoss and ride. Yo' massuh ain't gwine need dat hoss no more. Go on, if what you want is worth *dyin'* for."

With one agile leap Mingo was in the saddle. He gave Big Tom a last look, but even at close quarters he couldn't see anything of the man except is eyes—the longcoat seemed to gather the dark heart of the night beneath its folds, obscuring its owner's form and features. Mingo had never been scared of anything as he was of Big Tom at this moment, and the experience so unnerved him that he wheeled the Kentucky mare around and kicked it into a gallop and left the street as though the Devil himself were after his immortal soul.

CHAPTER TEN

The Quadroon

In a few moments the galling fear had abandoned Mingo, and he checked the thoroughbred, looking around to get his bearings—for a time he had been consumed by a single thought, to get away from Big Tom, to put as much distance as possible between the two of them, and he'd paid no attention to where he was going. Now he found himself on a street where several bordellos and gambling halls were in operation. Dark shapes moved on the unlighted sidewalks, and Mingo wondered if any of them thought it odd that a slave was astride a fine blooded Kentucky mare, a gentleman's horse. If anyone noticed, they would naturally assume he had stolen the animal—the thoroughbred was a rope around his neck.

He steered the responsive horse into an alley, dismounted, and leaned against a wall of peeling clapboard, wiping at the cold sweat on his forehead, and trying to decide what he should do next. One thing was certain—if he wanted any chance at all of getting out of Mobile, he'd have to do it on foot. This alley was as good a place as any to leave the mare. If he started now, he ought to be well clear of the city by daybreak. After that, eighty miles lay between him and Sadie. Eighty dangerous miles for a black man without papers. And if he made it, then what? Sadie would be willing to run away, but where would they run? Where could they go? Mingo didn't want to put Sadie and the baby she carried through the hardship and peril that a fugitive slave had to endure. He cursed softly. It was hopeless. He was trapped. There was no escape.

Unless . . . unless Pierce Hammond made him a free man. Manumitted him. Provided him with his freedom papers. Then, maybe, if he could somehow make enough money, he could buy Sadie from Marse Ambler. But maybe Marse Ambler wouldn't want to sell Sadie. Mingo shook his head. One thing at a time. He had to think. Make a plan. Pierce wouldn't free him for nothing. He'd have to make Pierce beholden to him somehow. So beholden to him that when he asked for his freedom, Pierce Hammond would have to oblige. Yes, that was it.

Like a river that flows first past one island and then another, the current of this thinking took Mingo from this idea to the next one—one that involved Big Tom. Hadn't Big Tom said that Pierce Hammond wasn't going to need the thoroughbred anymore? Of course Big Tom had just been trying to lure him into trouble by encouraging him to steal the mare. There were folks like that, who took pleasure out of getting other folks into hot water.

But what if a more sinister meaning attached itself to Big Tom's words? What if he literally meant that Pierce Hammond would *never* need this mare again? What if . . .

"Hey, you! What you doin' skulkin' like a dog in there?"

A burly shape filled the mouth of the alley.

"Come on out here where I can see you."

Mingo's first instinct was to run. But he reminded himself that the only way out of trouble like this was to use his head, not his feet. He stepped out of the deepest shadows, away from the wall.

"What you doin', boy?"

Mingo couldn't tell anything about the man, except that he was white, and that was all a slave needed to know, because every white man was an authority figure to whom a slave was answerable for his very existence.

"I be waitin' for my massuh, Pierce Hammond," said Mingo, as subservient as he could manage.

"Pierce Hammond, huh?" Suspicion lingered in the man's gruff voice.

"Yessuh. He tol' me to wait right here till he gets back. I don't know where he gone off to."

The man grunted. "Pierce Hammond, you say." Then he nodded and moved on.

Mingo started breathing again. Now he was convinced. He had no hope of reaching Sadie if he became a fugitive. He'd be captured for sure, and then there was no telling what would become of him. No, he had to stay with Hammond, because the Hammond name carried weight—and that name on his freedom papers would mean something. Somehow he had to manipulate the situation so that Pierce Hammond owed him those papers.

And Big Tom was the key.

Making up his mind, Mingo led the thoroughbred out of the alley, leaving by the back way, keeping to the shadows and side streets, hurrying as fast as he could, but not daring to return to the saddle, thinking that he might be able to explain himself if he was stopped and questioned as long as he was leading and not riding the mare. "Marse Hammond tol' me to bring this hoss back to that place where the Red Rovers be . . ." And they would probably believe it, because he was walking the mare and not sitting in his master's saddle.

But no one stopped him, and when he reached the meeting hall, he played his role to perfection, anxiously explaining to Gabe and Boone why he thought Big Tom was planning to murder Pierce Hammond.

"We'd best go," said Gabe, concerned.

Boone wasn't enthusiastic. "A man wanders into that part of town he's just asking for trouble."

"We'd better learn to stick together," said Gabe. "We're all Red Rovers now, remember? That means we stand with each other, no matter what."

"I suppose that is what it means," allowed Boone, acknowledging that Gabe's logic was, sadly, inescapable. They were Red Rovers, and whether they liked each other or not didn't figure into the equation. "Okay. Let's go."

"Reckon we might ought to bring some of the others."

Boone looked around the makeshift barracks.

He'd met a score or more of these men, but he didn't feel he knew them well enough to ask them to go down to the Lower Docks and possibly risk life and limb in the process. Besides, he wasn't sure that this wasn't a false alarm, a case of Mingo crying wolf. He didn't want to make himself the laughingstock of the company.

"I wouldn't have thought you'd care what happened to Hammond," he told the slave.

Mingo knew he had to be careful. Boone Tasker was nobody's fool.

"Somethin' happen to Marse Pierce," he replied, "I wind up back at Magnolia, and I don't last long then. Mr. Slade, he see to that."

Boone nodded. Mingo seemed to have his own brand of unarguable logic. He turned to Gabe. "This might be an incident your friend Pierce won't want to make common knowledge. The two of us can handle things."

"Right. Mingo, you'll have to take us there."

They left the meeting hall. Gabe and Boone fetched their horses; their mounts were being kept, along with those of the other Red Rovers, in a tannery yard only a block away. Shackelford had made arrangements to transport all the horses to Texas, too, since it was not known whether an adequate number of remounts would be available where they were going.

This time, in the company of two white men, Mingo could safely ride, and he led the way through the streets of Mobile in Pierce Hammond's saddle, astride the high-stepping thoroughbred, without fear of challenge from strangers. A quarter of an hour after leaving the meeting hall they were back at the street where Mingo had left Pierce, at the opposite end from the old cemetery. All was quiet. Mingo pointed out the house into which Pierce had disappeared. The windows were dark.

"Boone, we'd best go on foot from here," suggested Gabe. "You stay here with the horses, Mingo."

Mingo was happy to oblige. Big Tom was somewhere nearby, and that crazy scarecrow in his tattered black longcoat was too fearsome for Mingo's taste.

Convinced that this was a wild-goose chase, Boone reluctantly followed Gabe down the street. When they reached the front of the house, Gabe gestured for Boone to stay there while he circled around to the back. Boone shook his head. He didn't think splitting up was a very good idea, but Gabe had already turned away, and the darkness swallowed up the farmer as he made his way cautiously around the side of the house.

Standing there with a tight grip on his rifle, Boone strained to peer into the shadows. A night breeze, redolent with the smell of the sea, whispered in the trees and made the limbs of the moss-draped old oaks click and clatter like old bones knocking together. He was sure all this nonsense was the result of Mingo's overactive imagination, and that Pierce Hammond was perfectly safe—except, perhaps, from the diseases to which a man who frequented prostitutes exposed himself. Still, Boone felt uneasy. This *was* a spooky place, and either his imagination was just as active as Mingo's or there really was some kind of danger lurking here . . .

He heard a shout of surprise, cut short, then a grunt, a thud—all this came from around the corner of the house. Boone rushed forward; he saw an amorphous shape writhing on the ground, and then the shape separated into two men, and at that moment a lamp was lit inside the house and its weak yellow light escaped through a window and illuminated the scene. A black man in a longcoat was standing over Gabe, who lay sprawled, groaning, on the ground. Boone saw the dull glimmer of the light falling upon the blade of a knife—a stiletto—in the black man's grip, and Boone uttered an incoherent cry of warning meant for Gabe as he brought the rifle to his shoulder. He caught a glimpse of the black man's gaunt, wild-eyed features before he pulled the trigger.

The rifle's report ringing in his ears, Boone blinked at the sting of powder smoke in his eyes, fumbled with powder horn and shot pouch—Gabe had taught him that the first order of business after discharging your weapon was to reload. But he realized then that the black man was no longer standing there in front of him. Had he fallen to the ground? Had Boone actually hit his mark? No, there was only one man on the ground, Gabe. And Gabe was hurt. The black man had simply vanished. How was that possible? *I had him dead to rights at point-blank range,* thought Boone in stunned disbelief.

Concern for his friend caused Boone to disregard the hunter's cardinal rule; his rifle's readiness forgotten, he hurried to Gabe's side. "How bad are you hurt, Gabe? Gabe, talk to me!"

"Help me up," mumbled the farmer, his words slurred like a drunkard's.

"Did he get you with that knife?"

"Knife? What knife?" Gabe tried to steady himself on rubbery legs. "No, he hit me. I ain't never been hit so hard in all my days. Where's my long gun?"

They found the rifle, lying in the weeds that grew tall against the side of the house, and as Boone looked up from the search, he saw the pale oval of an indistinct face behind the thin curtains on a window. Then the face was gone. He grabbed Gabe by the arm. "Hammond!" he whispered.

"Let's go," said Gabe grimly.

They circled to the front of the shotgun house, and Gabe kicked the door in without a moment's hesitation. Another door, this one in the back of the house, slammed shut. Gabe rushed through the darkened front room into the next. Here a sputtering lamp on a table cast its flickering light on a rumpled bed where the thin, pale, naked body of Pierce Hammond lay facedown.

"Good God," breathed Boone, and gripped one of Pierce's wrists, searching frantically for a pulse. "He's still alive!"

They rolled him over and saw no wounds, and Gabe slapped him on both cheeks, slapped him hard, but Pierce was out cold. A bottle of cheap whiskey stood on a nearby table, with a shot glass half empty beside it, and something compelled Boone to lift the glass to his nose and sniff. A faint aroma of almonds was distinguishable from the sharp tang of the liquor.

"I think he's been drugged, Gabe. Or maybe poisoned."

At that moment Mingo entered the room, his brawny arms around a raven-haired woman in a gossamer-thin unmentionable of pink satin and lace. She was struggling to free herself, but to no avail.

"I come runnin' when I heard the shot," said Mingo, "and caught this one tryin' to slip out the back way."

"Get your black nigger hands off me," screeched the woman.

"Better do it, Mingo," advised Gabe.

Mingo chuckled. "She ain't no more white than I am, Mr. Cochran, suh."

"She sure looks white," said Boone, dubiously. He could see a lot of her—more than a gentleman *should* see. The satin and lace didn't keep too many secrets. He tried not to stare.

"She's quadroon," said Mingo confidently. "And she's a whore. Her name's Desiree. Ever'body in Mobile knows her."

She stopped struggling, peering at Boone with dark, smoldering eyes through a veil of disheveled hair. She was very pretty, thought Boone, and he decided Mingo had to be right about her. Were she white, one so beautiful would not be entertaining strangers in this part of town. At the very least she would be some rich man's kept mistress, or maybe even his wife.

"What did you give this man?" Gabe asked her, pointing at Pierce. "Did you poison him?"

"If I'd poisoned him, he'd be dead, now wouldn't he?"

"Must be laudanum," Boone told Gabe.

"I don't trust her," decided Gabe. Moving with swift purpose, he rinsed the shot glass with water from a pitcher, then filled the glass with water and proceeded to tear open cartridges taken from his shot pouch, pouring the gunpowder from a half-dozen cartridges into the water. With Boone's help he sat Pierce up on the edge of the bed and forced the contents of the glass down the unconscious man's throat. For a moment nothing happened. Boone glanced querulously at Gabe, but Gabe looked sure of himself. And then, abruptly, Pierce stirred, moaned, his eyes fluttering open, and with a great gasping heave he pitched forward onto his hands and knees and vomited.

"Never fails," said Gabe, pleased that his home-made purgative had worked.

Pierce got shakily to his feet, stumbled sideways, and fetched hard against a dressing table. So hard that the impact cracked the cheap mirror.

"Watch what you're doing, you clumsy bastard," said Desiree.

"What did you do to me?" asked Pierce, holding his head.

"I did everything you asked me to do."

"She drugged you," said Gabe. "Reckon she and that friend of hers were aimin' to rob you blind, or worse."

"Thanks for coming to help me," said Pierce.

"It's Mingo you ought to thank," said Boone. "He's the one who came and warned us you were in trouble."

Pierce glanced at Mingo, perplexed, and not knowing what to say.

"What are we going to do with her?" asked Boone.

"Hand her over to the constable," suggested Gabe.

Pierce was getting dressed. "The irony of it all, darling," he told Desiree, "is that I'm broke. I gave you all the money I had on me. There wasn't anything left to steal."

"Your father would have paid a pretty price to get you back safe and sound."

"So it was kidnapping, was it?" asked Gabe.

"You're incriminating yourself," warned Boone.

Desiree laughed. "I'll get off scot free. Just wait and see if I don't."

"She's probably right," said Pierce. "What judge would want to put a rope around that pretty neck? Thing is, my dear Desiree, my father doesn't put a very high value on my hide. You would have been disappointed."

Desiree shrugged a bare, seductive shoulder. "It was all Big Tom's idea, anyway. He made me do it. Threatened to hurt me, or worse, if I didn't go along with his scheme."

"You see, gentlemen?" asked Pierce. "A workable defense, don't you think? The worst they'll do to this little Jezebel is run her out of town, and I wouldn't count on that."

"Maybe they'll catch this Big Tom," said Gabe.

"No," said Mingo. "No, they won't catch him."

"How can you be sure?"

"'Cause he's the devil, that one."

Pierce asked them not to tell the other Red Rovers what had happened. He especially wanted Captain Jack to remain in the dark about the incident, for fear that the truth might prejudice Shackelford against him. Boone could see why. What he couldn't understand was why Mingo had saved his master's life. The schoolteacher from Illinois couldn't fathom how men could justify keeping others in bondage; even more unfathomable was why a slave would lift a finger to save the life of a man who denied him his freedom. There could be only one explanation: Mingo was too decent a human being to knowingly allow harm to visit another if it was within his power to stop it. From that moment on Boone had a new respect for Mingo.

They turned Desiree over to a constable that night. Pierce told the lawman that the courtesan had tried to rob him, and that her accomplice, Big Tom, had gotten away. The constable was acquainted with the "bloody scum" that populated the Lower Docks area, and he knew about both Desiree and Big Tom. He took the dark-haired beauty into custody and told Pierce to come to the courthouse first thing in the morning and swear out a complaint. Pierce said he would comply, but he had no intention of doing so. His destination in the morning was the *Mathilda*, Texas-bound. There was no point, he told Gabe and Boone, in pursuing the matter further. He wasn't going to stay behind in Mobile just to testify against Desiree, and without his testimony she would be acquitted. If she even went to trial. No, the best he could do was inconvenience her. Boone pointed out that if she wasn't stopped, her next victim might not be so lucky as Pierce had been. But Pierce Hammond's ears were deaf to that argument, and Boone had a hunch that in spite of everything Pierce had a soft place in his heart for Desiree.

They returned to the meeting hall for a few hours of sleep. At daybreak, following a hasty breakfast of coffee, bacon, and burgoo, Shackelford gave a brief and stirringly patriotic speech. Boone hardly heard him. His thoughts were on Sarah Ambler. He wondered how she would feel if she knew he was about to embark on a perilous adventure to Texas. After the speech they set out for the Lower Docks. Their departure had been advertised in the *Mobile Register*, and hundreds of curious spectators had gathered to cheer them as they marched by. They had no uniforms, no banners, no drum and fife, but Boone thought the Alabama Red Rovers looked very grand and martial, nonetheless. Stern and gaunt, the black-clad Captain Jack led the way, keeping his eyes fixed straight ahead. Boone and most of the others, however, waved and shouted back at the crowd. Everyone had a grand time of it.

There was a delay of a couple of hours at the Lower Docks as the horses were put on board the *Mathilda*. The Red Rovers waited on the wharf. At some point Gabe's blue tick hound changed its mind about going to Texas and wandered off. Gabe didn't seem to care, but Boone knew he was going to miss the old dog.

Mingo found a comfortable seat on a bale of cotton and gazed moodily at the coastal steamer that would carry him to Texas. Poor Sadie. What was she thinking at this moment? That she would never see him again. That her unborn child would never know its father. Mingo was of a mind to ask Pierce to free him, right here and now. After all, hadn't he actually saved the fool's life? His fabrication concerning Big Tom's evil designs had turned out to be the truth. The irony was not lost on Mingo. But he didn't ask; he knew Pierce would deny him. The ungrateful bastard was acting as though last night had never even happened.

It didn't matter. *Somehow, some way, I'll come back,* decided Mingo. It was a silent, heartfelt vow to the woman he loved.

CHAPTER ELEVEN

The Letter

As he watched the soldiers toss the bodies of the Alamo's defenders on a blazing funeral pyre, Captain Juan Galan was relieved that he had not been present during yesterday's final assault on the mission turned rebel fortress.

Santa Anna had ordered the enemy corpses burned, and now a towering black plume of smoke marked the site of final sacrifice by nearly two hundred Texans, including Travis, Bowie, and Crockett. Only a few women and children and an old black slave had survived. Galan understood that the latter had been the manservant of William Travis. Santa Anna had allowed these noncombatants to go in peace. Not, as some less familiar with the workings of the general's mind might suppose, from some chivalrous urge; His Excellency had given his troops license to rape and pillage and murder innocent people before, so great was his rage against the traitors of Texas. He had learned in the campaigns against the insurrectionists of the southern provinces that such merciless measures served to crush the enemy's will.

Galan didn't happen to agree. In his opinion,

such a policy simply made the rebels fight harder. But the only Texan civilians Santa Anna had treated with any courtesy thus far had been the Alamo survivors—because he wanted the word to spread among the rebels in arms to the east. Let them hear of the fate of Travis and his command. Perhaps they would realize that further resistance to the will of the Napoleon of the West was futile.

Galan doubted that this would be their reaction. He'd had grave doubts about many things these past weeks. Most of all, his faith in Santa Anna was severely shaken. Always before he had admired his commander in chief, had followed him, in the course of several campaigns, without question. Galan had first seen action fighting with Santa Anna to repel a Spanish invasion of Tampico. Santa Anna's brilliant defense of Galan's hometown had been inspired. He had long been of the opinion that Santa Anna had saved Mexico, from the Spaniards and from itself, and that no man was better suited to be president. He was no longer so sure.

Getting a whiff of the stench of burning flesh, Galan's horse began to act up, and he put the animal into motion, which brought him closer to the battle-scarred adobe walls of the Alamo. Here, at the northwest corner, two eight-pounders on a platform called *Fortin de Cordelle* had cut big bloody swaths through the ranks of Mexican soldiers advancing across the flat open plain yesterday. A little farther on, a three-gun battery on another platform called *Fortin de Teran* had done tremendous damage, as well; it was here, Galan had learned, that the valiant Travis had fallen, sword in hand, defiance stamped on his lean, sun-darkened face.

Travis and his men might be traitors, but they had perished bravely for what they believed in, and killing them had cost the Mexican army dearly.

At dawn yesterday—a bleak and chilly morning—Santa Anna had put his troops into motion. General Cos had led one column against this northwest corner. Three other columns moved forward from the north, east, and southeast. In the gray twilight the Texan cannoneers, lacking canister or grapeshot, had packed their ordnance with links of chain, nails, chopped-up horseshoes, and even small rocks, and fired this lethal blend into the Mexican ranks. A single cannon volley from the Texan batteries wiped out entire companies.

But though the Mexican troops faltered, they did not retreat. They could not. Santa Anna had ordered his lancers to follow in the rear of the infantry, with orders to execute any coward who turned and ran. In sheer desperation the soldiers had plunged forward. Sharpshooters picked off the defenders on the parapets, who were silhouetted against the fiery lightning of battle. Here at the north wall the mass of soldiers swarmed up and over the parapet, and once the wall was breached, the fate of the defenders was sealed.

Hand-to-hand fighting commenced. The soldiers had seen their comrades mown down by Texan cannon and rifles; now they showed no mercy. Their officers tried to stop the slaughter. General Castrillon managed to take Davy Crockett and six others captive. He had interceded on their behalf, telling Santa Anna that such valiant men had earned a reprieve from execution. But His Excellency was not moved by Castrillon's entreaty. His staff officers, eager to ingratiate themselves upon their commander, and having taken no part in the action, hacked Crockett and the other survivors to pieces with their swords. Castrillon and other front-line officers were outraged. Galan was, too, even though, praise God, he had not witnessed the atrocity.

Twenty-four hours had passed, and still the plains were blanketed with dead soldiers. Many of the wounded had remained unattended on the field of battle throughout the long, cold night. A large number of these unfortunate souls had not survived until morning. And what good would survival have done them, wondered Galan bitterly. There were only a handful of surgeons with the army, since Santa Anna had not seen fit to bring along an adequate medical corps.

Gazing bleakly at this scene of terrible carnage, Galan thought of the hundreds of widows and fatherless children whose husbands and fathers now lay on this field. Such brooding naturally brought his beloved Natalia to mind, and thoughts of her inhabited his heart with an exquisite anguish. Her love had quenched his desire for war. He was a soldier, and had been his entire adult life, and yet the profession no longer held any allure for him. Life, with Natalia, had become too precious.

Of course, only his friend Victor Benavides was privy to his true feelings in this regard. No one else would understand. Anyone else would call him a coward, a man who had let a woman emasculate him. But Galan was pretty sure his doubts about Santa Anna and this campaign stemmed from the realization that, because of Natalia, he looked at the world with new eyes. *Perhaps she has gelded me,* he mused as he watched the camp followers in their efforts to protect the dead and dying from a flock of insolent vultures. *She has bled every drop of warrior's blood from my veins.*

"I am still willing to lay down my life for my country," he had told Victor. "But I don't want to die for Santa Anna's glory. And this, you see, is not my country."

He meant Texas, and Victor knew it, nodding agreement. "I feel the same way as you, my friend. I have no love for the Anglos, but we invited them into this province, and they have made it their own. They have brought their traditions, their culture, with them. We lost Texas many years ago, the day the first Anglo settler crossed the Sabine River. But try persuading His Excellency of that, Juan. He will not give up Texas without a fight. He considers this part of his personal domain. So what can we do?"

Galan realized there was really nothing he *could* do. Except survive. Whatever it took, survive, and go home to Natalia. Perhaps when this campaign was over, he would resign his commission. This he could not do, though, until the campaign was finished. Santa Anna would have him imprisoned, or worse. Yes, probably worse; the Napoleon of the West had become increasingly bloodthirsty.

At least he had not been present at the fall of the Alamo . . .

For a week the Tampico Regiment had been patrolling the countryside to the east and south of San Antonio de Bexar. Santa Anna was aware that a large force of Texans—reports were that it numbered five hundred men—were concentrated in the area of Goliad, under the command of James Fannin. Travis had sent several appeals to Fannin, asking him to break the siege of the Alamo, and spies had indicated that Fannin was making preparations to march to the rescue of Travis and his men. The Tampico Regiment was charged with the responsibility of preventing Fannin from advancing toward San Antonio.

But Fannin had not sallied forth from Goliad, proving to Galan's satisfaction that there was a limit to Texan foolhardiness. In Fannin's place Galan would have abandoned Goliad and marched east, to join forces with the army Sam Houston was reportedly gathering in the vicinity of the Brazos River. That was why Galan thought Santa Anna so foolish to waste thirteen days in an effort to reduce the fortress of the Alamo. *In those thirteen days we might have crushed the rebellion, had we pushed eastward with vigor*. A single regiment of infantry could have kept Travis and his men bottled up, thereby protecting the army's rear echelon and lines of supply—such as those lines were. Galan was aware that many of his fellow line officers were privately questioning the wisdom of the siege.

And yet Santa Anna had spent his best troops in the assault, and now six hundred soldiers lay dead or wounded. Six hundred! Galan was appalled by the senselessness of it all. And to add to his grave misgivings was the rumor that His Excellency, having casually surveyed this field of carnage, had commented, "It was but a small affair."

Santa Anna seemed pleased with the progress of the campaign. General Urrea's column was sweeping along the coast, seizing one town after another, and destroying small rebel units at San Patricio and Agua Dulce Creek. If Fannin remained much longer in Goliad, he would soon be caught between Urrea's column and the main army.

Apparently, the Napoleon of the West expected the news of the Alamo's fall to so discourage the rest of the rebels that the insurrection would fall apart. He had now retaken San Antonio de Bexar, the most important town in Texas; by so doing he had also avenged the stain upon Mexico's honor occasioned by the surrender of General Cos a few short months ago.

A low moan reached Galan's ears, and he scanned the bodies near at hand. There! That man had moved—he was still alive. Galan leaped from the saddle and rushed to the man's side. He was a *cazador*, a light infantryman, clad in gray trousers and a dark blue coat with red facings and turnbacks. His shako and his Baker rifle—lots of the army's weapons and accoutrements were British military surplus—lay on the ground.

Galan gently rolled the man over on his back. It was then, at a glance, that he knew the soldier was doomed. The man had been shot in the belly and had lost a shocking amount of blood overnight.

Galan could scarcely believe he had managed to cling so long to life. Bloodshot eyes in a gray, ashen face, flecked with bloody sputum, fastened on Galan.

"Captain," wheezed the dying man, "did we take the mission?"

"Yes. You and your comrades were very brave."

"So was the enemy."

Galan nodded, too moved to speak.

"I . . . I have a letter. For my wife . . ." The soldier reached under his coat and drew out a bloodstained piece of paper. "I cannot write, so my lieutenant wrote this for me. My lieutenant, he lies over there. All my friends are dead . . ." He choked, drooled a pink froth, and drew a painful breath. "My wife lives in Saltillo. Her name is here. Do you see?"

"Yes, I see the name."

"Will you be sure that she gets this letter, Captain?"

"Of course."

"Captain . . ."

"I am here."

"Why is it so dark? Will this night never end?"

Galan glanced at the fiery golden sky to the east. The sun was rising, yet the soldier could not see its light, nor feel its warmth on his face.

"It will end soon," said Galan.

The soldier clutched blindly at Galan's sleeve; his body spasmed briefly in one last panicked struggle for breath, and then went limp. His grip slowly loosened, and then his hand fell away.

Galan drew a deep breath and stood, gazing at

the letter in his hand. This was the reason the *cazador* had clung so desperately to life through the long, cold night—he had wanted to be certain that someone found the letter to his wife.

Though he knew he was wrong to do so, Galan read the letter. In closing, the soldier had dictated a line that Galan knew he would never forget. *Death is one of the chances of the game I play, and if it is my lot I will not complain, and you should not regret.*

Brave man! thought Galan. A true soldier, who lay here with his comrades in the embrace of Death. And to what end? Galan knew it was not a soldier's right to know why he had to give his life. A soldier should never ask the reason why. But now, standing in this field of the dead, Galan asked that very question, even though he realized it might prove fatal to his sense of duty.

Because Santa Anna was wrong. The Texans would not give up. The rebellion would not collapse. Glancing at the pillar of black smoke that marked the funeral pyre where the mortal remains of the Alamo heroes were being consumed by flame, Galan was sure the Texans would have their vengeance, and he thought, with bleak despair, *I had better write Natalia a letter. A letter similar to this one. Because I may well never see her again . . .*

CHAPTER TWELVE

The Messenger

Sam Houston crushed the message from James Fannin in a big, blunt-fingered hand and turned his back on the young messenger who had just arrived on a foam-flecked, bottomed-out horse to deliver the bad news. He didn't want the lad to see the fury and dismay on his face. A pointless precaution, really—the boy knew. He had to know. It was there in his callow young face. There, too, was a query directed at Houston, for the young man sought an encouraging word from the general, something to restore his shaken faith in the future of Texas. From that, as well, Houston had turned away, if only for the moment he required to regain his composure.

For it was his solemn duty not only to save Texas but salvage the youth's faith. Houston knew, word for word, the instructions given him in writing by Richard Ellis, president of the recently adjourned convention at Washington-on-the-Brazos.

As commander in chief of the Texian army, you are ordered forthwith to repair to such place on the frontier as you may deem advisable, there to estab-

lish headquarters and organize the army. You will require all officers of the army to report to you. And, as it is impossible at this time to determine any particular point of concentration, you will act according to the emergencies of the occasion and the best dictates of your own judgment, for the purpose of protecting our frontier, and advancing the best interests of our country.

With this commission in hand, Houston had set out from Washington-on-the-Brazos six days ago, bound for Gonzales, and accompanied by the eighteen volunteers from Brazoria who had been mistaken by the skittish convention delegates as Mexican dragoons.

Yesterday Houston had sent two of his men on ahead with orders to find Fannin and deliver copies of the commission and the Declaration of Texas Independence, instructing the West Pointer to march at once to the crossing at Cibolo Creek, there to unite with the Gonzales volunteers.

He had sent several other couriers north, south, and east, each carrying the same proclamation, which he had penned in the saddle:

War is raging on the frontiers. Bejar is besieged by the enemy. The citizens of Texas must rally to the aid of our army. The enemy must be driven from our soil, or desolation will accompany their march on us. Independence is declared. It must now be maintained. Immediate action, united with valor, alone can achieve this great work. The services of all are forthwith required in the field. The patriots of

Texas are appealed to; in behalf of their bleeding country, Sam Houston.

He and his small band of brave men from Brazoria had met many Texas patriots on the road to Gonzales—all of them going, with haste, in the opposite direction, fleeing eastward and carrying their families and a few belongings with them, every last one stiff in the neck from peering anxiously over shoulder, keeping an eye peeled for the enemy. Not a single man opted to join up. Houston couldn't really blame them. Their first responsibility was to their wives and children. A massive exodus from the war-torn frontier was beginning.

Rumors abounded of Mexican patrols striking in all quarters. Houston had no way of knowing how much truth lay at the core of these rumors, and he realized that he was riding into the teeth of the storm, risking death or capture—which would be far worse—at every bend in the road. Still, he pressed on. Six hard days of travel in rain and cold, on heavy roads, crossing swollen creeks, and all he had to eat was parched ears of corn and an occasional rabbit or possum slain by one of the Brazoria sharpshooters. These were good men, stalwart and strong and determined to follow the "Old Chief," as they called him with fond respect, to the gates of hell if he should lead them in that direction.

Houston had no choice but to take such men into peril. Fannin had four or five hundred volunteers. Another three hundred men had reportedly gathered in the vicinity of Gonzales, led by Edward Burleson and James C. Neill, there to be recently joined by Captain Sidney Sherman, who had marched four hundred miles from Natchitoches Landing in Louisiana with a hundred Kentuckians and Ohioans. *If I can affect the juncture of those two forces,* mused Houston, *I will have in hand the nucleus of the army of the Republic of Texas.* An army that might be able to whip Santa Anna. But, at the moment, he was a general without a command.

Once more composed, Houston turned back to look at the exhausted young courier. Both the lad and his horse appeared to be on the verge of dropping in their tracks, and Houston felt a stab of pride cutting through the black fog of despair that the message had brought down upon him. By the Eternal, with such dauntless young men at her service, Texas still had a chance!

"The conduct of our brave countrymen at the Alamo has only been equaled by Spartan valor," he said. "God willing, we will avenge their deaths." Turning to the leader of the Brazoria volunteers, a man named Hardin, whom he had made a lieutenant the first day out of Washington-on-the-Brazos, Houston added, "Get the lad something to eat. Look in my saddlebags—there may be a little brandy left in the flask you will find there."

Hardin nodded and headed for the camp—a picket line of horses, a small, smokeless fire, and a tarpaulin, donated by a farmer headed east in a big hurry, stretched with rope between some trees to provide a modicum of shelter from the drizzling rain that had been falling virtually without cessation for a week.

The messenger didn't follow Hardin. Without

doubt he was famished, on top of being bone tired. But he had more urgent needs than food and rest. He stared earnestly at Houston.

"I'm obliged, Gen'ral," he murmured respectfully, "but I got to be gettin' back. All my friends are there in Goliad, and I'd sure hate not to be with 'em iffen somethin' happens."

"I understand. But I need you to take a message back to Colonel Fannin. To write that message I need some information from you. So, in the meantime, you surely won't object to a little something to eat."

"I'm as hungry as a Roman lion, sir."

"Well, we can spare no good Christians, but we do have some parched corn," said Houston with a smile. "So tell me. What is Fannin doing? Has he started for Gonzales, as per my orders?"

"No, sir. We're sittin' tight in Goliad. From what I've heard, Governor Robinson gave him express orders not to abandon Goliad."

Houston felt his temper flaring again. "Surely by now the colonel is well aware that Robinson is no longer in charge."

The boy shrugged. "Reckon he must be. Colonel Fannin's a right smart feller. But I ain't too clear on zackly who *is* runnin' the show, Gen'ral. So mebbe the colonel he's a mite confused, too."

Houston grimaced. How ironic that Fannin, who had always before acted as though he knew better than his superiors, and as a consequence of this hubris had blatantly disregarded orders in the past, chose in this crucial moment to adhere strictly to an outdated order by a man who was no longer in a position of authority, thanks to the wisdom of the delegates of the constitutional convention at Washington-on-the-Brazos. Surely Fannin knew by now that Robinson and that detestable council had been replaced. And even if he remained uncertain about the government, he, as a West Pointer, was bound to realize that his position at Goliad was no longer tenable now that the Alamo had fallen and Santa Anna was free to turn his attention elsewhere.

It was likely, mused Houston bitterly, that Fannin had lost his nerve. By all accounts, he had fortified Goliad, naming his stronghold Fort Defiance, and now was not inclined to leave the protection of his walls. He was rendered impotent by indecision, trapped in a possibly fatal paralysis by the knowledge that the various Mexican columns were on the verge of encircling him.

"You think you and your friends can hold on at Goliad, son?" asked Houston.

The lad nodded. "We've got enough supplies, I reckon. Why, a feller's even rigged up a thingamajig that'll fire sixty-eight muskets all at once. Shoot, Gen'ral, there be near on five hunnerd of us at Fort Defiance. I reckon we can whup the entire Mexican army, given the chance."

Houston nodded. He admired the boy's spunk—and he didn't have the heart to explain how dangerously naive such an attitude could be. Turning abruptly away, he shouted at Hardin to bring him his writing materials. A moment later, seated on a log, he was balancing a piece of wagon-board on his knees—a makeshift writing table—and applying pen to paper, working rapidly and in a bold, angry hand.

Colonel Fannin,
You will fall back to Gonzales with your command upon receipt of this order, and with such artillery as can be brought. The remainder must be sunk in the river. Every facility is to be rendered to women and children who may be desirous of leaving the frontier. Previous to abandoning Goliad, you will blow up all fortifications. Leave no foodstuffs or ammunition to fall into the hands of the enemy. What supplies you cannot carry must be destroyed. The immediate advance of the enemy may be confidently expected. More rain is also likely, and will cause a rise in creeks and rivers which may hinder your escape. Prompt movements are therefore highly important.
Your obt. svt., Sam Houston, General, Army of the Republic of Texas

"Son, you must get this through to Colonel Fannin," Houston told the boy, who had been chewing parched corn as he waited. "No matter what."

"You can rely on me, Gen'ral."

"I am. Lieutenant Hardin, provide him with a fresh mount."

Watching the boy ride west, Houston couldn't help but wonder if they would ever meet again. Odds were that the lad would get himself killed. Though he had expected the fall of the Alamo—an inevitable disaster from the moment Travis had willfully disobeyed orders and made a decision to hold the mission at all costs—Houston was still shocked and discouraged. Damn Travis. Damn his brave and noble heart. What good were dead heroes to the cause of Texas freedom? And what had their sacrifice accomplished? Would it demoralize other patriots, or make them even more resolved to see this business through to victory?

And what of Fannin? Houston felt keenly disappointed by the inactivity, the indecision of the West Pointer. Frankly, he'd expected more of the man. Fannin could have marched on San Antonio and tried to raise the siege of the Alamo. Or he could have used the thirteen days Travis and his men had bought with their lives to organize a withdrawal, uniting with the Gonzales volunteers and other independent units. Houston would have preferred the latter, but even the former would have been preferable to squandering those precious days and sitting in Goliad *doing absolutely nothing*!

Sam Houston shook his head. He had a bad feeling about James Fannin, a premonition that the man would lead his command to destruction. The Alamo's fall was a dark day indeed in Texas history. But darker days were coming.

"Beg pardon, General," said Hardin. "We're ready to move out when you are."

Houston realized then that the Brazorians had struck the camp and now stood by their horses, ready to ride. Ready to follow him to liberty or death. Houston flexed shoulders hunched beneath a terrible burden. These men were counting on him. He would not, could not, fail them.

"Yes," he said, long strides carrying him to his

horse, Saracen. "Yes, let's go, my friends. We must reach Gonzales with all haste, and I do not intend to stop until we arrive there. There is not a moment to waste. Texas depends on it."

"Texas depends on you, General," said Hardin. "That's why we know she'll pull through."

The others nodded, murmuring their full accord with Hardin's sentiments. Houston was deeply moved. *I only wish*, he thought, *that I had such faith*.

CHAPTER THIRTEEN

The Escape

On the fourth day out of New Orleans the steamer *Mathilda* sailed into Galveston Bay. Loaded to the gunwales with a hundred men and as many horses, the vessel had struggled through heavy seas for the duration of the voyage. Many men became severely ill, some from seasickness, others from drinking out of a barrel of rancid water. Pierce Hammond was one of those who was rendered completely incapacitated. He and a dozen others were destined to be left behind in Galveston to recuperate while the rest of the Red Rovers pushed on. Captain Shackelford made arrangements for Pierce and two others to be boarded with a kindly widow woman. "He's got dysentery," Captain Jack informed Boone and Gabe. "He can't come with us. Sorry, boys, but he and the rest of the sick would just slow us down."

Shackelford put Pierce in charge of the invalids. "When all of you are well enough to travel, come and find us. But remember, Red Rovers stick together. So leave no one behind."

Hammond was stunned by this sudden and unwanted responsibility. Why had Captain Jack singled him out? But he dared not ask, or give any indication that he was at all reluctant to do Shackelford's bidding. Besides, he doubted his chances of surviving the malady that had him in its grasp. Chills and fever, racking cramps, nausea, splitting headaches—he'd never been so sick in his life.

"He's paying the price for his waywardness," Gabe told Boone after they had said their goodbyes to Pierce. "This is God's way of punishing him for what he done back in Mobile."

"You really believe that?"

"Sure I do. Don't you? Nothing happens for no reason. If something good happens to you, it's a blessing from God. If something bad happens, don't you reckon the Almighty has something to do with it?"

"Well, I'm not sure," said Boone, dubious. "I never really gave it much thought."

Gabe glared at him. "Maybe you're just too educated to believe in God."

"What's come over you, Gabe? Of course I believe in God. I guess I've always thought bad things were the Devil's work. I never thought of blaming God."

"You didn't listen. I'm not blaming God. You only got yourself to blame. God gives, and if you ain't grateful for His blessings, He takes away. Sure, the Devil puts in his two cents worth, but he works in here." Gabe pounded his chest with a fist. "He's always trying to get you into hot water. And if you listen to him, the way Pierce did that night back in Mobile, well, then God punishes you.

When that happens, it ain't the Almighty's fault. It's your own."

Boone lapsed into frowning silence. He wanted to ask Gabe if he believed that Maggie and her mother had been taken away because of something *he* had done. If Gabe really believed this to be so, it was a crushingly heavy burden for any man to bear. But he couldn't bring himself to ask the question. The subject was too sensitive.

He knew Gabe was a religious man. Every Sunday, without fail, the farmer and his family had rolled into town in their wagon, bound for services at the plain, whitewashed church. Boone's attendance had been less than regular, to say the least. Fire and brimstone sermons had a chilling effect on him. He preferred to read the Bible or some other good book in the peace and privacy of his own quarters. In fact, if the truth be known, he'd only gone to church to catch a glimpse of Sarah Ambler. Feeling ashamed, Boone decided he wasn't qualified to engage Gabe Cochran, or anyone else, in a theological debate.

A short while later, they were leaving Galveston. That was fine with Boone. His first impression of Texas—a sandy, barren island dotted with a few scrawny palm trees and a seedy collection of weather-blistered buildings—was more than a trifle disappointing. He wasn't sure what he had expected Texas to be like, but he had expected it to be something more appealing than this; after all, a great many people were quarreling over possession of this land. Or maybe it wasn't really the land at all, but something bigger than the land, bigger and yet intangible, something like those inalienable rights Thomas Jefferson had so brilliantly and evocatively written about sixty years ago.

Boone was excited, but it was an excitement muted by dread. You couldn't say there was panic in the streets of Galveston, but there was definite concern—it was there plain to see in every Texan face. The Alamo had fallen, and Santa Anna's merciless army was on the march, leaving death and destruction in its wake. No one knew for certain where the dictator and his bloodthirsty troops would strike next. But no one could deny that the young republic's future looked grim. Very grim indeed.

Captain Jack was wasting no time. On the same day his Red Rovers landed they were on the march, ferried across shark-infested waters from Galveston Island to the mainland, striking the Victoria Road and turning west. He wasn't sure where General Sam Houston could be found at this moment, but he did know that Colonel Fannin was still at Goliad, and Fannin seemed the most likely target for the Mexican army. If there was to be a fight at Goliad, then by God the Alabama Red Rovers would be present and accounted for on the side of right when the first musket discharged.

Boone was ambivalent about the prospect of action. Going to Texas had seemed like a good idea back in Alabama, a fine adventure tailor-made to cure a broken heart. But he'd never given much thought to the possibility of dying badly, for instance at the end of a Mexican bayonet. The romantic in him decided it would be a nice touch if he wrote a letter to Sarah. *My dearest Sarah, if I should perish you must not grieve for me. Know only that my love for you was as pure as . . .* Or something along those lines. Something Byronic. And then, if he did die, wouldn't she be sorry she hadn't gone against her father's wishes and married him! Perhaps she would weep at the news of his untimely demise. Perhaps her sweet tears would fall like gentle rain upon the letter she would cherish for the remainder of her life. Perhaps she would always wear mourning black, and refuse to ever marry. Perhaps his memory, and thoughts of what might have been, would haunt her sleep forever . . .

But no—he decided it wasn't worth the effort. Alabama and Sarah Ambler and the anguish of heartbreak seemed suddenly very remote, and, well, relatively unimportant—part of a distant past. This was a new chapter in his life. He hoped it wouldn't be the last chapter.

Mingo Green was glad Pierce Hammond had fallen ill and been left behind on Galveston Island to convalesce. From the things he'd heard, it seemed obvious that Captain Jack Shackelford and his Alabama Red Rovers were marching gloriously off to certain destruction—and Mingo had no desire to die in Texas. The Red Rovers had talked about fighting for freedom, but they didn't mean freedom for black folk, so let them have their war and leave him out of it. Galveston Island was all of Texas Mingo would ever care to see.

Not that Galveston was a safe haven. Apparently a column of the Mexican army was working its way up along the coast, putting seaport after seaport to the torch and committing one atrocity after another, and no one could be certain whether the column would continue on its course to Galveston or turn inland at some point. And then there was the constant threat of an attack by sea. The Texas navy consisted of a handful of privateers, lightly armed schooners, and sloops, little more than licensed pirates really, who were so busy preying on defenseless Mexican merchantmen that they evinced no desire to protect the coast—there was no profit to be had in engagements with Mexican men-of-war. So lookouts were continually scanning the seaward horizon, and hardly a day passed that an alarm was not sounded upon a sighting of distant sail—always false alarms, as it turned out, but that didn't ease the tension, or mean that the next one wouldn't be genuine.

Mingo decided it was time to talk to Pierce, to persuade the man to give him his freedom papers. But first he had to help nurse Pierce back to health. While he was glad Pierce was sick, the worst thing that could happen to him was Pierce dying. So Mingo made himself very useful to the kindly widow woman who had taken Pierce and some of the other invalid Red Rovers into her care and keeping. Within a few days he had made himself indispensable to her, not out of the goodness of his heart, though he liked her well enough, but because he hoped she would put in a good word for him when the time came. Mingo even entertained the idea of staying on and working for the widow's wages; then he could save enough money to buy Sadie's freedom.

Gradually, Pierce's condition improved so that one morning, as Hammond sat in a rocking chair on a porch swept with cool, salty sea breezes, Mingo got up the nerve to pose the question.

"Reckon in a day or two you be headin' off to join up with yo' friends, Marse Pierce, and I ain't inclined to go, 'cause this ain't my fight. I got no stake in it. Want no part of it. I didn't come all this way to die for liberty when it don't count for me."

"So what do you intend to do?"

"I plan to stay right here, long as it's safe, and try to earn enough money so's I can go back to Alabama some day soon and buy Sadie free. I want my baby born free."

"Baby? Sadie's expecting? Why, I didn't know."

Mingo nodded. "I just figure you might feel obliged to give me my freedom papers."

"Because you saved my life in Mobile." Pierce nodded. "I see now why you went to so much trouble. I was wondering about that."

"Do it matter why I done it? Yo' still alive, ain't you?"

"I don't think my father would appreciate my freeing you."

"What Marse Hammond think ain't never stopped you before."

Pierce conceded the point, and he promised to give Mingo's request all due consideration. But Mingo came away doubting that he would. And, sure enough, on the next day, when he brought breakfast to Pierce's room—a rather bland gruel, which was all Pierce could keep in his stomach—Pierce told him his decision.

"I won't give you your papers, Mingo, because it will just get you killed. You'll go back to Alabama and you'll run afoul of Slade, and my father wouldn't acknowledge any paper with my signature on it anyway. I'm telling you, just forget that woman. No woman's worth dying for."

"A man like you can't find nothin' worth dyin' for. Or livin' for, neither."

Pierce smiled wanly. "Who would I have to talk back to me if you were gone?"

"I'm as good as gone."

Pierce shook his head. "You're not that big of a fool. If you were going to run away, you would have done so in Mobile. It's too late for you to run now. Besides, I need you here. I promised ol' Jubal I would try to locate his boy. He might be here in Texas. You remember Jubal's son?"

"I worked right alongside him in Marse Hammond's cotton fields, so I reckon I know him."

"I'll write you out a pass. Go and ask around. Maybe something will turn up."

Pass in hand, Mingo proceeded to roam the length and breadth of Galveston Island. Several times he was stopped and questioned by suspicious whites, but the pass saw him through safely every time. Pierce Hammond's name carried little weight here, in and of itself, but he had appended *Alabama Red Rovers* to his signature, and everybody in town knew by now about the gallant Red Rovers.

Mingo heard rumors of a slave insurrection on

the mainland, in the vicinity of the lower Trinity River; apparently twenty or thirty slaves from several neighboring plantations had killed an overseer and made an attempt on the lives of several other white folk. They had vanished into the swamps, and the local citizenry were urging the provisional government to detail a company of militia to track them down. Problem was, most of the men of fighting caliber were off to the frontier to meet the Mexican threat. It was said that Mexican spies were circulating among the slaves, inciting them to turn against their masters. In exchange, Santa Anna had promised every slave his freedom once the insurrection was quelled and Mexican rule reestablished over the province of Texas.

This was bad news for Mingo. He recognized that if this country was up in arms over a slave insurrection, it just made what he had to do even more dangerous. But his resolve would not be shaken. He'd made up his mind. In a couple of days Pierce Hammond would be going off to war, and Mingo wasn't going with him. Somehow he had to get away. Somehow he had to get his hands on fake freedom papers. He had no inclination to join a slave revolt, but every fugitive slave apprehended in Texas would have a hard time convincing a bunch of white men that he wasn't a participant in the insurrection.

He made only a token effort to find ol' Jubal's son. Chances were extremely remote that the boy was in Galveston. He could be anywhere in Texas—or not in Texas at all. He could be dead for all Mingo knew. Mingo felt sorry for Jubal, and under other circumstances would have liked to help locate the old man's prodigal son, but he had his own problems to deal with.

Mingo tried not to let his growing desperation get the better of him. Only a matter of days was left to him. Once Pierce Hammond was up and around, they'd be headed for the frontier, and the big scrape, and the big killing. But Mingo kept telling himself he had to make a plan. He couldn't just take off running and trust blindly to fate. Fate had never done him any favors. He had to use his head. He had to be cunning, like a fox.

So he kept his eyes and ears open, covering the island, using the pass signed by Pierce Hammond like a shield. If only he could write! Then perhaps he might have been able to make his own freedom papers and forged Pierce Hammond's signature. Why, he had that signature right here on the pass. But of course that was exactly why masters forbade their slaves to learn how to read or write.

He noticed that Galveston was a bustling harbor. Even with a rebellion on, there were many ships coming and going, and they flew many different flags. Mingo lingered at the docks for the better part of an entire day, calculating his chances of stowing away on one of those ships. He would have to make sure it was going back to Mobile, or at least New Orleans—it wouldn't do him or Sadie or his baby any good if he ended up in some foreign land. The prospect of another sea voyage was not at all appealing; the trip over on the *Mathilda* had been about all he could stomach. And what would they do to a stowaway nigger if they found him? Mingo decided he didn't want to find out.

He even considered running off to join the Mexican army. Maybe it was true that Santa Anna had promised all slaves their freedom. Once he was a free man in a Texas ruled by Santa Anna, though, how would he get Sadie here from Alabama? Once he stepped foot out of Texas, he'd be a slave again. Not likely any Alabama slave catchers would care spit that Santa Anna had made him a free man. And if Santa Anna lost, as unlikely as that seemed, why then he'd not only be a runaway but a turncoat to boot, wanted for raising his hand against his masters. They'd put a rope around his neck for sure. Besides, Mingo didn't want to get anywhere close to the big fight.

Finally, on the day that he returned to the widow woman's house to find Pierce Hammond up and about, and declaring his intention to be off in a day or two to catch up with the rest of the Red Rovers, Mingo knew he had to act. He was out of time. Of the other twelve men left behind in Galveston, one had died, and all but one of the remaining eleven were fit to travel, or very nearly so.

The next morning Mingo was walking along the beach, gazing across the mile-wide inlet to the mainland, wishing he were a strong enough swimmer to make it across. Were that the case, he would have tried, despite the sharks that were very common in these waters. This island had become his prison, and he had to break out. He no longer bothered trying to figure out what he would do once he reached the mainland; he had no idea how many miles lay between him and Sadie now, but he knew his chances were slim to none of getting back to Alabama, so why worry about that? One step at a time. In the end, that was all a man could do.

Prowling the beach, he rounded a point and saw two barefoot boys bringing a rowboat to shore through the gentle surf. Mingo ducked down behind a sand dune and watched through tufts of yellow saltgrass as the pair of youthful fishermen left the boat and set out for town with their catch. His first impulse was to leap into the boat as soon as the two boys were out of sight. But he decided his chances of crossing the inlet undetected would be much improved if he waited until nightfall. He could only pray that the boat would still be here when he got back.

Returning to the widow woman's house, he managed to steal a little bread and cheese and a pair of shoes belonging to one of the Red Rovers. These items, along with a hand ax taken from the shed out back, he put into a burlap sack and secreted the sack beneath the back steps of the house.

He waited until the house was still that night. Trusting that everyone was asleep, he stole away, the burlap sack slung over a shoulder. He had to reach the beach unseen—no pass would save a slave caught lurking about town at such a late hour. The boat, praise God, was right where he'd last seen it. Without hesitation he pushed off, climbed in, fit the oars into their locks, and began to row, his muscles, hardened from a lifetime in the master's fields, rippling across his back as he steered a course straight and true for the mainland a mile away.

When he reached the other side, he pushed the boat out to let the tide carry it away. Taking a moment to check the stars, he put on the stolen shoes and headed due east. *I'm comin', Sadie,* he thought, wondering if somehow he could think it hard enough so that Sadie would hear him in her mind. *I got a lot of ground to cover, but I'm comin' to take you away, and ain't nothin' and nobody gonna stop me.*

CHAPTER FOURTEEN

The River

In the ten days since his enlistment in the Alabama Red Rovers, Boone Tasker had gotten to know quite a few of the men who followed Captain Jack Shackelford. They were backwoodsmen and ploughmen for the most part, rough-hewn, resilient, self-reliant men with a streak of independence a mile wide. They were full of confidence in their ability to fight the Mexican—most of them sincerely believed their foe came from inferior stock. Many had been the obstacles life had thrown in the paths of these men, and Santa Anna was just one more hurdle. Conditions were such that no place in Texas was safe, but Boone *felt* relatively safe in the company of the Red Rovers. Their supreme self-confidence was contagious.

With a fight imminent, he spent a lot of time wondering how he would acquit himself. It occurred to him that in all his twenty-six years he had never heard a shot fired in anger. There had been some Indian troubles up in Illinois during his boyhood, and a time or two his father had gone off with the militia to tangle with the redskins. But Boone had been too young to go to war at his father's side, and though as a youth he had dreamed of a career in the military—anything but farming!—as he grew older he'd lost all martial inclinations. He had much preferred a book in his hand to a musket. His only hope was that some of the gruff courage exhibited by the Red Rovers would rub off on him.

The march to Goliad was not a pleasant one. The weather made it so; a cold rain fell day and night, turning the road they followed into a morass of mud, soaking them to the skin, so that at night when the temperature dropped to near freezing, they huddled shivering in their sodden blankets without so much as a fire to warm them. Even assuming they could have found dry kindling, Captain Jack sternly forbade any fires. No one knew for certain where the enemy would turn up next. The civilians who crowded the road, fleeing to the east, were of no help in this regard. Boone figured that if every rumor he heard was true, Santa Anna had an army of fifty thousand troops—and not ordinary men, mind you, but hulking barbarians as savage as the Vandals and Visigoths who had destroyed Caesar's legions and sacked the city of Rome.

At the end of the fifth day out of Galveston, Captain Jack summoned Boone Tasker. They had made camp in a stand of timber—an "island," as the locals called it—on high ground surrounded by the gently rolling prairie. Shackelford straddled a log, and he was writing while his son stood over him, shielding his work with a blanket from the rain that dripped down through the trees.

"Tasker," said Shackelford, "you were a schoolteacher, weren't you?"

Boone reluctantly confessed that it was so. He was afraid that Captain Jack had decided he wasn't suited, after all, for the task confronting the Red Rovers. With action on the horizon maybe Shackelford was separating the wheat from the chaff.

"Good. I have here a message for General Sam Houston. It's come to my attention that he is north of here, at a place called Gonzales. You remember the river we crossed today?"

Boone nodded. He'd be hard-pressed to forget it, having very nearly drowned crossing that rain-swollen stream.

"That was the Guadalupe, I believe. Follow it north, and it will take you to Gonzales. You will read this message, committing it to memory, and then you will destroy it."

"Sir?"

Shackelford stood up and put a hand on Boone's shoulder. "Listen, son. I believe there are two columns of Mexican troops, one to the north of us and the other to the south. Should you run into an enemy patrol and get yourself killed, I do not want this message to fall into their hands."

"I see," said Boone, and cleared his throat of some mysterious obstruction.

"You being a schoolteacher, I assume you have a good memory. I don't want a hopelessly garbled message delivered to General Houston. I know you will keep it straight in your mind. And I am confident that you will get through."

"I'll do my best, Captain Jack."

"You're damned right you will. You're an Alabama Red Rover. And a Red Rover never does anything by halves."

Boone wondered if that was meant to inspire him. He took the message and read it.

General Houston,
Information I have received leads me to conclude that Colonel Fannin is still at Goliad and is threatened by the enemy. Therefore I and my volunteers, who number about ninety brave men, are on the march to join Fannin, with the expectation of arriving at Goliad tomorrow night or the following morning.
Yr obt svt
Dr. J. Shackelford
Captain, Alabama Red Rovers

"Can you deliver that message, Tasker?"

"Yes, sir." Boone had no doubt he could remember it, word for word. There was, however, some question in his mind whether he could actually reach Gonzales alive. But now was hardly the time to give voice to his lack of self-confidence.

"Fine. You'll need a better mount than the one you brought from Alabama. Pick your horse, and off with you."

"Yes, sir."

Boone went in search of Gabe and told his friend what had befallen him. "I'm to be Joshua to Captain Jack's Moses," he said, bemused. "I'm sure there are better men for the job. I'm not even that good of a horseman. And I didn't tell him I'm no judge of horseflesh."

"I'll pick you out a good mount, Boone."

"Thanks. Maybe I could talk him into letting you come along with me."

"Don't fret. You'll do just fine on your own. Besides, I don't hanker to go to Gonzales. It's Goliad for me. That's where the big scrape's gonna be. I reckon you'll miss out altogether."

Boone frowned. "You think that's why Captain Jack chose me? Because he knows I'd be worthless in a fight?"

"He wouldn't have given you the responsibility he did if he thought that. There's a chance you might run into dragoons."

"I know." That was just what Boone was afraid of.

"I just mean that if you're with Sam Houston you won't see much action," said Gabe. "From what I hear, he'd just as soon retreat all the way back to Louisiana rather than make a stand against the Mexicans."

"Captain Jack seems to think pretty highly of him."

"All I'm saying is some folks are beginning to wonder if Sam Houston's got enough backbone."

Boone shrugged. He knew little about Houston. The man had fought the Indians under Andrew Jackson. As Old Hickory's protégé he had become governor of Tennessee. People expected big things from him in the political arena. He was destined for the United States Congress at the very least. But then a scandal had brought him low, some unsavory business with his young wife, and Houston had resigned the governorship and gone into self-imposed exile among his Cherokee friends. The tribe had adopted him, giving him the name Raven. Later he had shown up in Texas and established a legal practice. Now he was commander in chief of the Texas Army. Could he be a coward? Boone doubted it. But since he didn't know the man personally, he couldn't be certain. Still, if the big fight was going to be in Goliad, what was Sam Houston doing in Gonzales?

Gabe picked out a good horse for him, a fine-looking buckskin, but upon further reflection the animal struck Boone as a little too headstrong. He'd become comfortable with the lackadaisical roan he'd brought from Alabama. The roan wasn't very energetic on the best of days, but at least Boone could count on it not to get too rambunctious to handle. One look at the buckskin and he knew docility was not one of its virtues. But Gabe assured him the buckskin was the better horse for the task ahead, and Boone reluctantly agreed.

Feeling tremendously inadequate for the mission he was about to undertake, Boone said farewell to his friend.

"Don't go getting yourself killed, Gabe."

Gabe was startled. "What? Why do you say such a thing?"

"I don't know," murmured Boone, looking down at his mud-caked boots. "I've just got this funny feeling that I won't be seeing you again. That you're going to get yourself killed. Maybe I'm wrong."

"I'll say you are."

"Lord knows I hope I am. I know you're hurting because of Sally and Maggie. But life is still worth living, isn't it, Gabe?"

"Don't go worrying about me," replied Gabe woodenly. "You've got other things to worry your head about."

"It's just that you're about the only friend I've ever had."

Gabe was deeply moved. "Yeah, well . . . you'd better get a move on. Reckon I'll be seeing you in a few days." He stuck out a hand.

Boone gripped it, shook it, and turned away.

Leading the buckskin, he returned to Shackelford. Captain Jack took one look at the horse and nodded his satisfaction.

"That one will surely get you there. Now listen, Tasker. Just go back to the Guadalupe River and turn left. If you ride all night, you ought to reach Gonzales by tomorrow midday. Cross over to the east bank of the river where you're able. Good luck and Godspeed."

When at last he reached the Guadalupe River, Boone figured it was hours after midnight. He was cold, bone-tired, and saddle sore. But he was a lot less anxious than when he'd started out. For one thing, with each passing mile he was becoming more comfortable with the buckskin. The horse was strong and fast and intelligent, and Boone was grateful that it hadn't tested him, even though it was bound to know that its rider lacked a firm hand.

And after four hours on the trail Boone had stopped seeing Mexican cavalry in every vague shape looming up out of the wet black night. He decided he really didn't have much to worry about until daylight. The night would act as his shield.

He dared not attempt a crossing of the high-running river until morning, so he turned north and followed its west bank. The dripping darkness closed in around him, and he began to think he'd left the war behind him, that he was alone and safe in another world, far removed from danger. He thought that maybe he'd been very lucky after all, to be the one chosen by Captain Jack for this mission. Because in that other world, where danger lurked, it seemed to him inevitable that the Red Rovers were hell-bent for trouble. That made him start worrying about Gabe all over again. He tried to convince himself that it was just his imagination that Gabe wanted to die. The Lord knew he was plagued with an overactive imagination. Anybody who could have imagined that Sarah Ambler would marry a church mouse–poor Yankee schoolmaster, or that going off to Texas would be a glorious adventure, had to be too much of an imaginer for his own good.

But, as for Gabe, the man was bound to have a survival instinct, and that instinct would be so strong that no temporary imbalance—and that was what it was, a mental imbalance brought on by grief too great to overcome—would compel him to intentionally court destruction. Yes, if Gabe got into a scrape, he would do what had to be done to survive, and he would not be able to help himself because that instinct would constrain his rashest impulses.

One dark mile was indistinguishable from the next. The night wore on. Would it never end? Eventually, Boone was too mentally exhausted to think. He focused all his attention on keeping the river on his right, and that slowed his progress somewhat because the overcast night limited his vision and the incessant drizzle muted the voice of the river, and regularly he had to turn the buckskin and confirm that the river remained near at hand.

Dawn came stealing up behind him, the blackness fading to gray so surreptitiously that he only belatedly realized his range of vision was enhanced. Then, as the sun rose, the eastern sky was painted in a fiery explosion of orange, and Boone realized that the overcast was breaking up, and he could see promising spots of pristine blue sky, and the maddening drizzle had finally ceased. Just the prospect of feeling the warmth of the sun again brought a smile of weary joy to his face.

But his elation was short-lived. He had to cross the raging river. He had no idea how much ground he had covered during the night and could only presume he hadn't passed Gonzales in the darkness. Captain Jack had said by noon today, but Shackelford might have made a mistake with the distance. Following the riverbank, Boone searched for a likely crossing. The swift and roiling chocolate brown waters of the river frightened him. He'd been hungry long before dawn, but now the knot in his stomach was not from lack of sustenance. There seemed to be no hope of swimming the river. His only hope would be a ferry—surely there would be a ferry crossing at Gonzales. True, he was in greater danger on the west side of the Guadalupe than he would be on the east; it was highly unlikely that any Mexican patrols were east of the river. But the danger presented by the river was more immediate, more tangible. He decided to take his chances on the western side. His mind made up, he urged the buckskin into a loping canter, eager to reach his destination. The commander in chief of the Texas army was bound to rate a fire, beside which a lowly, worn-out messenger could warm himself!

A few minutes later, a dozen horsemen emerged suddenly from timber several hundred yards ahead of him. Boone checked the buckskin and stared, momentarily paralyzed with fear and indecision. There could be no doubt that these men were Mexican dragoons—their green uniforms and plumed helmets made them instantly recognizable.

The dragoons paused, too, seemingly as startled as Boone by this unexpected confrontation. Then one of them gave a shout, and the whole lot charged forward, and Boone wheeled the buckskin around and kicked it savagely into a gallop, bending low in the saddle as the sharp crackling of Mexican muskets reached his ears.

The buckskin had spirit, but there were limits to its stamina, and the overnight journey had sapped some of its strength. The horses of the dragoons, on the other hand, were rested. Boone figured the Mexicans had camped for the night in those woods, and had just broken camp, in fact, when he appeared on the scene. So it was inevitable that this race would end badly for Boone Tasker. He could see that this was so before they had gone a half mile. The dragoons were definitely gaining on him. They could see this, too, and they stopped shooting—a fairly futile waste of ammunition, anyway—since obviously they would catch their prey without having to kill it first.

With great reluctance Boone concluded that the river was now his only hope. At such a moment action had to be quick as thought. He steered the buckskin toward the Guadalupe. The horse nearly balked at the brink of the embankment, but another hard, decisive kick by Boone sent it plunging bravely over. The buckskin twisted as it struck the water, and Boone came out of the saddle as the muddy waters closed over him.

CHAPTER FIFTEEN

The Darkness

Boone tried desperately to hold on to the buckskin's reins. He was not the best of swimmers and figured the horse might have strength enough for both of them. But the shock of sudden immersion in the ice-cold water made him gasp, and his mouth filled with water. He panicked, flailing to get to the surface and losing the reins in the progress.

As he bobbed to the surface, his first instinct was to swim for shore, but he quickly realized he was too weak to fight the current. The only thing for it was to let the current carry him downstream. He caught a glimpse of the buckskin, doggedly making headway in its determined effort to reach the bank and quit the river; unfortunately, the horse was swimming for the west bank—where the dragoons were riding along the edge of the river in an attempt to keep pace with Boone's progress. Now they were shooting at him again, but Boone could do nothing about that. Their bullets were the least of his worries.

He felt sure the river would take his life, and he was powerless to prevent it. A spectator to the process of his own destruction, he concentrated on keeping his head above water and conserving his energy. He noticed that the dragoons were falling farther and farther behind. The treacherous and uneven bank of the river, dotted here and there with impenetrable thickets, was slowing them down. Before long Boone was well downstream of the pursuit, out of range of their short muskets, and soon he lost sight of them altogether. He saw the buckskin finally realize its goal and clamber out of the river. He was confident the dragoons would find and confiscate the horse.

Ahead, a small island split the river, and Boone had a brief ambition that he might be able to save himself there, but the current quickened and hurled him into the whitewater chute between the island and the west bank. As he hurled down the chute, half drowned, he struck a submerged object—a rock, perhaps, or a log—and the impact almost knocked him unconscious. He fought desperately to cling to life then, one last paroxysm of rebellion against the inevitable.

Beyond the island he struck another object, this one *not* completely submerged. A tree had fallen into the channel, anchored by its roots to an embankment. Boone clutched at the stubs of broken limbs as the current tried to drag him away. With a final expenditure of all the strength remaining to him, Boone managed to pull himself, inch by laborious inch, up the slanting trunk of the tree. An excruciating eternity later, he was on the embankment, clawing at the red mud to reach the crest, where he rolled with a long groan onto his back and passed out.

When he came to, he just lay there for a while, dazed and disoriented. Then the pain hit him. Gritting his teeth, he sat up and saw that his trouser leg was soaked with blood, and the panic began to rise in him again. He slipped a finger into a ragged hole in the fabric and ripped the trousers so that he could see the wound, for at first he couldn't tell if he had been shot or if he'd suffered some other injury in his battle with the river.

It was definitely a bullet hole. The bullet had struck the inside of his leg six inches above the knee and exited. Thank God for that, thought Boone—at least he wasn't going to have to carry an ounce of lead around. Ripping the trouser leg to the bottom, he tore off a long strip and used this to bind the wound. Then he got to his feet and tested the leg. It hurt like hell, but at least he could walk.

Yes, but walk where? Boone looked about him, trying to get his bearings, wondering how far the river had carried him—wondering, too, if the dragoons had given up searching for him. How long had he been unconscious? The sun was still hidden behind the clouds, but the overcast was thinning out, and he could see that it was still morning. There was no sign of the Mexicans. He was on the east side of the river, and could only hope they had been unable to cross over. He couldn't see how they would have, but then, with his luck . . .

He put his mind to work. Deal with one problem at a time. First, the enemy. It was likely they had by now assumed that the river had taken his life. How much time and effort would they expend prowling the bank, searching for some sign of him? Not much, he decided. But just to be on the safe side, he left the rim of the embankment and took shelter in a nearby thicket. This little bit of exertion exhausted him. Dropping to the ground, he considered his prospects, which were bleak, and cursed himself for a fool.

What had ever possessed him to join those damned Alabama Red Rovers in the first place? He was a schoolteacher, for crying out loud, not some swashbuckling adventurer, nor some noble patriot ready to lay down his life for the cause of freedom and republican government.

And damn Captain Jack Shackelford, too, for choosing him, of all people, to carry the message to Sam Houston. That only proved that Captain Jack had less sense than one Boone Tasker. Next time Shackelford could deliver his own damn message.

Next time? Boone seriously doubted that there would be a next time. If he didn't bleed to death, or get caught by the dragoons, or perish from exposure in this godless country, he'd turn himself right around and head for the Sabine River and not stop until he was back in the good old United States of America.

What did he care about Texas, anyway? Men like Shackelford cared—Southern men, men of honor, of property, of standing and ambition, slaveholding men who had a vested interest in expanding their slave empire by wresting Texas from the Mexicans. Who were they trying to kid with their high-flown claims that they loved liberty more than life itself and were willing to make the greatest sacrifice of all for the sake of principle. And here he lay, Boone Tasker, a Northerner, a nobody, but a nobody who at least had the decency to disapprove of the institution of slavery, and now on the verge of dying for the slave power. He shook his head, consumed by bitter self-reproach. *My father always said I didn't have a lick of common sense. Too many books, he'd say, and not enough of life. Well, I guess this proves he was right.*

So what was he supposed to do? Just lie here and die? Of course not. He had to at least make an effort to keep on living. But he had lost his horse and, yes, his rifle. All he had in the way of weapons was an old hunting knife Gabe Cochran had given him a long time ago, back when they'd first gone out searching for game in the woods across the creek from the Cochran farm. The blade was thin from many years of sharpening.

Well, he had to do something. What were his options? He could head upriver. Gonzales was somewhere north of here. He could deliver Captain Jack's damned old message and get some medical treatment. And then, when he had recovered sufficiently from his wound, he could say a fervent fare-thee-well to Sam Houston and Texas and strike out for Louisiana and just let anybody try to stop him.

But the dragoons had been camped upriver. And where there were a dozen Mexican, there had to be dozens more nearby. Santa Anna might be marching on Gonzales even now, seeking to bring Houston to battle and crush this misbegotten insurrection once and for all. Now wouldn't that be ironic—if

Gabe Cochran, who had been dead set on rushing off to Goliad to fight, were to learn that his foolish friend, Boone Tasker, had wandered into the big scrape at Gonzales, no doubt getting his hash cooked for a cause he didn't care a whit for!

On the other hand, the Guadalupe River would lead him southeast, away from the war—like all the other major rivers in Texas it emptied into the Gulf of Mexico. So if he followed it downriver, he would come eventually to the coast, where there was bound to be a boat tailor-made for taking him to Mobile, or New Orleans, or some other civilized place. That was a very appealing prospect.

Of course already a little voice had begun a persistent nagging at the back of his mind. A man, the voice said, was supposed to see things he started through to the end. And a man was supposed to keep his word, too. By accepting this mission from Captain Jack, he had, in effect, made a solemn promise. Was he a quitter and a liar as well as a coward?

At that crucial moment, as Boone wavered between duty and survival, he heard the Mexican dragoons. Crawling to the margin of the thicket, he saw them—on the other side of the Guadalupe, thank heavens!—heading upriver. North, back toward the spot where Boone had first seen them. One of them had the buckskin in tow. Evidently they had spent all morning searching downriver for Boone. Even before they were out of sight, Boone had made up his mind. They were going north. He was heading north. That was all there was to it.

He started on his way, dragging his wounded leg behind him, and keeping to the open ground because that made the going easier. He would just have to trust to luck that there weren't any Mexicans east of the river. Sooner or later he was bound to get at least a little lucky. Every step was an ordeal. He just didn't have the strength. The all-night ride, the ordeal in the river, coupled with the fact that he hadn't eaten since yesterday morning—and then only a day-old biscuit and a handful of parched corn—all this conspired to slow him down. Finally he came across a limb that had fallen from a towering pecan tree; breaking off a piece that looked to be just the right length, he used more scraps of cloth from his ruined trouser leg to pad one end of it—the end that would go under his arm and upon which he would put his weight. This makeshift crutch proved an instant success, and he made much better time because of it.

Except in a very general sense Boone didn't know where he was. Somewhere to the south was the road the Red Rovers had taken in their march from Galveston to Goliad. If he could just reach that road, then surely he could find transport to the coast. It seemed to him that he and his comrades in arms had passed more than two hundred civilians fleeing eastward along that road. Yes, if he could just reach that road, his worries would be over.

Most of his worries, anyway. That little voice, his conscience, was nagging him again. The very least he could do, it said, was turn west on that road and try to find the Red Rovers. He could inform Captain Jack that the way to Gonzales was blocked by the enemy. That was true, more or less. But loyalty to Shackelford, or to the Red Rovers as a whole, or even to the cause they were fighting for wasn't Boone's reason for thinking twice about making tracks out of Texas. It was his friend, Gabe, and not just that Gabe would be disappointed in him if he ran away, but because Boone thought that somehow he might be able to prevent Gabe from getting himself killed.

Boone brooded over his dilemma all day. It gave him something to occupy his mind, helping him ignore the constant pain lancing through his entire body from the bullet wound in his leg, never giving him a moment's respite. He lost track of time—time meant nothing to him anymore, the past and the future of no consequence to a man who focused his entire being on taking the next step, and then the next—so that the darkening of the day caught him by surprise, and he was shocked to realize that night had come. It was cold, frightfully cold, and he shivered violently, but at least the rain had stopped, the clouds were gone, and stars blinked like frosty pinpricks of light through the indigo cloak of the night sky.

He spent that night in a brush-choked ravine, curled up in a tight ball to conserve his body heat, and in spite of his ravenous hunger and the cold wind and the pain of his wound he managed to sleep. Exhaustion overcame him, and as he drifted off, his last thought was to wonder if he would ever wake up.

But he did awaken, the warmth of the morning sun on his face, and with fresh resolve he set out again. His leg was extremely stiff and painful, and yet he hardly noticed the pain anymore—it had become part of him. He could scarcely recall what life without pain was like. Onward he stumbled. His horizons shrank, and so did his goals. All he wanted to do now was reach the road, any road; that was the only thing that mattered, and he couldn't have said why it did, but he knew that reaching a road would be the crowning achievement of his life.

And he did reach that road near midday. He was sitting on a rock beside it when a wagon trundled into view, heading east, and the man driving the wagon stopped the brace of oxen in their traces when he saw Boone. He and his wife and three children—the oldest a boy of about twelve, the youngest an infant girl in her mother's arms—gathered around the dirty, bloody, tattered scarecrow, who at first hardly seemed to notice them.

"You look like you been through hell, son," observed the farmer, laconic.

"Oh, it wasn't so bad."

Noticing Boone's leg, the farmer said, "Reckon you've run into them Mescans."

Boone nodded and explained that he had been on his way to Sam Houston at Gonzales, only to run afoul of an enemy patrol. The farmer offered to find him a berth in the crowded wagon, but Boone shook his head.

"I've got to get to Goliad," he sighed.

"You'll never make it, not in your condition."

"Probably not. But I've got to try."

The plowman glanced at his wife, scratched his

head, and worked on the chew of tobacco that bulged his beard-stubbled cheek. "Well, reckon you can take the horse, then, if that's the way you feel." He nodded at the swayback plow mare tied to the wagon's gate. "Won't never see that nag again, but what the hell."

"I'm obliged to you."

"I ain't one to stand in the way of a feller if he's dead set on gettin' hisself kilt."

He helped Boone get aboard the horse, and his wife handed Boone a sack.

"A few corn dodgers and a little salted meat," she said. "God bless and keep you, young man."

Boone nodded his thanks and rode west. He rode all that day and into the night. The old plow mare was as different from the buckskin as black is from white. It had one pace—slow and methodical—acquired from a lifetime in front of a middle-buster, and no manner of coaxing or threats on Boone's part could compel it to a faster gait. Eventually Boone just gave up trying.

As the day waned—and he wasn't sure what day it was, or how much time had passed since his parting from Gabe and the rest of the Red Rovers—Boone began to feel progressively worse. His wound burned like the dickens and throbbed with pain more intense than any he had yet suffered. One minute he was burning up, the next shivering violently, chilled to the bone. Even his eye sockets burned, and his eyes watered mercilessly. He realized that the wound had become infected, and his imagination leaped into gear, terrifying him with thoughts of gangrene and amputation. But what would that really matter? He was going to find Gabe and try to keep his friend from getting killed, and in all likelihood he would get himself killed in the process, so why worry about infection. It really made no sense at all, and Boone was thoroughly disgusted with Texas and Gabe and the Mexican Army and Captain Jack and the Alabama Red Rovers and most of all with himself.

Several times during the night he passed cook fires marking the campsites of civilian refugees, but he did not stop to ask for help, even though he knew his only hope was to have the wound cauterized, because such treatment would incapacitate him, and he would never rejoin the Red Rovers then. So he pressed doggedly on, stubbornly ignoring the panic-stricken little inner voice of self-survival screaming at him to forget everything else and for God's sake just save himself.

In the early morning hours he drifted off to sleep—only to be rudely and painfully awakened as he hit the ground. He lay there, dazed, dimly aware that the old plow mare was plodding on down the road, and Boone had just enough energy left in him to curse it and all of its ancestors before a darkness much deeper than the night closed down upon him. . . .

When he woke, he realized it was daylight. He was being lifted into a wagon, but his vision was blurred, and he hadn't the strength to speak. He felt his heart flutter with alarming irregularity in his chest, and he knew then that he was dying. He flailed out in blind panic as the darkness closed in on him again—a soft, cool hand on his fevered brow—a soft, lilting female voice, heard as though from a great distance.

"Don't worry. Just rest yourself. I'll take good care of you . . ."

And Boone relaxed, accepting the darkness with some equanimity, because he knew intuitively that he could trust that voice.

CHAPTER SIXTEEN

The Prairie

Captain Jack Shackelford and his Alabama Red Rovers arrived in Goliad on the morning of March 18th. He was immediately ushered into the presence of Colonel James Fannin.

Fannin was a darkly handsome, square-featured man from Georgia. He had entered West Point in 1821, only to withdraw after two years. It was said that he had entered the United States Military Academy under false pretenses, using an assumed name; his abrupt departure from that institution was shrouded in even more mystery than his entry into it. Coming to Texas, and engaging in the lucrative slave trade, he made important friends, spent freely, and dabbled in politics. Being one of the few patriots with any formal military training, he'd been one of the first to receive a commission from the provisional government's general council—that less-than-august body that had been such a thorn in Houston's flesh.

"I have received orders from General Houston to fall back toward Gonzales," Fannin informed Shackelford, "and I am anxious to do so."

Shackelford was puzzled. He had seen no evidence to indicate that Fannin's command was preparing to withdraw from their fortifications near Goliad. He asked Fannin when he had received those orders from Houston.

"Several days ago. But I could not act upon them at that time. You see, I had dispatched Captain King and his Kentucky Rifles—some thirty in number—to assist in the evacuation of settlers at Refugio, as an enemy column commanded by General Urrea, who is by all accounts the most capable officer at Santa Anna's disposal, was advancing on that town from Matagorda."

"And King has not yet returned, I take it."

Fannin went to the window of the small adobe house he had commandeered and made his headquarters. His hands were clasped so tightly behind his back that the knuckles were white.

"King and his men are dead. I received the news yesterday. He notified me that he was engaged with the vanguard of Urrea's cavalry. I sent Colonel Ward and his Georgia Battalion to reinforce him. Ward arrived in time to scatter the enemy force. But instead of assisting the Refugio civilians, King and Ward set off in search of a fight." Fannin shook his head. "They got more of a fight than they had bargained for. The two commands became separated. Urrea arrived with his main force and engaged both. Ward's Georgians took refuge behind the walls of Mission Rosario and repulsed several strong attacks. Under cover of night, Ward and his men managed to escape by heading south, rather than north toward Goliad, which is what Urrea apparently expected them to do. I regret to say that

King was not so lucky. He and his men were captured and shot down in cold blood in the streets of Refugio."

Shackelford grimaced. This was why the cause of Texas independence had suffered one reverse after another. Small independent commands led by impetuous men who refused to act in concert with one another were allowing themselves to be destroyed in piecemeal fashion. Fannin had made a colossal blunder in sending King and Ward to Refugio in the first place, splitting his forces in the face of a superior enemy. Apparently the good colonel hadn't learned his lessons during that sojourn at West Point.

"Then why, may I ask, do you still tarry here?" asked Shackelford. "You say you received word of King's fate yesterday. You know Ward cannot make his way back to Goliad. Urrea's entire army now stands between him and this place."

"Yes," murmured a bemused Fannin, still gazing out the window. "Yes, I realize that."

"Then we must make all haste to join General Houston at Gonzales. If only we can accomplish that, Colonel, Texas will finally have its army and its one chance to defeat Santa Anna."

Fannin glanced dryly at the Alabamian. "You don't know my situation, Captain. My command is composed of several volunteer companies, like your own. Despite all the evidence to the contrary, every man here is convinced that one Texan can whip ten Mexicans. They don't cotton to turning tail."

Shackelford was starting to fume. "This is not

running away, but rather a strategic withdrawal. It also happens to be the direct order of our commander in chief. And frankly, Colonel, you shouldn't give a tinker's damn what your men want or don't want. By God, you're in command here—*aren't you?*"

Fannin refused to rise to the bait, and Shackelford was disappointed that he didn't. *Where was the man's pride? Where was his spirit?*

"It just isn't that simple. That is what I am trying to explain to you, Captain. This morning I called a council. I was obliged to win all of the leaders of those independent commands over to my way of thinking, so that they in turn could persuade their own men."

"Good Lord," gasped Shackelford, disgusted. "I do not endeavor to *persuade* my Red Rovers to do anything. I give orders, and woe unto the man who fails to obey them without question."

"It has been agreed that the time has come to withdraw. Mexican scouts have been spotted roaming about this vicinity. Captain Horton and his Mounted Rifles went out this morning to engage them. But those *rancheros* are as cunning as foxes. When Horton charged them, they melted into the woods. Then, when Horton regrouped his men, the *rancheros* dashed out and nipped at his heels, only to scatter again when he turned on them."

Shackelford grunted. "Sounds like they are having great sport at our expense. It also sounds like it's time to leave. Those *rancheros*, as you call them, are obviously trying to detain us here until their reinforcements arrive."

"I thought you came to fight, Captain."

"My Red Rovers and I *will* fight, sir. But this is neither the time nor the place. Surely you must see that."

"Yes, of course," said Fannin with an ambivalence that struck Shackelford as odd. "We will march at dawn. During the night such provisions and armaments as we cannot carry with us will be destroyed. But the Mexicans are no doubt watching us, and we must not give them any indication that we are abandoning our position until the last possible moment. If they knew today that we intend to march on the morrow, Santa Anna and Urrea will rush their troops forward during the night and cut us off."

This seemed dubious in its logic to Shackelford, but he didn't take issue with Fannin. He left the colonel's office, deeply disturbed. Fannin's odd lethargy could only be attributed to indecision. Shackelford hoped that this indecisiveness would not have tragic consequences.

The next morning enemy dragoons were spotted north of town near the old Mission Aranama. Once again Horton and his Mounted Rifles sallied forth to engage them. The dragoons withdrew into an island of timber, and Horton, impetuous as always, gave chase, only to be struck by more Mexican cavalry, who had rushed forward to reinforce their comrades-in-arms. Horton was in trouble, and Shackelford expected Fannin to issue orders to effect his rescue. When no such orders were issued, Shackelford requested permission to lead his Red

Rovers out to help Horton. Fannin gave it, perhaps realizing that Shackelford was going out one way or the other.

The Red Rovers were eager to clash with the enemy. They had come a long way for this moment. In high spirits they left the defenses of Fort Defiance. No one was more prepared for battle than Gabe Cochran. All night he had thought about the old maple tree and the two graves beneath its sweeping branches. He had heard Sally's sweet voice and Maggie's lilting laughter, and the memories were driving him mad. He missed them so, and couldn't wait to see them again.

But the Red Rovers were disappointed in their quest for action. The Mexican dragoons retreated. Captain Jack's Alabama boys jeered at the withdrawing horsemen and shook their fists at them and even sent a few bullets flying after them. Then they and Horton's rescued riflemen returned to Goliad.

Expecting an attack at any moment, Fannin had his cannon, previously made ready for transport, wheeled back to the walls, and for the rest of that day he had his men standing to, waiting for an assault that never came. It was another decision with which Shackelford privately disagreed. Fannin feared being caught in the open, but Captain Jack didn't think it mattered where they were caught; once Santa Anna and Urrea combined their forces, the whole command was doomed whether they were in Fort Defiance or on the road to Gonzales.

The following morning, the 19th of March, a reconnaissance reported the road was still clear, and

Fannin gave the orders to march. A heavy fog clung to the ground, and Shackelford hoped it would work to their advantage by masking their movements from enemy eyes. They were bringing ten pieces of light artillery with them. The heavier cannons were spiked and buried. The last men out set fire to the buildings containing the provisions for which there was no transport. At ten o'clock that morning the rear guard crossed the San Antonio River.

At noon Fannin called a halt on the banks of Manahuilla Creek, only six miles out of Goliad. The teams of oxen, having been kept in the fort all yesterday, needed to be grazed. Shackelford remonstrated warmly against this delay. He argued that they should push on at least to Coleto Creek, where there was heavy timber that they could use for cover in case of attack; the ground around Manahuilla Creek was too open for his liking. Fear of being caught on the road had caused Fannin to tarry in Fort Defiance. Suddenly, he had come to the conclusion that the enemy would not attack him, but rather linger for a day or two in captured Goliad.

Forward scouts reported no enemy in sight. Fannin led his men across Manahuilla Creek, through a line of post oaks, and onto an open prairie about four miles in diameter, undulating toward the distant woods that marked the course of Coleto Creek. A few *rancheros* were seen on the edge of the prairie to the south, but they quickly vanished when fired upon. Suddenly, the four rear-guard scouts galloped up. The enemy was crossing Manahuilla

Creek in hot pursuit! Soon a dark mass of men were seen emerging from the post oaks to the west.

A column of dragoons, their helmets and the tips of their lances gleaming in the sun—the fog had by now dissipated—came forward at the gallop. Fannin ordered the cannon unlimbered. A few rounds were fired. The Mexicans withdrew. Fannin ordered his command to march at double-quick time for the timber along Coleto Creek about a mile and a half away. They moved in the formation of a hollow square, with artillery at each corner, and Shackelford could see that Fannin had done a good job of drilling his men. Small comfort now, though. More Mexican cavalry circled to the north in an attempt to cut Fannin off from the trees.

Then an ammunition wagon broke down. Again Fannin called a halt. Shackelford couldn't believe it. The Mexicans were swarming on three sides of them, and some of their snipers were now in action. Bullets buzzing like angry bees all around him, Captain Jack rode to Fannin's side.

"We must push on at all hazards until we reach the woods, Colonel!"

Fannin had been wounded in the thigh by a sniper's bullet. Yet he seemed remarkably self-possessed. "I will not abandon this ammunition. We may have need of it before long."

"I should say we will if we don't reach Coleto Creek."

But within moments it was too late. They were completely surrounded. The enemy attacked from all sides. Fannin's men mowed the Mexican soldiers down as they advanced in ranks afoot or charged forward on horseback. Dozens fell, and the Mexican dragoons were especially hard hit, so much so that eventually they dismounted and fought like infantry. Several times a handful of Mexican soldiers actually reached the hollow square, plodding doggedly forward in the face of the withering Texan fire, and then the fighting became hand to hand. But Fannin's men fought like demons. Again and again the Mexicans were driven back, and the square remained intact. Soon the open prairie was carpeted with the dead and the dying. A pall of powder smoke lay so heavily on the field of battle that it lingered for hours.

The fighting continued until nightfall. Then the Mexicans withdrew into the woods on all sides of the prairie and made their night camp. In the murky twilight of early evening Urrea's Carise Indians from Yucatan crawled close to the Texan square and practiced their sharpshooting skills. Shackelford, with his Red Rovers forming the north side of the square, sent some of his men forward to scatter the Indians. The sharpshooters were eventually rooted out and silenced, one by one.

Captain Jack was proud of his men. These volunteers, many of whom had never experienced battle before, had acquitted themselves like veterans of a dozen campaigns. The enemy had been repulsed with heavy loss of life. But the situation was grim. The command was without water. A wagon containing barrels of water had been wrecked by dragoons, and every last barrel smashed. Lack of water was particularly hard on the wounded, of which there were many in the Texan ranks.

A trench about four feet deep was excavated during the night; the carcasses of horses and oxen killed during the battle were used to strengthen this fortification. Shackelford scanned the ring of campfires that encircled them. He calculated that the enemy numbered at least two thousand men. Fannin called a council, and the suggestion was made that at dawn an attempt be made to reach the woods along Coleto Creek. But the wounded, about sixty men, would have to be left behind if the breakout was to have a chancc to succeed. Shackelford and most of the commanders voted against leaving the wounded. The Mexicans were marching under the red banner of no quarter. No one doubted that the wounded would be butchered if they fell into enemy hands. No, they would stay and fight to the bitter end, said Fannin, and all those present concurred.

CHAPTER SEVENTEEN

The Valiant

Captain Juan Galan gazed bleakly out at the open prairie as the slow gray light of dawn stole across the face of the earth. He could not yet distinguish the Texan square, but the bullet-torn banner of the enemy was silhouetted against the orange streaks of the eastern sky. Somewhere between that square and the margin of the woods where Galan stood lay Victor Benavides.

Whether his friend was dead or wounded Galan did not know, but he feared the worst. It had happened yesterday in the thick of the battle. Galan and Victor had participated in a gallant charge against the Texan square. They had been met by a hail of small arms fire and canister fired by the enemy cannon. It was as though the regiment had run into an invisible stone wall. Men fell by the dozens, among them Benavides. Of course Galan didn't know this until later, when the bloodied regiment had withdrawn from the field.

The fate of the Tampico Regiment had resulted in Urrea's order that his cavalry fight on foot. Again and again Galan had led his company forward through the tall grass. It wasn't that Galan wanted to reach the Texan square. All he cared about was finding his friend. But the initial mounted charge had carried them to within a few yards of the Texans, and as the day dragged on, Galan could never get that close again. Of course Victor had been at the forefront of the charge. He was very brave; perhaps he did not look like a warrior, and maybe he'd had his doubts about Santa Anna and the way El Presidente was prosecuting this war. That did not, however, mean that he would not do his duty. Victor Benavides was loyal to the regiment and to his comrades-in-arms. He took his duty seriously. Yes. Victor had fallen very near the enemy entrenchments, and a frustrated Galan could not reach his side.

He had even tried under cover of darkness, crawling through the tall grass, over the bodies of dead soldiers, until he was so close to the Texan square that he could hear them talking to each other in low voices. He'd found several wounded men and dragged two of them back to the trees. One had been in too much pain to be moved, his belly opened up by a load of "blue whistlers" fired from both bores of a rebel's blunderbuss. And one of the two men Galan took back died silently, without so much as a whimper, somewhere along the way. But after a long night of heroism Galan still had not found Victor. There were so many dead in that blood-soaked field! And so many wounded!

An exhausted Galan had gone to his commanding officer, requesting that the colonel go to General Urrea and ask that a truce be arranged with the enemy, so that in the morning the wounded could be retrieved from the field. The colonel honored Galan's request, but Urrea had replied that the attack would resume at first light. The enemy was low on ammunition. He was without water. Most of his oxen and horses had been slain—Urrea had given his sharpshooters specific instructions that they must shoot down all the Texan livestock—so that now Fannin was immobilized. "The general is confident that if we press the attack in the morning, the rebels will break," the colonel informed Galan. "Time enough then to see to the wounded."

Galan was not pleased. Neither was his colonel, who was a good man, a good soldier, a commander who cared about his men. But what could be done? The wounded would have to suffer, would have to hold on somehow until the battle was won. Orders were orders. It was not a good soldier's place to question them.

But Galan *did* question them—silently, to himself. Victor had been pleased when General Sesma, Santa Anna's cavalry commander, had dispatched the Tampico Regiment to join Urrea's column temporarily. When it became evident that Urrea alone would be able to handle Fannin at Goliad, Santa Anna had decided to march on Gonzales, where another large force of rebels was reportedly encamped. "General Urrea is a good commander," Victor had told Galan. "He will not sacrifice us for no reason, as His Excellency saw fit to do when he sacrificed six hundred men attacking the strongest points of the Alamo fortress—a fortress, I remind you, my good friend, which did not even have to be stormed."

And yet now Urrea seemed as insensitive to the plight of the wounded who lay with pain unalleviated in that tall grass as Santa Anna would have been in his place.

So, this morning, an emotionally drained and physically exhausted Juan Galan stood at the edge of the trees and watched the eastern sky brighten and wondered how many more good men would see the sun rise for the last time. He wondered, too, why God had spared him. He had come through yesterday's carnage without a scratch. He had been but a few yards from the enemy lines, with bullets and buckshot and canister filling the air all around him with death, cutting men down to the left and to the right of him as a scythe cuts through tall, ripened wheat. But he had been spared. Would God shield him again today? Or perhaps it was Natalia's prayers that protected him. Still, would this be his last sunrise?

A few minutes ago he had tried to write a letter to his bride, one of those letters that a man-in-arms writes to be delivered to his loved one in the event of his death. Yet words had failed him. The letter remained unwritten.

All Galan could think about now was how much he hated war. He despised it with an unbridled passion. He knew what this hatred meant. He could no longer be a good soldier. He was, in fact, a traitor, because it mattered not in the least to him whether the Texan rebellion was crushed or not. He wanted only one thing—to live. He had to survive, to love Natalia with all his heart and soul. That was his only ambition. He made a silent vow. *I will re-*

turn to you, my love. He could not write the letter, so he had to survive. He resolved not to die for a cause he didn't believe in.

During the night three fieldpieces had arrived—two four-pounders and a howitzer. These were immediately employed in bombarding the Texan square as soon as it was light enough for the cannon crews to find their range. The rebel cannon did not reply. Galan's colonel expressed his opinion that the enemy must be low on ammunition. Galan thought otherwise. He believed it was entirely likely that many of the Texan cannon had been rendered useless; the Texans had had no water with which to sponge the barrels of their fieldpieces in the heat of yesterday's action.

"I hope you're right," said the colonel. "If so, we may not lose the *rest* of the regiment when we resume the attack."

"We don't need to attack at all," said Galan. "We need only continue the bombardment. The Texans will surrender."

"I remind you that the rebels at Bexar did not surrender."

"They were not commanded by James Fannin."

The colonel glanced sharply at him. "Do you know this man?"

"Of course we have never met. But I know he has been sitting idle in Goliad for weeks."

"Are you saying he is a coward, this Fannin?"

"No, not a coward. But he is no Travis. He is not willing to lay down his life if it is to no avail."

And neither am I, thought Galan. *I know Fannin, because we are alike. We are too much in love with life to court death.* It was that love of life that had made Fannin fatally indecisive.

"If he is going to surrender," said the colonel grimly, "he had better hurry. General Urrea will not wait long. If he does, he will have to answer to His Excellency."

Why, wondered Galan, the sudden urgency? It had been Santa Anna, after all, who had squandered thirteen days in the siege of the Alamo. It seemed as though El Presidente considered the capture of San Antonio the climax of the campaign, and that from now on they had only to do a little mopping up.

Galan's prayers were answered. An hour later, James Fannin himself limped across the prairie toward the Mexican lines, carrying a flag of truce, to ask for terms. Urrea informed him that if he wished to "surrender at discretion," the matter was ended. Otherwise, the attack would be renewed immediately.

After a brief conference with his subordinates, Fannin accepted the terms.

A meeting was held between the lines, attended by Fannin and several of his officers as well as several English-speaking officers representing Urrea. One of these was Galan. The terms of the capitulation were written out in both English and Spanish. These instruments were then signed and exchanged.

The terms included a stipulation that the Texans would be received and treated as prisoners of war, that the officers and men would be paroled and shipped to the United States after swearing that they would never again take up arms against the Republic of Mexico. Urrea promised that the wounded would be treated with all possible consideration.

As the Texans were disarmed, ringed now by watchful cavalry, Galan searched for and finally found his friend. Victor Benavides was dead, saber clutched in his hand, lying only a few yards from where the Texan square had stood on the previous day. His horse, also dead, lay across his legs. Galan could tell by the wounds Victor had sustained that his friend had died instantly. That was some consolation. At least he had not suffered.

Kneeling beside the body, Galan gazed at the ragtag rebels now being divested of their weapons. They were a sorry-looking bunch of freebooters, clad in buckskin and homespun, bearded and dirty, hungry and thirsty and bloodied. But they stood proud and defiant, and Galan silently gave them their just due. They were fighting men. Of that there could be no question. He held no malice toward them, did not blame them for Victor's death. If anyone was to blame, it was Santa Anna.

Carts were found for the purpose of transporting the Texan wounded, and then the prisoners were put on the road to Goliad. The Mexican wounded were left behind, along with a detail charged with the grim task of burying the dead. Galan had to leave Victor to their care; the Tampico Regiment was assigned to guarding the prisoners. He took Victor's watch and saber and a few other personal belongings. Why leave them to the gravediggers?

They would strip every body of anything that might have value.

And so, with a heavy heart, Galan put the site of *La Batalla del Encinal del Perdido*—the Battle of the Lost Woods—behind him.

When the column of prisoners reached Manahuilla Creek, the Texans, most of whom had been a day and a half without a drop of water, plunged into the cold, chocolate brown stream like cattle that had just survived a long desert crossing. Some of the cavalrymen prodded the prisoners with their sabers and lances, trying to get them to move on, but Galan stopped them. Only when the colonel sent word that it was time to press on did Galan seek out one of the rebel leaders and politely request that his men quit the creek and fall in line to continue the march.

"I'm obliged to you for your kindness," said the Texan in a slow Southern drawl. "You are obviously a man of honor. I hope your commanding general is, too. The men have heard that Santa Anna marches under the red banner of no quarter."

"General Urrea is an honorable man," said Galan. "He will abide by the terms of the surrender. Of that you can be assured."

At Goliad, Fort Defiance was transformed into a prison camp, ringed with several hundred soldiers. There the prisoners languished for several days, four hundred of them, cold and weak and hungry, most without blankets, some without shoes. Their daily ration was a pittance of beef and a little bread when it was available. The fare of their captors was no better. Most of the civilians had fled Goliad and the surrounding area, leaving very little in the way of provisions for the invaders.

On the 23rd of March, eight Tennessee volunteers, captured at Copano, were added to the other prisoners. Two days later, Ward's Georgia Battalion, one hundred strong, captured at Las Juntas, were also incarcerated in Fort Defiance. That brought the total number of prisoners to nearly six hundred.

Fannin was escorted to Copano to secure a vessel to take the prisoners to New Orleans. On the day he returned, with news that no ships were available for that purpose, Galan's colonel received orders from Santa Anna. The colonel had been left in charge at Goliad until Urrea pressed on toward Victoria. Galan was called to headquarters and allowed to read His Excellency's orders.

With growing horror, Galan read:

As the supreme government has ordered that all foreigners taken with arms in their hands, making war upon the nation, shall be treated as pirates, I have been surprised that this standing order has not been fully complied with. I therefore order you to give immediate effect to the said ordinance in respect to all those foreigners who have had the audacity to insult the Republic and shed the precious blood of Mexican citizens. I trust that, in reply to this, you will inform me that public vengeance has been satisfied, by the execution of these detestable pirates. I zealously hope that in the future the provisions of the supreme government may not for a moment be infringed.

"You cannot execute them," said Galan. "Remember, sir, the details of the surrender instrument which General Urrea himself signed. His Excellency is obviously unaware of the terms . . ."

"His Excellency will be completely indifferent to the terms," sighed the colonel. "I have my orders, Captain. The prisoners must die."

CHAPTER EIGHTEEN

The Massacre

"You can't do this," insisted Galan, desperation rising within him. "It is . . . dishonorable."

The colonel looked surprised. "I am a soldier, and I have been given a direct order."

"You will still be held accountable. All of us will be."

"Held accountable? By whom?"

Galan shook his head. "By all humanity, Colonel. How will you explain this to your family and friends back home?"

"If I do not obey His Excellency's orders, I will never see my family and friends again."

"This is insanity. No act could be more calculated to stiffen the resistance of the rebels. From this point on they will surely fight to the death. And that means many more of our own brave men will never see home or family again."

"I respect Colonel Fannin and his men for their courage," said the colonel, gazing morosely at Santa Anna's orders, which Galan, after reading them, had cast down with a wholly warranted disdain upon the table between the two men. "I have no desire to play the role of executioner. But I am a professional soldier, and as such I am obliged to obey the official dictates of the Republic of Mexico and its president."

"The Mexican people would not ask you to do this. Santa Anna is the only law."

"Yes. And you would do well to remember that, Captain."

"If we prosecute the war in this way, we will lose. God Himself will abandon our cause."

"I never took you for a religious man, Galan."

"I have begun to see things with new eyes."

The colonel rose from his chair, circled the table, then put a hand on Galan's shoulder. "I have always held you in high regard. You are a gifted soldier and a natural leader of men. I am aware that you lost your good friend, Lieutenant Benavides, a few days ago. I would like to spare you further . . . difficulty. For that reason, I am sending you and your company to General Urrea at Victoria. I wish to make a report to the general, and I want you to take it to him."

"Will you at least delay executing your orders until General Urrea can be informed?"

The colonel regretfully shook his head. "Urrea will not countermand His Excellency's orders, Captain. If that is what you are hoping for, it is a forlorn hope."

Galan realized that the colonel was trying to spare him, his company, and Urrea from having to participate in this ugly business. Their souls, at least, would not have to bear the burden that his would carry to the end of his days. It was a noble gesture, but a futile one; Galan felt that the execution of Fannin's command would be a crime for which every man who wore the uniform of the Army of Mexico would have to bear responsibility. As for the Tampico Regiment, its honor would be forever sullied.

"I have always respected you, sir," said Galan as a feeling of helplessness overwhelmed him. "But never more so than at this moment."

"Prepare to leave at once, then. I will have the dispatch ready in a half an hour."

Leaving the colonel's quarters, Galan had to pass near the low, makeshift walls of Fort Defiance, now a prisoner of war camp, as he made his way to the place where his company was camped. One of the prisoners was playing a fife. The tune was "Home, Sweet Home." The mournful melody floated across the ramparts to Galan, leaving a bitter melancholy in his heart. There did not seem to be another sound in all of Goliad; only the soft plaintive wail of the fife and the crunch of dirt beneath Galan's booted feet broke the strange stillness. It was, mused Galan, as though the whole world had caught its breath in anticipation of the horror about to be perpetrated.

Before dawn of March 27th, Captain Jack Shackelford was awakened by one of his Alabama Red Rovers, who informed him that a Mexican officer, a Major Garay, had requested the presence of all rebel surgeons and their hospital attendants.

Rubbing sleep out of his eyes, Shackelford tried to collect his thoughts. He was mentally and physical exhausted. Only a couple of hours ago he had stretched his aching body out on the ground in the corner of the shed made of wagon tarps spread over cedar poles, which served as the hospital for those held prisoner in Fort Defiance. For days of unending toil and misery Shackelford and several other men with medical training had done their best to save the wounded. Their best had seldom been good enough. They were disastrously short on the necessary medical supplies. Their captors would not or could not provide them with anything. As a consequence, the seriously wounded one by one worsened and died. Even now, in the chill darkness before dawn, the moans of the suffering packed into the shelter, lying on the cold ground, most of them with only a tattered blanket, tormented Shackelford, as they had for every waking moment since their return to Goliad. Only in sleep could he find respite.

"To hell with Major Garay," he growled. "And damn your eyes for waking me."

"Sorry, Captain. But maybe it has something to do with our release."

On the verge of telling the man he was a fool for thinking the Mexicans would just let them go, Shackelford thought better of it. If such delusions made this situation easier for the poor fellow to bear, so be it. Captain Jack knew better. He wasn't sure how he knew—but he did. This business was going to end badly.

"Sure," he said with a sigh. "Or maybe we'll finally get some medical supplies."

He took a moment to search out his son. Tom Shackelford had been in the thick of the fight a few days ago and had done himself proud. Praise God, he had emerged without a scratch. Captain Jack told Tom he had been summoned by a Major Garay. Tom was worried, and Shackelford tried to reassure him.

"Likely they need help with their own wounded," he said. "Apparently, Santa Anna forgot to bring any doctors along with him. Don't worry about me, son. In war physicians are worth their weight in gold." He started to turn away. Then, moved by some indefinable dread, he hugged Tom to him. His son was surprised and a little embarrassed by this display of affection. Jack Shackelford was not a demonstrative man. "Whatever happens," said Shackelford, his voice husky with emotions, "I'll always be with you. Never forget that."

"And I with you, Father."

Shackelford was escorted to Garay's tent, along with Dr. Barnard and two other men who had acted as hospital attendants.

"I have been instructed to inform you gentlemen," said Garay, a polite, impeccable, and pleasantly-disposed officer, fluent in English, who had been acting as a liaison with the Texan officers, "that arrangements have been made to send your men to New Orleans on vessels now berthed at Copano Bay."

"Joyful news!" exclaimed Barnard, vastly relieved.

"I was under the impression there were no vessels available for that purpose," remarked Shackelford.

"The arrangements have been made," repeated Garay, smiling warmly. "Those prisoners who are able to march will leave immediately. The wounded will be transported as soon as sufficient wagons are collected. You gentlemen must remain with the wounded until such time as they are evacuated."

"My son is among those who are to leave this morning," said Shackelford. "I would ask that you allow him to remain with me."

Garay stared at Captain Jack. Was that pity in his eyes? Shackelford couldn't be sure, but his suspicions were aroused.

"I regret that I cannot fulfill your request, Captain. The orders are very clear. All able-bodied prisoners leave immediately. There can be no exceptions."

"It's just that I promised him we would remain together and see this through to the end."

"I am sorry." Garay was eager to leave the tent. "You gentlemen will please remain here for the time being. I must attend to a few details, and then I will return."

After Garay's hasty departure, Shackelford paced the confines of the tent like a caged animal. For his part, Dr. Barnard seemed quite content with the situation.

"Cool your heels, Jack," he urged, good-naturedly. "We'll all be back in the United States in a few days."

"You're an utter fool if you believe that," snapped Shackelford.

Before long they could hear the tramp of marching men. Peering out of the tent, Shackelford saw Fannin's command leaving the fort-turned-prison, guarded by Mexican dragoons, and followed by several companies of infantry. When Captain Jack spotted his son among the other captives, his heart seemed to twist painfully in his chest, and without thinking he barged out of the tent—only to have his way blocked by a pair of stern-faced sentries. They pushed him back, but he resisted, and one of the struck him with the butt of a Brown Bess rifle, knocking him to the ground. As Shackelford got back to his feet, eyes blazing with fury, Barnard rushed forward and clutched his arm.

"In heaven's name, Jack! Do you want to be killed?"

"We're all going to be killed," rasped Shackelford, watching with empty eyes as his son was marched away. "I just want to die at my boy's side, that's all."

The word that they were being taken to the coast and from there to New Orleans by boat swept through the ragged ranks of Fannin's command. But Gabe Cochran remained aloof, unaffected by the contagion of high spirits among his compatriots. He seemed to be in a kind of trance, and those who walked along beside him assumed he had a touch of madness brought on by the emotional and physical stress all had suffered in the past few days.

Some of the men noticed a group of Mexican women, *soldaderas,* standing outside Fort Defiance and gazing at them with pity in their dark eyes, wringing their hands and murmuring, *"Pobrecitos! Pobrecitos!"* Those prisoners who understood Spanish knew that the camp followers were calling them "poor fellows," but assumed the kind-hearted women were lamenting their wretched condition.

A short distance from the fort the prisoners were divided into three groups of approximately one hundred and fifty men each. One group was taken down the road to San Antonio, another put on the road to San Patricio, and the third on the wagon trace that would bring them to the lower ford of the river.

Gabe Cochran was in the last group. The sun had just risen in all its crimson glory, but he could feel no warmth from the sunshine on his bearded face. He paid little attention to what occurred around him. Instead, he concentrated on listening hard for a sound he thought he heard above the shuffle and tramp of marching men. It sounded very much like singing—a little girl singing, somewhere far away, singing the way his precious daughter Maggie used to sing. His dead wife and daughter had been much on his mind. A few days ago, as he participated in digging the trenches around the Texan square during the battle, he had so lost himself that for a moment he was back in Alabama, digging graves beneath the old maple tree . . .

The Mexican guards called a halt. The infantry company that had been tagging along behind filed abreast of the column of prisoners and turned, left face, while the dragoons moved to the front and rear of the column. At that moment there came a sound like distant, crackling thunder in the direction taken by one of the other groups.

Fannin stepped out of the ranks, limping badly on his wounded leg. Gabe hadn't realized the colonel was with them until then. Ashen-faced but stiffly composed, Fannin turned to face his men.

"Boys, it looks like they're going to shoot us."

A Mexican officer approached Fannin, flanked by a squad of soldiers. Fannin smiled wanly at the officer and handed over his watch.

"I ask only that you send this watch to my family, that you shoot straight, and that we are all given a decent Christian burial."

The Mexican officer bowed stiffly and walked quickly away. Gabe heard the clicking of musket locks all along the Mexican ranks. Several prisoners broke and ran. The dragoons had been expecting this; they galloped after the runaways, lances lowered. Gabe didn't look back to see how the fugitives fared. There was no escape. Even if there were, he didn't *want* to escape. He noticed how the banners of the Mexican infantry were silhouetted against the red sky in the east, and he remembered the dream he'd had on the road to Mobile with Boone Tasker.

Boone! Thank God Boone wasn't here. That was the one thing he would have regretted . . .

The enemy muskets spoke, a crashing volley. All about Gabe men cringed helplessly and fell dying. Gabe stood tall, gazing at the red sky above the Mexican ranks, brows knit as he listened hard to the singing that grew louder and louder until it drowned out the din of gunfire, and then he knew it was Maggie singing, his sweet dear Maggie, calling him home, and a look of contentment was frozen on Gabe Cochran's face as he fell with a bullet through his heart.

CHAPTER NINETEEN

The Serpent

Following his successful escape from Galveston Island, Mingo Green made up his mind to travel by night, hoping to reduce the odds against him. He realized those odds were high. Realistically, he didn't have a prayer of getting all the way home to Alabama and Sadie. There was no way for him to know how many miles lay between him and his destination, or how many white men, all of whom were now his mortal enemy. He dared not let himself be seen by a white man, especially in Texas, with rumors flying as they were about a slave insurrection. In such a fear-charged environment any white man he met would probably shoot first and ask questions later. He was going to have to live—and think—like a hunted animal.

Nonetheless, Mingo never for an instant regretted what he had done, and not once did he even contemplate turning back. He was committed to getting back to Sadie, not to mention his unborn child, or die in the attempt.

At least the rain had finally stopped, and the days got warmer. He steered his course by the stars in the night sky. Keeping as much as possible to the woodlands and swamps, he spotted a lot of game. He killed some squirrels and a rabbit by using his belt for a slingshot; he could hurl a stone twenty yards with pinpoint accuracy, a skill he had acquired as a child. Laid up during the day, he dug a hole in the ground and built a small fire, using wood that didn't produce a lot of smoke. Fires were risky, but he preferred his game cooked, and he never stopped anywhere near a road or a farm. There weren't very many roads or farms in these parts; Texas was still a largely unsettled country. What he most feared was crossing paths with a white hunter. The only weapons he had were his belt-slingshot and the hatchet he had stolen. They weren't sufficient if he tangled with a Texas backwoodsman. But for two days and nights Mingo traveled east and never saw a living soul.

The swamps worried him the most. This was a country of numerous bayous and sloughs. He had to keep an eye out for water moccasins and gators and quicksand. The swampland that lay between Magnolia and Ravenmoor, which he'd had to traverse every time he slipped away to visit Sadie, was nothing compared to these Texas swamps, which seemed to go on forever.

On the third night, deep in the heart of one of those seemingly endless swamps, Mingo saw the flicker of a campfire directly ahead. His first impulse was to steer wide of the fire, thinking that it must belong to white hunters. Or maybe a band of cutthroats hiding out in the swamp. And yet, in spite of the danger, Mingo felt an irrational urge to slip in closer and see what he could see. For three days now he hadn't set eyes on another human being, and Mingo longed to hear a human voice again—even a white voice. Besides, he might be able to steal a firearm or some food or even a horse, once the inhabitant—or inhabitants—of that camp went to sleep. He could go a lot farther a lot faster if he was mounted on a good horse.

It was crazy, utterly crazy, but Mingo threw caution and logic to the wind. Creeping closer, he saw that there were four or five dark shapes hunched around the fire, which was located on a hummock of sawgrass and deadwood rising above the level of the swamp. Mingo could hear voices, but he could not yet distinguish the words being spoken, so he moved closer still, keeping a clump of cypress trees between him and the hummock, wading through the black water that rose almost to his knees, moving very slowly because the slightest sound might give him away. Reaching the cypress trees, he crouched among the massive knees beneath the moss-draped limbs. He was very close now, maybe thirty yards from the hummock, and he could tell that the men around the fire were all Negroes. They were looking up, raptly attentive, at another man who stood before them, and who gestured dramatically as he spoke.

This man was tall and wiry—clad in a long, tattered black cloak and a stovepipe hat, the crown bent, on his head.

An icy dread seized Mingo.

It was Big Tom—the man who had been in league with Desiree, that Mobile prostitute!

Mingo thought he had to be dreaming. Big Tom

had fled Mobile then to escape the authorities. Mingo hadn't figured they'd catch him. But by what quirk of malicious fate had Big Tom ended up here, in a Texas swamp? And not just any Texas swamp, but the very one that Mingo happened to be crossing in his desperate odyssey. No, it couldn't be. Fate could not be that cruel. Yet there he stood, Big Tom, with his shoulder-length locks and blazing eyes and Sugar Islands accent—the man Mingo had met only briefly, and yet feared more than anything or anyone else in the world.

Mingo tried to calm himself. Big Tom was just a man, he told himself. A mere mortal. *And I am a man, too. I am his equal. I can handle him if I have to.* But such reasoning failed to restore to Mingo even a modicum of self-confidence.

Peering cautiously over the cypress knees behind which he crouched in the stinking black water, Mingo watched and listened as Big Tom addressed his audience.

"'And he dat stealeth a man, and selleth him, he shall surely be put to death.' Dat's what de Good Book says, brothers. Exodus, chapter 21. And in Deuteronomy, chapter 24, it say, 'If a man be caught stealin' any of his brothers, and makin' merchandise out of dem, or sellin' dem, then he should die, and thou shalt put dat evil away from among you."

"Amen," murmured one of the others.

"I seen a vision," said Big Tom. "I seen white spirits and black spirits locked in a life-or-death struggle. The sun was dark, and the sky was filled with thunder, and blood it flowed like a river. I have seen strange writings on leaves in de forest. I have seen a rain of blood fallin' from de sky. And den I heard a voice sayin' dat Serpent was loose among us, and dat Jesus had done laid down de yoke he bore for the sins of man, and dat I should take up dat yoke, and when I did, I saw de future, and I know now I have been chosen, like Moses hisself was chosen, to lead my people to de promised land. De time is fast approachin', my brothers, when de first will be last, and de last first. The Day of Judgment will soon be at hand."

"Amen!"

Big Tom leaned forward, his angular face illuminated by the firelight, and he pointed at the others, one by one, with a long, crooked finger.

"You will be my disciples. De signs in de heavens have told me it is time to begin my great work. We must arise and slay our enemies with their own weapons. And den will come de Year of Jubilee, and we will be de masters, and de white folks will be our slaves. The Serpent will be defeated. We are de weapons of God's vengeance, my brothers."

"But what we goin' do?" asked one of the others. "Dere's so few of ussen, and so many white folk."

"Ye of little faith," said Big Tom, his tone one of gentle scolding. "Jesus had only twelve disciples, and yet dey changed the world. We will strike, and a host will gather around us, as the slave bursts his chains and joins our cause. It is for us to show de way, and all our people will follow. Dey be waitin' for our call. We must not fail."

Mingo didn't like the sound of this. Big Tom was preaching slave rebellion, and the others—runaways, no doubt—were eating it up. Fleeing Mobile, Big Tom had fallen in with these fugitives, and right away he had proceeded to bend them to his will. Mingo wanted no part of it. It was time to leave.

As he began to ease away from the clump of old cypress knees, he heard a sound overhead and looked up in time to see something drop out of the moss-draped limbs—something big—and when it landed on his back, its weight drove him down into the black water. Mingo was strong, and panic made him stronger. He flipped the weight off his back and came up out of the water, sputtering, and staggering backward. A man rose up before him, the biggest man he had ever seen, a black man who had to stand at least seven feet tall and weigh in at three hundred pounds if he weighed an ounce, and all of it muscle and sinew. The man grinned at him, displaying big yellow teeth.

"Come here, boy," rumbled the giant. "Come here to Friday . . ."

Mingo turned to run, knowing the goliath could crush him with his bare hands. He had lost his sack when Friday had dropped on him, and the hatchet—along with the stolen shoes, which he did not wear in the swamp—was in the sack. Not that Mingo thought the hand ax would be effective against a giant like Friday. So he made up his mind to flee, but for a man so large, Friday was remarkably quick and agile. He lashed out with his long arms, and one of his hands closed on Mingo's arm like a vise. Then Friday lifted Mingo into the air and slammed him into the trunk of the nearest cypress tree, and Mingo blacked out . . .

When he came to his head hurt so much he figured his skull had been split wide open. As his vision cleared, he could see Big Tom leaning over him.

"We met once, and dat was chance," drawled Big Tom. "Now here we be meetin' again, and dat's coincidence. I don't put no faith in coincidence."

Big Tom's hand came into Mingo's view, and in the hand was a stiletto knife.

Mingo got to his feet in a hurry. The other runaways, including Friday, stood in a grim, suspicious circle around him—all but one who sat by the fire, a blanket over his head and shoulders, his back turned.

"You best talk fast and sweet," advised Big Tom, "or I'll cut you up like a Christmas hen."

"I stole the horse, like you said to do," replied Mingo. "And I run. I want to be free. Only place to go was Texas. So here I am. But what are *you* doin' here?"

"I run, too. I stow away on a boat. Didn't know where dat ol' boat would take me. But de Almighty sent me here, and now I know why—to lead dese brothers to freedom."

Mingo didn't believe for a moment that Big Tom was the least bit interested in these men or their future. But he tried to *look* like he believed.

"I heard what you said. I was fixin' to come in and ask if I could join you—and then *this* one jumped me." He looked at Friday, who grinned yellowly at him again.

"Dat Friday, he got eyes like a cat. He can see at

night as good as you or me can see in de daytime. Dat's why he be up in dat tree. Keepin' a lookout."

"Why is he called Friday?"

"'Cause he cain't 'member a t'ing past a year ago—except dat he was born on a Friday. Dat's all he know."

Mingo glanced at the other runaways. All of them carried a weapon of some sort—a knife, a hatchet, a length of rusted chain, a club. He realized that if Big Tom gave the word, they would fall on him and tear him to pieces. He turned his attention back to Big Tom and tried to keep the fear out of his eyes.

"So what you goin' do? Kill me? Or let me join up?"

Big Tom turned to the blanket-draped figure sitting by the fire.

"We'll let Marriah decide."

The girl stood, then turned and looked deeply into Mingo's eyes. Astonished, all Mingo could do was stare back at her. She was tall and willowy with a heart-shaped face and big, doelike eyes. She was bewitching rather than beautiful, with an exotic woman-child quality about her. When she lowered the blanket to her shoulders, he could see that her hair was cut short like a man's. But there was no mistaking her for a man.

Still gazing into his eyes, Marriah opened her left hand and let the small bird bones she had been holding fall to the ground. Big Tom looked down at them, as did Mingo and all the others. They gazed at the tiny, fragile white bones. Marriah merely glanced at them, then returned her gaze to Mingo's face.

"What do de tell you?" asked Big Tom eagerly. "What do de bones say?"

"They tell me that God sent him to help us," replied Marriah.

A glance at Big Tom convinced Mingo that the man put great store by this voodoo fortune-telling. Marriah, then, was a seer, who could "read" the truth in the pattern made by the bones strewn on the ground.

"De bones say you live," Big Tom told Mingo. "Brothers, we have a new disciple."

The other runaways introduced themselves to Mingo, one by one. There was Gus and Jules and Kimbo, the first in his fifties or sixties, the last barely twenty, and Jules somewhere in between. And, of course, there was Friday, who nearly crushed Mingo's hand in his own and flashed his big yellow teeth.

"You come at a good time," said Big Tom. "Tomorrow we begin the uprisin'. Tomorrow we will go to a place not far from here, where a family of white folk keep some of our brothers in bondage."

"Then what?" asked Mingo.

"Den we start dat river of blood to flowin'. No white man, woman, or child be spared."

"Children, too?" Mingo was aghast.

"Dat's de only way to save dere souls. Dere blood will wash away de sins dey have done."

Mingo nodded as though he understood and accepted this madman's logic, but he *couldn't* accept it, and wanted no part of the madness.

Problem was, how was he going to get out of it?

CHAPTER TWENTY

The Fugitives

Pierce Hammond was angry at Mingo Green for running off. But in a way he was glad the slave was gone. That ungrateful wretch had been more trouble than he was worth. Pierce had been trying to do him a favor—well, actually, he had been doing Jubal a favor—and if Mingo wanted to go back to Alabama and be branded, or worse, then that suited Pierce, who was determined to wash his hands of the whole affair. Not that he expected Mingo to get anywhere near Alabama. No, Slade would never get Mingo in his clutches again, would never be afforded the opportunity of satisfying his sadistic cravings at Mingo's expense. There was no chance that Mingo would get that far. Somewhere along the line he would be caught and sold into slavery, or, if he resisted capture, which Pierce thought likely, he would be killed. So Pierce was secure in the knowledge that old Jubal would never know that he had let him down.

Nonetheless, Pierce was obliged to file a notice in the local newspaper, describing Mingo as a runaway slave and offering a modest reward for his return. This was expected of a slaveholder, and others would think something was amiss if he failed to go through the motions. He was confident that Mingo was not hiding out somewhere on the island. No, the boy was headed east. Just as well, for Pierce was not possessed of the means to pay the bounty if Mingo *was* returned. He was practically penniless.

The lingering effects of severe dysentery kept a couple of the Red Rovers bedridden for longer than Pierce had anticipated, and so while he was eager to be on his way, he had to tarry a while longer in Galveston. Captain Jack had made it clear that he was not to leave anyone behind. So Pierce found himself with time on his hands. He whiled away that time exploring the island, which he found bleak and uninteresting. Remembering his pledge to old Jubal, he asked around after Jobe. He talked to several men engaged in the slave trade and attended the local slave auction. No luck. His description of Jobe fit a hundred slaves.

So it happened that he was still on the island on the 22nd of March when word came that Fannin's command had been captured in a battle near Goliad. Captain Jack Shackelford and his Alabama Red Rovers were in the hands of the enemy, and no one doubted for an instant what their fate would be.

Pierce was stunned by the news. At first it did not even occur to him how fortunate he had been that dysentery had incapacitated him. The other eleven Red Rovers looked to him now for leadership. Not that they would necessarily do his bidding, no matter what. Pierce knew these men, knew how their minds worked. They were frontiersmen for the most part, an independent bunch. They gave their allegiance conditionally, and any man who hoped to lead them had to prove he was worthy of their loyalty.

It was a responsibility Pierce gladly would have forsaken, except that if he did, and one of the other Red Rovers took over the leadership role, disaster might befall them all. It was clear to Pierce that most of the others wanted to ride hard for Goliad in a gallant bid to free their comrades-in-arms. A completely ludicrous idea, of course, and at first Pierce could hardly believe they were serious. But they were, and Pierce had no intention of sacrificing himself in an act so fatally quixotic.

He understood that the others were more steadfast in their loyalty to the company than he. And most of them had friends—and, in the case of one of them, a brother—among the Red Rovers who had fallen into enemy hands. So he could not simply *order* them not to go. He had to reason with them. And he tried to, because he wanted to save their lives, as well as his own.

We just join General Sam Houston's army at Gonzales, he told them. That had been, he thought, Shackelford's intention, and why Captain Jack had so foolishly changed his mind and marched to Goliad and disaster instead, he would probably never know. But the only way they could help the other Red Rovers, not to mention Texas, was to avoid throwing their lives away.

His arguments worked on all but a few of the men—one of them the man whose brother was now a prisoner of war. That man slipped away during the night, and Pierce never expected to see him again. He would ride for Goliad and lose his life. It made no more sense to Pierce than Mingo's determination to go back to Alabama.

Pierce and the others were preparing to depart the island themselves two days later when a deputation of concerned citizens, including the mayor of Galveston, called upon them. The meeting took place in the parlor of the widow woman's house, and Pierce insisted that all the Red Rovers be present.

"I am sure," said the mayor, "that you gentlemen have heard the rumors circulating about a slave revolt in this vicinity. Santa Anna, damn his hide, has issued proclamations urging the slaves to take up arms and turn against their masters. In return, he promises them their freedom. His spies are known to be active in encouraging insurrection among the Negroes, not to mention our Mexican population. Well, gentlemen, it is my solemn and distasteful duty to inform you that the rumors have been proven true. Yesterday a man's body was found on the road to Sabine Town, about fifty miles east of here. Not far from that place, a farm was burned, the farmer and his wife butchered. A small band of Negro runaways was spotted on a plantation near Black Bayou. The owner of the plantation, his two sons, and the overseer confronted the runaways. Shots were fired. Some of the runaways had firearms, no doubt taken from the dead hands of the man found on the road, and the farmer.

"This is a grave business, gentlemen. Very grave,

indeed. There are reports of increasing unrest among the slaves in these parts. If this insurrection picks up steam, the whole of Texas could be bathed in blood within a fortnight."

"What do you want of us?" asked Pierce.

"Why, sir, you and your men are the only army unit left in Galveston. It is your duty to protect the citizenry. And we are in peril, sir, make no mistake about that. I, too, have a duty. The maintenance of order is my responsibility. I do not wish to see vigilante mobs take to the streets of Galveston, or patrolling the roads in the surrounding countryside. Once panic sets in, and vigilantes take the law into their own hands, innocent blood will be shed. Mark my words, that unless I can assure the populace that the gallant Red Rovers of Alabama are actively engaged in putting down this insurrection, we will have panic. Panic, sir, and murder."

Pierce nodded and turned to his men. "Boys, I don't like the idea of innocent women and children being butchered. Seems to me Captain Jack would want us to do this. These runaways, for all intents and purposes, are fighting for Santa Anna. This is just what that so-called Napoleon of the West wants. I think it's our duty to put out this fire before we go off to join Sam Houston."

The others readily agreed. They appreciated the way Pierce seemed to be involving them in this decision. And they were all Southerners. Slaveholder or not, a white Southern man lived with the fear of slave revolt in his heart. That sort of thing simply could not be permitted. An insurrection here might trigger others, perhaps even in Alabama, where some of these men had wives and children.

Pierce was surprised that they went along so readily. He had expected insistence on their part that some effort be made to save Captain Jack and the other Red Rovers. Not that a single one of them really thought this was possible. But honor would demand it. After all, honor was not the exclusive property of the Southern gentleman—even though Southern gentlemen would have liked it to be so.

Giving the circumstances careful consideration, Pierce concluded that the slave revolt had saved these men from the horns of a dilemma—satisfying honor on the one hand and sacrificing themselves in a suicide mission on the other. Now they had an excuse to avoid Goliad and certain death, and their honor would remain intact, because putting down a slave insurrection, thereby saving who knew how many innocent men, women, and children from slaughter, was also an honorable thing to do.

Taking this line of reasoning one step further, Pierce realized that he was no different from these men. His honor, too, was at stake; he, too, had resolved to ride to the rescue of the captured Red Rovers not because he wanted to, but because he had to. This was a quite shocking revelation. Pierce had always scorned the concept of honor as practiced by men like his father and Charles Drayton. Now here he was making his decisions according to the dictates of a code of personal honor of which they would heartily approve!

Then how could he explain to himself that refusal to demand satisfaction for Drayton's insult by meeting the man on the field of honor? There seemed to be only one explanation. His father had been right. He was a coward. He hadn't refused out of scorn for the code of honor, but rather to save his own skin. This explained why he had come to Texas, even knowing there was danger here. He'd come to prove to himself—and to his father—that he was not a coward.

And so far he wasn't succeeding in that endeavor.

With these sobering conclusions weighing heavily on his mind, Pierce and the Red Rovers left Galveston Island and headed east into the bayou country to pick up the trail of the fugitive slaves.

As he watched the runaway called Jules die by slow inches, his belly full of buckshot, Mingo's mind was racing. He knew that if he didn't get away from Big Tom somehow he'd be dying soon, too. Just like Jules. He'd die here in Texas after all, never to see Sadie again. He had to get away. But how?

They were back in the swamp now. They'd ventured out, and before Mingo knew what to think, the traveler had been waylaid, the lone white man who had been on the road to Sabine Town. Big Tom, Friday, and Kimbo had done the killing, and it hadn't been pretty. Friday had jumped out of the bushes and grabbed the man's horse by its bridle check straps and bent the animal's neck, wrestling it to the ground the way one would a calf; Kimbo had hurled himself at the rider and carried him out of the saddle and to the ground and held him there while Big Tom drove the stiletto to the hilt beneath the man's chin. The point of the blade had pierced the man's brain, killing him instantly.

Big Tom had taken the dead man's flintlock rifle, and Kimbo took his pistol. They offered the knife to Friday but he didn't want it, so it was offered next to Mingo because he didn't have a weapon—he hadn't been able to find the sack with the hatchet, which had fallen into the black water of the swamp. But he didn't want the knife. He didn't want anything to do with any of this. And yet, because of the way Big Tom was watching him, he took it.

And then Big Tom led them to a nearby farm, and before Mingo could figure out a way to warn the folks who lived there without getting his own throat cut, it was too late. Big Tom had paired him up with Friday, and it seemed to Mingo that Big Tom could read his mind and knew he was thinking turncoat thoughts, so he had put Friday to the task of keeping an eye on him.

The memory haunted Mingo and made him sick. He knew it would always be with him, and that it would never fade, and that even though he hadn't lifted a hand against anyone, he would still have to answer for this at the pearly gates, and there was no excuse he could give that would save him from the fires of hell.

If they'd just killed that farmer and his wife, it would have been bad enough. The farmer had died quickly—one shot with that rifle and Big Tom had dropped him in his tracks. But Kimbo and Jules had raped the woman before they killed her. Mingo almost acted then. Almost. Until he saw that Big Tom was watching him again, watching him with those hellish eyes, *and to my everlastin' shame I just stood by and let them have their way with that poor woman and just tried not to puke,* because any sign of weakness on his part and Big Tom would have killed him, too. The man liked to kill. He was pure evil, that one. The Devil owned Big Tom's soul—*and he's made a down payment on mine, too.*

Next they had moved on to the plantation. Big Tom said if they killed the master and the overseer, all the plantation slaves would join their cause, and the day of reckoning and redemption would be upon them. But they'd been routed instead, and Mingo was glad. Jules had been shot, and Mingo was glad of that, too. After what Jules had done to that poor woman, Mingo couldn't feel sorry for him, not one bit.

So now they were back in the swamps, and Jules was dying, Big Tom was brooding, and Mingo was wondering how he could escape this nightmare. He had a hunch Gus was having second thoughts, too; the old graybeard hadn't cottoned to the killing and raping, either. But one look deep into the old man's eyes and Mingo knew he couldn't count on Gus for help. Gus appeared more scared of Big Tom than Mingo was—if that were possible.

Night came, seeming to rise up out of the black water, a heavy, oppressive darkness full of the stench of rotting vegetation and swamp noise. They did not dare risk a fire. No one said anything. Everybody but Mingo was waiting for Big Tom to say or do something. Mingo was just waiting to get up enough nerve to make a run for it.

He had even thought about trying to kill Big Tom. He had the knife. But he wasn't sure he could do it. Wasn't altogether sure that Big Tom would die if his throat was cut or a blade ruptured his heart. Because Mingo wasn't entirely certain that Big Tom was human. He thought the man might be the Devil himself in human form.

Finally, Jules drew his last tortured breath, and Big Tom seemed to have been waiting for that. He lay down on the ground as if to go to sleep. Kimbo, Gus, Friday, and Marriah did likewise. Mingo continued to sit there, knees drawn up to his chest, watching Big Tom's longcoat-draped body, wondering if Big Tom was tricking him, pretending to be asleep, but waiting for Mingo to make his move.

So deep in thought was Mingo that Marriah's voice, a whisper in his ear, nearly made him jump out of his skin.

"You can go ahead and run out now," she said, "but you got to take me with you."

"What makes you think I want to run out?"

"I just know these things."

Mingo glanced warily at the dark shapes on the ground—Big Tom, Kimbo, Gus, Friday, and the dead man, Jules.

"Don't fret," she said. "They won't hear us."

"How can you be so sure?"

"I put a spell on them, that's how."

Mingo peered at her.

"You don't believe me," she said, pouting, and

before he could stop her, she clapped twice, very loudly.

"Lordy!" muttered Mingo.

But none of the others so much as stirred.

"You see?" she asked with a smug smile.

"Yeah." But Mingo wasn't convinced. Maybe it was a trap to lure him into playing his hand. Maybe Big Tom was just using Marriah. Such a diabolical scheme would be just the kind of thing Big Tom would do.

"How come you want to get away?" Mingo asked her. "I thought you and Big Tom were . . ."

"We are. But I'm still scared of him. I don't expect you know what I mean."

In fact, Mingo knew exactly what she meant. Any person in his or her right mind would be afraid of Big Tom.

"He doesn't care about me," continued Marriah. "He's just using me. And when he gets tired of me . . . well, I don't want to be around for that to happen. He'd just hand me over to Kimbo and Friday. Jules wanted me, too. Real bad. Least he's dead now. I ain't no whore, to be passed around from man to man like a jug of corn liquor."

Mingo didn't trust her. Still thought it might be a game orchestrated by Big Tom. He wasn't sure of anything, but he decided if he waited until he *was* sure, it would be too late. So he took a chance.

"Okay," he whispered. "Let's go."

They stood up, he took her hand, and they left the camp, venturing into the night-shrouded swamp, but Mingo wasn't afraid of the swamp anymore. The dangers of snakes and gators and quicksand paled in comparison to the much graver danger represented by Big Tom.

They didn't stop moving until nearly dawn. Marriah had stamina; she never faltered or complained. And as the sky began to lighten, they emerged from the swamp and rested in a stand of timber from which they could see the road to Sabine Town a few hundred yards away, across a mist-shrouded field of tall grass and wildflowers.

"You got someplace to call home?" he asked.

Marriah shook her head, watching him intently with those big doelike eyes of hers.

"Well, you cain't come with me, girl," he said. "I've got me a wife and child back in Alabama. That's where I'm bound. I don't reckon to have much chance of gettin' there, but I'd have even less of a chance with you along."

"Neither one of us has got a chance, so long as Big Tom's alive."

"You should have used your voodoo on him."

"Hexes don't work on a man whose soul is so black. I'm going to find the white men and lead them back to Big Tom. The white men will hang Big Tom, and then we be safe."

"Like as not they'll hang you, too."

"Would you be sorry if they did?"

"Like I said, I got a wife . . ."

She leaned over and cupped his face in her hands and kissed him on the lips. Mingo felt himself weakening, then caught himself with a fierce shake of the head, grabbing her wrists and pulling her hands away.

"No, I'm leavin' Texas fast as these old feet can

carry me. You do what you want. Just leave me out of it."

She smiled coyly. "I could make you love me. I could put a spell on you."

"There's somethin' I been wantin' to know. How come you led Big Tom to believe I'd been sent by God to help him?"

"God *did* send you. But to help me, not Big Tom. I knew you'd run out, and you'd take me with you."

Mingo started to say something. But then he saw movement back in the swamp from whence they had just come, and he stared hard, trying to see in the gray twilight that lingers before dawn . . .

Fear stabbing at his heart, he shot upright and pulled Marriah to her feet.

"Run, girl! Run for your life!"

She looked back and saw what he had seen.

Big Tom and Kimbo and Friday, splashing through the black water, coming after them, and it seemed even at this distance that one could see the hellfire in Big Tom's eyes.

CHAPTER TWENTY-ONE

The Hanging

When Big Tom and Kimbo started shooting at them, Marriah threw herself to the ground, but Mingo yanked her back on her feet and started running, towing her along behind. He knew that at this range it was unlikely they'd be hit, and there was no time to waste on the ground; their only hope was to flee. They had to reach the road and hope for a miracle.

By the time they reached the road, Marriah was winded. She'd been on the move for hours without respite, and had just about come to the end of her rope. Mingo paused only long enough to glance back at their pursuers. Big Tom and Kimbo had pulled out in front of Friday, who was lumbering doggedly along. Even so, Big Tom and his young disciple had not gained on their prey. They'd made the mistake of trying to reload their weapons on the run, which had slowed them down.

Still, Mingo wasn't encouraged. He hadn't lost any ground, but neither had he gained any. Without Marriah he could make better time. He was strong and could run like a deer, all day if need be. And yet he refused to leave the girl behind. He wasn't going to let Big Tom get his hands on her. There was no telling what that devil would do to her, but whatever it might be, it wouldn't be pretty, and Mingo didn't want to live with that on his conscience. Since falling in with Big Tom, his conscience had been burdened enough.

He turned down the road, pulling Marriah along behind him, giving no thought to the direction he was taking. Again Big Tom and Kimbo fired their weapons. Marriah stumbled and fell. Mingo thought at first that she had been hit. But she hadn't been—she just couldn't go on, and told him so. "Run!" she cried. "Leave me and save yourself!" But Mingo swept her up and threw her over a shoulder and kept going.

And then riders appeared where the road curved through a stand of timber up ahead, and Mingo couldn't believe his eyes because the man in the lead was Pierce Hammond, astride his Kentucky thoroughbred! So miracles did happen. The riders spotted them and broke into a gallop. Mingo kept running until they were almost upon him. Then, exhausted, he stopped and fell to his knees and rolled Marriah gently off his shoulder and just sat there for a moment, chest heaving, blinking sweat out of his eyes as he looked up at Pierce, who had checked his horse while the other Red Rovers thundered past.

Mingo looked back. Big Tom and Kimbo and Friday were running away now, but they didn't have a chance. A few of the Red Rovers cut loose with whoops and hollers as they ran their prey down. Shots were fired. Kimbo had turned at bay, raising his pistol. Mingo doubted the boy had had time to reload. But that didn't matter to the Red Rovers closing in on him. They gunned him down without hesitation, several pistols barking and spitting flame, and Kimbo performed a bizarre, jerky pirouette, then crumpled. Friday also turned to face his attackers, lunging at the nearest rider, taking the man's horse down just the way Mingo had seen him do with the mount of the lone traveler on the Sabine Town road. But before the giant could get his hands on the fallen rider, another Red Rover galloped up and clubbed him with the barrel of a pistol, knocking Friday to his knees. An instant later, three of the Alabama men were swarming all over him, like wolves on a wounded elk. They overpowered him, but it took all three to get the job done.

As for Big Tom, he tossed his rifle away and just stopped running as his pursuers closed in. He held his hands out away from his sides and put up no resistance as one of the Red Rovers dismounted and hit him hard in the face with a pistol. Big Tom went down, and a moment later his hands were tied behind him.

Relieved, Mingo glanced up at Pierce, who was still in the saddle. Pierce was aiming his pistol at him.

"You damn fool. I told you you'd never get back to Alabama."

"I ain't done tryin'," gasped Mingo, and hung his head.

Mingo came close to hanging that day.

There was no question in the minds of the Red Rovers that they had captured at least some of the fugitive slaves they were after. Questions were put to Big Tom and Friday, but neither said a word. Mingo, however, was forthcoming.

"Are there any more of you?" asked one of the Red Rovers, a man named Gregg.

Mingo wondered what had happened to Gus. Had Big Tom left the old man behind? Or had he merely fallen behind during the pursuit through the swamp? Old Gus hadn't taken an active role in any of the killings. In fact, he'd been as sickened by the bloodshed as Mingo had been. So Mingo decided not to mention him, and answered in the negative.

Some of the Red Rovers weren't inclined to believe him. They had expected a much larger force.

"Well, what are we gonna do with them?" a man named Martin asked Pierce.

"We hang them, of course," said Gregg. "That goes without saying. Nobody expects us to drag them back, just so's they can stand trial. We hang them from the nearest tree and leave their bodies as a warning to other slaves." He looked expectantly at Pierce.

"But ain't this one your boy?" Martin asked Pierce, nodding in Mingo's direction. "I remember him from Galveston."

"Yes, he is. And I'd like to know how he came to fall in with this crowd."

"What does it matter?" asked Gregg, impatiently. "Let's stretch their worthless necks and get it over with."

"I'd just like to know," said Pierce. "What do you have to say for yourself, Mingo?"

And Mingo told him the unvarnished truth—how he had stumbled upon Big Tom and the others in the swamp, how he'd been compelled to join them, knowing they wouldn't let him live otherwise, how he had stood by helplessly and witnessed the ambush of the lone traveler on the road to Sabine Town, and then the brutal murders of the farmer and his wife and then described the confrontation at the plantation. He concluded with a brief summary of his and Marriah's attempt to escape Big Tom.

"It doesn't matter none whether he was trying to get away or not," said Gregg. "He was there when the killings were done, and he's just as guilty as the rest."

"Leastways let the girl go," said Mingo. "She ain't had no hand in none of this."

"You lie down with dogs you get up with fleas," said Gregg, glaring at Marriah.

Martin was watching Pierce. "So what do you say?"

Pierce knew he was standing on thin ice. These men would not obey an order if they didn't agree with its premise. He could either stand by and let them hang Mingo or come up with a convincing reason for them not to. The easy way out would be to let the executions commence.

But he couldn't do that. Couldn't, because he recognized Big Tom as the associate of Desiree, the Mobile courtesan, and now that he knew what Big Tom was capable of, he was beginning to wonder if

Mingo hadn't saved his life after all, that night back in Alabama when he'd come to heaving his guts out on the floor of Desiree's bedroom, with Boone and Gabe and Mingo there. Mingo had claimed that Desiree and Big Tom were scheming to cut Pierce's throat, but he hadn't been so sure. Rob him, yes. But murder him? Now, looking at that crazy bastard Big Tom, knowing he had the blood of innocents on his hands, Pierce had to accept the possibility as real that Mingo had actually saved his life back in Mobile.

And if there was any chance that this was true, he couldn't stand by and let the Red Rovers hang the slave.

"I say I believe Mingo is telling the truth," said Pierce, choosing his words carefully. "I happen to know this one," he added, pointing a finger at Big Tom. "I know for a fact he attempted murder in Mobile. He's a bad character, and I have no doubt he's the leader of this insurrection."

"I say the only reason you don't want to see your boy hanged is because he's worth money to you," said Gregg. "You planters are all alike. Always putting profit ahead of everything else. Including justice."

"I didn't pay two bits for Mingo," replied Pierce, unruffled. "He is my father's property, and he's no particular friend of mine. But I can assure you of one thing. He is no liar. And he isn't a cold-blooded murderer, either."

"Well," said Martin, "it was plain enough he and the gal were tryin' to get shed of these others. We all seen that."

"That doesn't mean he didn't take part in the killings," snapped Gregg. "We got no proof he didn't, except his own word. And what's a nigger's word worth?"

"My word is worth something, I should hope," said Pierce icily, feigning indignation. "And I gave you my word that Mingo is no murderer."

Truculent, Gregg glared at Pierce, and Pierce wondered if his bluff would work. Gregg knew he was a Southern blueblood, and had to assume that he was exceedingly sensitive about his honor. Pierce had managed to turn this discussion into an issue of honor, hinging on whether Gregg and the other Red Rovers accepted his word as a gentleman. If Gregg pressed the issue now he would be questioning Pierce's integrity, and he would have to wonder if Pierce would demand satisfaction for the affront. Of course, Pierce had no intention of challenging Gregg. But Gregg couldn't know that. So it all depended on how important it was to Gregg to see Mingo hang.

"All right," growled Gregg, sullen. "But these others are gonna hang."

"Not the girl," said Pierce.

Gregg glanced at the faces of the other Red Rovers. Pierce thought he had Martin on his side. But he couldn't be sure of the rest. How sure could Gregg be of them?

"I say we turn her over to the authorities," continued Pierce. "I don't cotton to killing a woman."

Most of the others seemed to think this was an acceptable compromise, and Gregg nodded, reluctantly conceding another victory to Pierce.

"No," said Mingo.

"Be quiet," snapped Pierce.

"She don't have a prayer in no white man's court."

"If you ever want to see Sadie again, you'll shut your mouth," advised Pierce, exasperated.

Mingo knew this was good advice. He glanced at Marriah, who sat on the ground beside the road, hugging her knees to her chest, her eyes downcast. Mingo felt sorry for her, wanted to help her, but he realized that Pierce was right—he had to think of Sadie and his unborn child.

"It's settled then," said Gregg. "Boys, get some rope and pick a good tree."

Big Tom's hands were bound behind his back. So were Friday's. Friday just stood there like a big dumb ox as though he didn't comprehend what was about to happen to him. And as they put the rope around his neck, Big Tom grinned at Mingo.

"You ain't never gonna be free, boy, till de day you die."

"Take 'em up," growled Gregg as the ropes were tossed over the stout lower limb of a big elm. He and two other men took hold of Friday's rope and hoisted the giant off the ground. It took only two men on Big Tom's rope. As the pair danced on air, dying by slow strangulation, Pierce turned away. He had no stomach for this kind of justice. It would have been better, no matter how heinous the crime, to shoot them dead.

Mingo forced himself to watch Big Tom die. He watched until that hellish light in Big Tom's eyes flickered out, and the corpse twisted slowly on the rope. He wanted to be certain Big Tom was dead.

When the Red Rovers emptied their guns into the two bodies, he breathed a sigh of relief.

"Now we're even," said Pierce, standing nearby.

"Give me my freedom papers."

"No."

"Let me go back. Sadie needs me."

"It's no good, Mingo. Even if you go back, how would you get Sadie away from Ravenmoor? You think Ambler is going to give her her freedom papers just because you ask nicely? No, he wouldn't, and you'd run off with her, and they would hunt the both of you down."

"I'm goin' back and you cain't stop me."

"You're going to stay and testify on behalf of that woman yonder, if need be. Then, when the fight is over, we'll *both* go back, and I'll try to buy Sadie."

"With what? Yore daddy's money? It was Marse Hammond who sold her away in the first place."

"I'll think of something."

Mingo scoffed at that. "You can stay here and die for Texas if you want to. But not me."

Pierce gave him a long, angry look, then turned sharply on his heel and walked away.

CHAPTER TWENTY-TWO

The Communion

When Boone Tasker regained consciousness, the first thing he remembered was that soft, lilting female voice. *Don't worry. Just rest yourself. I'll take care of you.* There had been something in that voice so reassuring, so comforting, that the fear of dying had left him. Belatedly, he recalled the rest of it—the patrol of Mexican dragoons, the river, the seemingly endless ordeal of his long walk south. He remembered very little after that, just bits and pieces—except for that voice. He would never forget that voice.

He opened his eyes and looked around. He lay on a narrow bed in a small room, a wall of well-chinked, square-cut logs beside him, and a small window in the wall draped with pale yellow muslin curtains, and the golden sun was streaming through the window, a warm and welcome sight. He was covered with a patchwork quilt and lay on a luxurious feather mattress, and he was so warm and comfortable that he decided to drift off to sleep again.

"How do you feel this morning?"

Boone's eyes snapped open again. She had been

sitting in a chair at the head of the bed, and now she rose to lean over him, smiling. He knew this was the owner of the voice that had been of such comfort to him. She was slender and fair-skinned, her auburn hair long and tied back, her eyes bright and bottle green, as green and limpid as a pool of spring water.

"I thought you were an angel talking to me," he said.

She laughed. "Oh, I'm no angel. Just ask my father if you don't believe me."

"Where am I? How long have I been unconscious?"

"We found you three days ago."

"Three days!"

"You had an awful fever. The wound in your leg had become infected."

"My leg . . ." Boon groped under the quilt, felt the bandage, and breathed a sigh of relief as the panic left him, quick as it had come. "I thought for sure I'd lose my leg."

"It was a near thing," she replied gravely. "The wound had to be drained and cleaned and dressed twice a day. I used an elm poultice to draw the poison out." She fussed with the quilt, tucking it in tight against his sides.

"You did all that for me?" Boone blushed, realizing he lay naked beneath the covers.

Again she laughed softly, seeming to read his mind. "I've lived with a pair of brothers all my life." Then the smile faltered. "The oldest is . . . is dead. The Mexicans killed him."

"God, I'm sorry."

She shook her head. "He died for a cause he believed in. That's good, isn't it? If you must die, it's best to give your life for something important."

"Of course." Boone didn't know what to say. His heart went out to her. "What is your name?"

"Jessy. Jessamine Reynolds."

"You're Irish?"

"You noticed." The smile was back in full force. "I do have a bit of a brogue, don't I? And you?"

"Boone Tasker. From Illinois, by way of Alabama. I came to Texas with Captain Jack Shackelford and the Red Rovers—"

"Oh." She drew back, brows knit above those now-troubled green eyes.

"What's wrong?" asked Boone. "Have you some news of the Red Rovers?"

"Bad news, I fear," replied a man who stood, unnoticed by Boone until that moment, in the doorway. He was a short, stocky man, his rust-colored hair graying, his craggy features stern, almost sour.

"This is my father," said Jessy, "Alton Reynolds. His name is Boone Tasker, Father. He was with the—"

"I heard, girl. The Red Rovers were with Fannin, my friend, when they met the Mexican Army at Coleto Creek. They went down in defeat three days ago. We just got word of it ourselves."

Boone was stunned, his thoughts turning to Gabe Cochran. "Heavy casualties?" he asked.

Alton nodded. "I've heard it was so. The rest be in the care and keeping of the Mexican army. Which is to say that they would be better off dead."

"Father!"

"Well, they brought it on themselves," snapped Alton crossly. "The bloody fools."

Alton Reynolds's attitude perturbed Boone. Gabe could be dead, along with a lot of other Red Rovers, and this man was sneering at them.

"Those were good, brave men," he said, sitting up in bed. "They came here and fought and died, some of them, for you and yours, Mr. Reynolds."

"No, not for me, lad. I didna want this war."

"Apparently your son felt differently."

Boone instantly regretted his words. Grief sprang like a tiger into Alton's eyes, its claws ripping at the man's heart.

"Aye. He went off to fight, against his father's wishes, and they killed him. He was a bloody fool, as well."

"Well, this is one fool who won't be a bother to you a moment longer," said Boone. "I'll have my clothes, please, miss, so that I can be on my way."

"You're not going anywhere," said Jessy. Now she was angry, and her eyes shot emerald sparks at him and at her father. "I've gone to a lot trouble to keep you alive. Father, tell him he must stay a while yet. If he tries to travel, that wound will open up again, and likely become infected once more. And that will be the end of him."

"If he wants to go, let him. It'll make trouble for us if the Mexicans find him here."

"Oh!" Jessy was furious now. "Men! Stubborn as mules, the both of you." She opened a cedar-lined chest at the foot of the bed and took out Boone's clothes. They had been washed and mended and neatly folded. She threw them at him. "There. Be gone with you then, I wash my hands of you."

She stood there, fists clenched, and Boone could see that her eyes betrayed her. She was afraid that he really would go, and she wanted so badly for him to stay, and not entirely because of his delicate condition. He realized, too, that he didn't really want to leave, after all, and the risk of opening and infecting the wound again had nothing to do with that either.

"No, lad," said Alton, with a sigh. "You must stay, at least for another day or two. Jessy's right, of course. You'd lose your leg, for certain, and probably your life. We'll forget all about our differences on the war."

Boone nodded, quite willing to accept a truce. "I apologize. It's just that my best friend was with Fannin, and now I don't know if he's dead or alive."

"Many good men will die before this is done," said Alton sadly, and left the room.

Jessy gathered up Boone's clothes, folded them, and put them back in the trunk. She was quite composed, as though nothing had happened. He watched every move she made, and she smiled a little self-consciously under this intense scrutiny, a shy but pleased smile, and it made Boone smile, too. He couldn't help himself.

"Now we've had our first quarrel, and we're none the worse for it, she said. "You lie back down, and I'll go fetch you a bit of soup and some tea."

Boone did exactly as he was told.

Jessy told him everything he wanted to know. He

was in Brazoria—she and her father had found him on the side of the road and brought him home in the wagon they had taken to Refugio for the purpose of retrieving the body of her older brother, John. He had died in a skirmish with Mexican cavalry a week earlier, and they had only just gotten the news. So Boone had traveled in the back of a wagon beside a week-old corpse, and he was glad he'd been unconscious. Alton Reynolds had been sure they would have to dig two graves when they got back to Brazoria, but Jessy had vehemently disagreed; she'd made up her mind that she was going to save Boone—and Boone got the distinct impression that when Jessamine Reynolds made up her mind she was going to do something, it usually got done.

Alton had come to Brazoria eight years ago. He was a shopkeeper by trade, and his business back in Georgia had suffered during the hard times brought on by the Panic of 1819. When his wife died of lung fever, that was the last straw, he sold his struggling store, loaded his daughter and two sons in a wagon, and headed west for a new beginning. He had heard that the new Republic of Mexico was inviting Americans into the province of Texas. Mexico knew it needed to populate its northern province if it hoped to hold onto it—and keep the Comanches at bay—and its own people had not thus far demonstrated much interest in relocating to the fringes of civilization. Bringing Americans in was a gamble, but Mexico hoped to win the loyalty of the Anglo emigrants with generous grants of land, few restrictions, and no taxes.

The policy was successful—at first. Impresarios like Stephen F. Austin were given land grants to establish colonies, and most of them were sincere in their desire to become good citizens of the Mexican Republic. Alton Reynolds was more than willing. Born in Ireland, he'd come to the United States as a child, seen his parents fall on bad times, and had suffered tragedy and travail himself. Forsaking his United States citizenship had not been a difficult decision for him. No patriot to any flag, his loyalty was to his family. He established another store in Brazoria and prospered. The Texas settlers were in desperate need of goods and supplies. And even the requirement that all Anglo settlers become good Catholics was no hardship for Alton, for he was and always had been a Catholic, and had suffered for his faith in the United States, where prejudice against "popery" ran strong.

All in all, Reynolds was quite content with his new life in the Republic of Mexico, and he had opposed the move for Texas independence from the very beginning. He saw it as a scheme by Southern slaveholders who wanted to add a new state to the Slave South. Alton had a powerful aversion to slavery—another reason he hadn't prospered in Georgia. But his oldest son, born in Georgia—and thus born a citizen of the United States—saw things in an entirely different light. John Reynolds had become an ardent rebel and gone off to fight for freedom, against his father's wishes. Now he was dead, and Alton blamed the rebellion's ringleaders—men like Houston and Bowie and Travis and Burleson. He was frankly glad that Bowie and

Travis had perished at the Alamo. Served them right, he said.

Of course, such sentiments did not stand him in good stead with the majority of his neighbors. Brazoria turned against Alton Reynolds. By now, though, most of the town's inhabitants had joined the "Runaway Scrape," fleeing before the advance of the Mexican army. Good riddance, was Alton's defiant opinion. He wouldn't run. Had no reason to flee. He was a loyal citizen of the Republic of Mexico, and after Santa Anna had crushed the insurrection—as he was bound to do—Mexico would reward those who stood with her during the crisis.

Like her brother, Jessy supported the revolution, and she hated it that her father steadfastly opposed the noble cause for which John had given his life. Her younger brother, Seth, was of like mind. John's death had hit them all very hard, but Seth was perhaps the one hit the hardest. Seth had idolized his older brother. The news of John's death seemed to knock all the youthful innocence out of him. Seth had been a happy, carefree boy of fourteen. Now he was very grave, very moody, never smiling, and Jessy had a feeling the change was permanent in nature. Worst of all, Seth was very upset with his father. While Jessy tried to understand Alton Reynolds's point of view, Seth refused to acknowledge any mitigating circumstances. He despised his father now, with every bit as much passion as he hated the Mexicans. The estrangement of father and brother was a source of profound distress for Jessy.

Boone was surprised to discover that Jessy's feelings were important to him. He tried to analyze his own feelings. From the very start he felt strongly attached to her. At first he thought this was merely because she had saved his life. But he soon came to realize that there was much more to it than that. For one thing, he felt very comfortable in her presence. More than comfortable—when she was near he experienced a kind of giddy warmth that seemed to rush madly through his veins and made him feel more alive than he had ever felt before. Her smiles made her skin tingle.

What was more, he felt completely relaxed in her presence. Their being together seemed to him to be the most natural thing in the world—and being apart the most unnatural. He could talk openly to her, confident that she would understand him, even if words failed. It was as though there existed an invisible connection between them that allowed one to know completely the other's heart. This kind of communion with another human being had never happened to Boone before. Always before he had been thoroughly tongue-tied around women. This had been particularly upsetting to a person like Boone, who in every other circumstance would seldom be caught at a loss for words. Even around Sarah Ambler he had been nervous and conversationally inept. Not so with Jessy. He could tell her anything, speak his mind, even bare his soul, certain that she would comprehend his true meaning, and, most important, accept him unconditionally. It seemed that they had known each other all their lives.

He thought she was beautiful, though her beauty

was entirely different from Sarah's. Sarah was a delicate, doll-like young woman, Jessy was tall and willowy. Her face and arms were tanned, and that made the dusting of freckles on her cheeks more pronounced. The freckles and the fine blond hair on her forearms Boone found especially beguiling. There was nothing really dainty or delicate about Jessy. She was strong, both physically and emotionally. Boone was bewitched by her eyes, too. They were very candid eyes, and very intelligent, too. They were the mirrors to her soul. One could tell by looking into her eyes whether she was angry or sad or happy or pensive. Boone realized he had never really looked deeply into Sarah's eyes the way he could look, unabashedly, into Jessy's. A proper young Southern belle, Sarah had always averted her gaze, somewhat coquettishly, Boone thought. But she would certainly have been offended had a young man been so bold as to gaze at her. Not so with Jessy. In fact, quite frequently she and Boone caught themselves staring for long moments at one another—and during those moments Boone was filled with a quiet, contented kind of joy and wonder all the more complete because he knew Jessy was feeling the same as he.

Alton Reynolds could not fail to notice the strong attachment between the stranger and his daughter, and in the days to come he became increasingly anxious for Boone to leave. It was quite likely that Mexican soldiers would appear in Brazoria at any moment, and he feared that Boone's presence would jeopardize his family. The word was out that Sam Houston had withdrawn from Gonzales, and that Santa Anna had effected an unopposed crossing of the Guadalupe River and was pursuing Houston's ragtag army of rebels eastward. "I expect that drunkard will retreat all the way to Louisiana," said Alton. "He's a big talker, like the rest of the so-called leaders of this rebellion. But when the times get tough, Houston fades into the brush like a scared rabbit."

Boone was offended. "Sam Houston is no coward."

"Oh? I suppose you're well acquainted with the man."

"I've never met him, but I can assure you that he has never run from danger in his life. He had demonstrated his courage on many occasions. Why, everyone knows that at Horseshoe Bend, when he was but a young ensign in the United States Army, he suffered two serious wounds while leading attacks against the Red Stick Creeks. His bravery was so conspicuous that it brought him to the attention of Andrew Jackson himself."

"Legends are wonderful things," said Alton dryly. "Especially when the gullible swallow them, hook and all."

"What I have told you is well-established fact, sir."

"Then why is he running like a scalded dog now? Why doesn't he stand and fight? He and his cohorts claimed they would gladly give their lives for the cause. Now they have their chance. Let them give their lives, and we'll be done with this tragic business."

"When the time is right, Sam Houston will fight."

"And I suppose you'll be there when he does," sneered Alton.

"I will be if it is humanly possible."

"And why are you willing to die for Texas? You're from Alabama."

"Illinois, by way of Alabama."

"I will repeat my question."

"No need, sir. It isn't just Texas. It's an idea. A principle called liberty."

"Bah!" said Alton, disgusted. "A fancy word that means nothing. I'm free enough under Mexican rule. I'll have no more liberty under the Stars and Stripes than I have now. You don't have a clue why this war is being waged. Men like Houston and Travis and Fannin—Southerners all, mind you—are fighting to make Texas another slave state. If you're from Illinois, you ought to know that."

Boone shook his head. He refused to believe he was the pawn of the Southern slave power. "That may be the motive for some," he replied, "but it is not why I came to Texas."

In fact, Boone was hard-pressed to understand why he felt so compelled to defend Sam Houston and the revolution. He knew full well he hadn't come to Texas dedicated to fight and maybe die for freedom. It had simply been a lark, an adventure, and an avenue of escape from heartbreak. Following his clash with the Mexican dragoons, he had been determined to forsake Texas. But now he felt entirely different. Maybe it had something to do with Jessy, and Jessy's brother, who had died for what he believed in. And maybe there was some revenge, too, because he had a hunch Gabe

Cochran was dead, too. If so, it didn't matter that Gabe had wanted to die, had perished for the wrong reason. Gabe had been a friend, the only true friend Boone had ever had—until Jessy, for he knew that Jessy was a friend—and this nurtured in him a strong animus against the Mexican Army in general and Santa Anna in particular.

He realized that Alton Reynolds was right about one thing. At any moment Mexican soldiers might appear in Brazoria. Of course he didn't want to fall into enemy hands. But more than that, he didn't want Jessy to be here when they came.

"I'll go," he told her when they were alone. "But only if you'll come with me."

"I can't do that. I couldn't leave. Not unless my father and Seth do."

"I've heard some awful stories about Santa Anna's soldiers and what they do to civilians," said Boone. "You can't count on your father's sentiments to protect you. The Mexicans may not be too discriminating, if you know what I mean."

She nodded, and he could tell that she was frightened.

"It's you I'm most concerned about," she replied. "I . . . I want you to go. Not because I'm afraid you'll make trouble for us. I just want to know you're safe. And when this is all over, then . . . well, maybe then you'll come back and see me . . ."

For the first time she was shy in his presence.

"Please, Jessy," said Boone, distraught. "Please come with me. We'll take Seth with us. I'll talk to your father. I know he won't leave, but I'll make him see that sending you and Seth away is a precaution he ought to take."

"He won't do it. He's convinced that his loyalty to the Republic of Mexico will protect us."

"No. He's just trying to prove a point," said Boone, getting angry. "And he's putting his children at risk in doing it. He's trying to prove he's right and those who have chosen rebellion are wrong. I can see now why Seth is so mad at him."

"Promise me you'll leave in the morning."

Feeling empty, Boone gazed into her green eyes, and the knowledge that he *had* to go subjected him to the most profound melancholy. Unable to say the words, he nodded, absolutely miserable.

She put on a brave smile for his benefit. "I'll miss you," she whispered. "And now you must make me one more promise—that you'll come back after the fighting is over. I want you to come back to me, Boone Tasker, safe and sound."

"I promise."

That night, after Alton and Seth had gone to bed, Boone and Jessy sat near the hearth fire, sat close together but not touching, and not talking, either, because there was no need for words. They treasured these last moments together, enjoyed one another's nearness, and wondered if it would ever be so again. There were a lot of things Boone wanted to say—that he would miss her, that he wouldn't, couldn't be happy unless they were together. He wanted to explain how she made him feel. So content, so complete, so full of hope for the future, and so full of life for the present. How his whole life had been but a preface to his meeting her, and that nothing that had happened before, or would happen after, would be nearly as important to him. She had become the pivot of his life, the hinge of his fate.

But he didn't say any of those things, and he knew he really didn't need to, because Jessy understood everything, knew exactly how he felt and—the most wonderful part of it all—she felt the same way.

Finally, she sighed and with a sad smile told him good night and left him, and Boone sat there for another hour or two, staring morosely into the fire, dreading the dawn, wishing it would never come, that the earth would stand still. That was the problem with life, though. You couldn't stop it at a certain point, that most magic moment, when you knew it would never get any better, and had every reason to fear it would get only worse. Those moments came and went just like the night, and you could never recapture them. All you could do was try to preserve them in memory, for the memory had to suffice to get you through the dark times you knew lay ahead . . .

An hour before dawn Boone fell asleep on the floor by the fireplace.

It was Jessy who shook him awake.

"Jessy," he said, still groggy with sleep, and with pain in his heart. "Please come with me . . ."

"It's too late," she said very quietly. "The Mexicans are here."

CHAPTER TWENTY-THREE

The Prisoners

Boone entertained some hope that it might be just a small patrol. He'd eluded one before, and maybe he could do so a second time. But it wasn't a mere patrol. In a matter of minutes an entire regiment of dragoons filled the muddy streets of Brazoria. They obviously knew what they were doing; clearly this was not the first Texas town they had invaded. Instead of coming from one direction, they swarmed in from all sides, without warning, so that there was no chance of organizing resistance or fleeing.

Not that there was any organized resistance in Brazoria. About half of the population had already departed, joining the "Runaway Scrape." Those who remained were not prepared to put up a fight. Most of the able-bodied and hotheaded men of Brazoria had already gone off to "hit a lick" for independence.

But Boone knew there was at least one man in town who was eager to tangle with the Mexicans. Or rather, one boy who thought he was man enough. Seth Reynolds grabbed his squirrel gun and made for the door, an expression of cold fury stamped on his face. Alton yelled at him to stop, and grabbed at him, but Seth eluded his father and was at the door when Boone got to him.

"I know how you feel, Seth, but don't go out there with a gun in your hands. This isn't the time or the place to avenge your brother's death."

"Let me go!" rasped Seth. "Get out of my way."

Boone held on to the lad. Fortunately, Seth Reynolds was a bantamweight. Still, he made up for his size with his fervor and bold courage.

"Use your head, boy! You'll just bring harm to your sister. I know that's not what you want."

Seth looked at Jessy—and stopped trying to bull his way through Boone, who slowly pried the squirrel gun out of the youngster's grasp.

At that instant he heard horses right out front of the cabin, and then boot heels beating a stern tattoo on the weathered planks of the porch, and Boone knew he was doomed if the soldiers barged in and found him with a gun in his hands. He tossed the old smoothbore to Jessy, who stood over near the fireplace, and Jessy, without hesitation, racked the gun in the iron hooks above the mantel. Boone marveled at how well they knew each other's mind; she'd known somehow what he wanted, just as *he* had known, without question, that she would rack the smoothbore.

The soldiers didn't bother to knock. The door cracked open on its hinges, and three men entered, two dragoons with pistols and sabers in hand, their dark, lean features hawkish beneath the brass visors of their plumed helmets. This pair was followed by a third man, obviously an officer.

Boone took Seth by the shoulders and stepped

back, taking Seth with him, putting some distance between them and the Mexicans, and ready to restrain Seth should the boy, God forbid, allow his rage to get the better of him. It was obvious by the looks on the faces of the dragoons that they would not hesitate to respond violently to one wrong move. They were ready and willing to kill. All they needed was an excuse. And maybe they didn't even need that.

The officer swept the room and its occupants with cold eyes, which finally came to rest on the squirrel gun above the fireplace. He snapped a command and one of the dragoons brushed past Boone and, firing a cruel glance Jessy's way, confiscated the rifle.

"Any other weapons here?" asked the officer in halting English.

"No," said Alton. "We are not rebels, sir. My name is Alton Reynolds. I am a loyal citizen of the republic. I have always stood adamantly opposed to this insurrection. I—"

"Be silent." The officer swung his attention to Seth. He saw the hate in the boy's eyes, and a faint, unpleasant smile curled his lips. "And you? Are you a loyal citizen, as well?"

"He's just a boy," said Boone. "He can do you no harm."

"I have seen younger than this among the rebels. And who are you?"

"He's my brother," said Seth. "My brother, Johnny."

"That's right," said Alton. "This is my oldest son."

Surprised, Boone glanced at Alton. Then he realized that Reynolds was trying to protect his family, not him.

"And how do you feel about this insurrection?" the officer asked Boone.

"I'll be glad when it's all over with."

"It *will* be over, soon." The officer turned to the dragoons and gave them a curt order before leaving the cabin. The dragoons motioned with their pistols, making clear their wish that Boone and the Reynolds family go outside. Boone's trouser leg had hidden the bandages that remained on his leg, but he could not conceal his limp. The dragoons gave no indication, though, that they thought anything of it.

The residents of Brazoria were rounded up and herded into the building that served as the community's church, schoolhouse, and meeting hall. It was the only structure large enough to hold them all. No one was permitted to leave. A squad of dragoons encircling the place made certain of that. The rest of the Mexicans proceeded to ransack every cabin.

A short while later, another officer entered the meeting house, flanked by a pair of dragoons, to address the forty-odd men, women, and children incarcerated there.

"My name is Juan Galan, captain in the Tampico Regiment. I regret that you people have been inconvenienced."

Alton stepped forward. "We can see from the windows that your men are looting our homes,

Captain. Why are you doing this? We are loyal citizens of—"

"Speak for yourself, Alton," growled someone from the back of the crowd that had gathered to hear what Galan had to say.

"We are not looters," said Galan. "We are looking for food. Our army's supply lines are stretched thin. The rebels have left very little behind as they flee to the east. My men are hungry. I must requisition as much in the way of supplies as I can. But rest assured that we will not take everything. I do not want you to go hungry. I am sure, as loyal citizens, that you will not object to sharing your food with the army, which has come to punish the rebels in your midst."

"Well," said Alton, "I guess that's all right."

"All right for you, maybe," said a man who pushed to the forefront of the crowd. He was a burly, sandy-haired man wearing a blacksmith's leather apron. He looked very strong and very belligerent—but Boone noticed that Galan did not seem the least bit wary of the man, and his lack of fear had nothing to do with the pair of dragoons backing him up.

"Who are you, sir?" asked Galan.

"Ed Hardin. And I say your men are gonna rob us blind. It ain't just food you're after. We're a poor people, and we ain't got much, and we won't have anything left when your vultures get finished."

"Not so," said Galan calmly. "We have express orders not to take anything but supplies. I repeat, there will be no looting. You have my word as an officer that any looter will be severely punished."

"Your word don't float any boats with me," said Hardin.

"The captain seems to be an honorable man," said Alton.

"Thank you," said Galan. "I assure you that your inconvenience will be brief."

Another officer entered the hall with urgent strides and spoke in hushed tones to Galan, who promptly turned and went outside, followed by the brace of dragoons, who closed the doors behind them. At that moment a woman cried out, and a man shouted, "Look there!" The crowd pressed to see through the windows on the north side of the hall. Having taken a seat on a bench near one of those windows, Boone had a clear view. A detail of dragoons were coming into town, trailing a pair of dead men draped over a single mule.

"That's Titus Pittman's mule," said Hardin. "So I reckon it must be Titan and his boy. They must have put up a fight. Brave men, and may God rest their souls."

"Idiots," said Alton angrily. "What could they hope to accomplish besides getting themselves killed—and putting the rest of us at risk?"

"Better hold your tongue, Alton," advised Hardin, scowling. "I'm of a mind to wring your scrawny neck with my bare hands, and you know I can do it, too. Beg pardon, Jessy, but your pa just gets my goat."

It was obvious that most of the others shared Hardin's sentiments concerning Alton Reynolds, and Alton was smart enough to know when to shut his mouth.

Watching through the window, Boone saw Galan approach the two bodies, listening to the other officer who was clearly reporting what had happened. Galan nodded, turned, and looked at the meeting hall—and it seemed to Boone that he was looking right at the window where he sat. The expression on his face alarmed Boone.

"We've got to get out of here," he muttered.

Jessy was right beside him, her face close to his, and only she heard him.

"Why?" she asked. "That captain strikes me as an honest man."

"I guess he is, for one of Santa Anna's soldiers. But a good soldier follows orders, even if he doesn't agree with them. And Galan is a good soldier. It's been bred in him from the day he was born. You can look at him and tell."

"But there are innocent women and children here."

"From the stories I've heard, that won't make any difference to Santa Anna."

"There *is* a way out," whispered Seth, who had slipped up behind Boone and overheard the conversation. "But we'll have to wait until dark to have any hope of getting away."

Boone nodded. He hoped they would still all be alive at sunset.

"The orders are clear," the colonel told Galan. "Should there be any resistance in a town, that town is to be burned to the ground and all its inhabitants executed. You can see for yourself, Captain. This bears His Excellency's signature."

Galan did not take the document the colonel held out to him. He couldn't believe this was happening. Didn't want to believe it. Standing stiffly at attention, he stared at the colonel until the latter, discomfited, cleared his throat and rose from his seat at the table to walk to a window, hands clasped behind his back. The colonel had taken the house of Alton Reynolds as his headquarters in Brazoria, and from this window he was afforded an excellent view of the town, and of the dragoons busily loading sacks and casks of foodstuffs into confiscated wagons. From here he could not see the meeting hall, where the town's inhabitants were being held—but it, and its occupants, were very much on his mind.

Galan couldn't believe this was happening, and yet it came as no surprise to him that such a situation had arisen. Ever since the execution—the massacre—of James Fannin and his men, Galan had been praying that another such tragedy would not confront him, that it had just been an isolated incident. But of course he'd known in his heart that he was only fooling himself. And he had witnessed Santa Anna's war on noncombatants during the campaigns against the rebels in Mexico's southern provinces, so he knew how His Excellency operated.

"This is sheer madness," he told the colonel.

"War is madness, Captain."

"None of our men were killed, and only one slightly wounded. The two Texans responsible are dead. Nothing can be gained by murdering the rest."

"Murder?" The colonel rocked back on his heels. "When a soldier carries out his orders to execute someone, he is not committing murder. He is simply doing his duty."

"I trust you do not sincerely hold to that view, sir. Surely, you must be aware that this *is* murder that you propose. Murder, under any circumstances."

"I have always encouraged my officers to speak frankly. But take care that no one else hears you refer to His Excellency's commands as madness and murder."

"I will not carry out such an order."

The colonel looked over his shoulder at Galan, and Galan could not decipher his expression. Was it pity? Or pride?

"You take great liberties with my warm regard for you, Juan."

"Neither will my company take part."

"I wonder if they would if I relieved you of command."

"Please do, Colonel. I came to Texas to fight rebel soldiers, not to make war on innocents."

The colonel returned to his perusal of Brazoria. He was thoughtfully silent for a moment.

"I wish someone would relieve *me* of this duty," he murmured ruefully.

"Refuse to carry it out."

"I wish to see my family again. If I refuse, I will stand before a firing squad. That fate may befall you, Captain, if you are not more careful."

"I have made my decision."

The colonel nodded. "I could send you dashing off to Urrea again. But this time I don't think you would go."

"No, sir. I would not."

"Very well, then. You have my permission to inform the prisoners of their fate. The executions will commence at dawn tomorrow. However, I do not feel it is necessary to strengthen the guard around the meeting hall. In fact, I should think that a detail of four or five men will be sufficient for the night, as I do not anticipate the prisoners attempting to escape. Do you understand what I'm saying, Captain?"

Galan understood perfectly. "God bless you, sir."

"You told me once before that God would abandon our cause," said the colonel, pensively. "I believe He has already done so."

CHAPTER TWENTY-FOUR

The Chosen

Galan returned immediately to the meeting hall, where he picked out Alton Reynolds, Hardin the blacksmith, and Boone Tasker, requesting that the three men follow him outside. Jessy was alarmed, but Boone tried to reassure her, telling her not to worry, that no harm would come to him. Inwardly, he could only hope that his assessment of Galan as an honorable man had been accurate.

A pair of dragoons escorted them outside, out into the warm midday sunshine, and Boone was relieved to see no evidence of a firing squad being formed. A few strides from the meeting hall Galan stopped and turned and ordered the dragoons to return to their posts, leaving him alone with the trio of prisoners. Once the dragoons were out of earshot, he informed the three of Santa Anna's orders.

"Good God!" gasped Alton in stunned disbelief. "This can't be. These are innocent women and children we have here! And I for one have always been loyal to the Republic of Mexico."

"You see now where that got you, Alton," said Hardin with a certain grim satisfaction.

Boone stepped forward. "Captain, I am the only one among your prisoners who has ever taken up arms against your country. Execute me, if you will, but please spare the others."

"A truly admirable gesture," said Galan with genuine respect. "But I cannot save you. You must save yourselves."

With a curt gesture Galan summoned the watchful dragoons. Without another glance at Boone and the others, he walked away.

"Bastard," growled Hardin. "I wish I'd gone off with my boy to kill some of them Mexican sons of bitches. Now it don't look like I'll get the chance." He shook his head. "Bad enough they're gonna murder us. But them tellin' us in advance, just so's we can suffer a little more—that's a devilish way of doing business if you ask me."

"I don't think that's why he told us," said Boone.

He looked at Alton. Jessy's father was shattered. All the color drained from his face, he stood there slump-shouldered, staring at the ground. Boone couldn't help feeling sorry for the man. His loyalty had been misplaced, and now it had been betrayed.

The dragoons marched them back into the meeting hall. Jessy was so relieved to see Boone—she'd been afraid that she wasn't going to see him alive again, and the last few minutes had been some of the worst in her young life—that she threw her arms around his neck. Alton was so consumed by his own bitter reflections that he didn't even notice.

The others in the hall gathered round to hear what Hardin had to say. They could tell by the look on Alton Reynolds's face that something was terribly wrong. When the blacksmith gave them the news, a woman let out a stifled sob as she clutched her two-year-old daughter to her bosom. A man muttered an angry curse. These were the only audible reactions. Boone was watching Jessy's face as Hardin revealed the fate that lay in store for them.

"Don't be afraid," he told her.

"I'm not afraid. Not with you beside me. I'm only sad. Sad that we won't have more time to spend together."

"We will have all the time in the world, Jessy. Because we're going to get out of here."

Hardin overheard him. "And just how do you aim to do that? We've got guards all around us. We try to make a break, they'll shoot us down, and I don't reckon they'll worry about hittin' the children and womenfolk. Not with what they've got in mind for us. And we cain't leave the children and womenfolk behind, if that's what you've got in mind."

"I'll tell you what I think," said Boone. "That captain, and probably his commanding officer, have got orders from Santa Anna that they don't have the stomach to carry out. But they can't just let us go, even though they might like to. Because if they did something like that, they'd end up court-martialed. Or maybe even in front of a firing squad themselves. So they're going to make it as easy as they can for us to escape, without giving themselves away."

"You're as daft as a knob-head mule if you believe that," replied Hardin.

Boone turned to Seth. "You mentioned something about a way out of here."

"There's a trapdoor in the back corner. This place is built up on brick piers. We can drop down under the floor and crawl out."

"Sure," said Hardin. "Me and a lot of the men here helped build this place. We know about that trapdoor. It was cut into the floor on account of if there was an Injun raid we all agreed to bring our families here and fort up. We could maybe hold the savages off while the children and womenfolk went through that trapdoor and slipped off into the woods under cover of night. But that ain't gonna help us none now, not with all them soldiers out there."

"We'll wait until dark," said Boone. "Then we create a diversion at the front while the women and children slip out through the hatch. If we're lucky, all the guards will be up front as they go out the back."

Hardin scanned the grim faces of his neighbors as they mulled over Boone's scheme.

"What choice do we have?" asked Boone.

Hardin nodded. "Reckon you're right. It's either that or we all go like sheep to the slaughter in the morning."

"I'm not leaving here without you," Jessy told Boone. "If you don't go through that trapdoor, neither do I."

"If we do like you say," said Seth, "I'm going out the front door."

"No," said Alton.

They all looked at him. He was slumped on one

of the split-log benches lining the walls of the meeting hall. Boone was surprised that he was at all aware of his surroundings, but obviously he had heard every word.

"No," he said, "you're not going to die here, Seth. I have already lost one son. I won't lose another."

"You can't stop me," replied Seth. "I'm going to finish the job Johnny started, and you'd better not get in my way."

"Seth!" cried Jessy. "That's no way to talk to your father!"

"You're going to get away," said Alton flatly. "Both of you. And you, Mr. Tasker. You are going to make sure that they do."

"Now wait a minute," said Boone. "The diversion was my idea. I ought to be a part of it."

"Why are all you young men so eager to throw your lives away?" Alton shook his head. "No, I will lead the diversion, and the three of you will escape."

"You?" gasped Seth in disbelief. "You won't lift a hand against Mexican soldiers. I've heard you say that many a time."

"Santa Anna has compelled me," said Alton with bitter irony in his voice. "And I will do anything I have to in order to save my family." He gazed earnestly at Boone. "I must have your word that you will see my children to safety. I know I can rely on you. You do love Jessy, after all, don't you?"

Boone didn't hesitate. "Why, yes. Of course I love her." It seemed the most natural thing in the world to make that confession—so different from all the times he had strangled on "I love you" in the presence of Sarah Ambler. Three simple words he hadn't been able to say then, but now they, or something very much like them, just rolled off his tongue, and he so calm and matter-of-fact that one might have thought he was commenting on the wholly unremarkable and unalterable fact that the sun had risen in the east this morning. Perhaps he'd had so much trouble with those words in Sarah's case because he hadn't truly understood what love was.

"Then it's settled," said Alton. And so it was. There was nothing more to be said.

Boone moved to one of the meeting hall windows, and Jessy stayed by his side. No words passed between them as they waited and watched, because no words were necessary. They loved each other, and they would stick together, and if they had but one day or the next fifty years, they would share the time allotted them with one another. No one and nothing was going to come between them. It was perfectly natural, and perfectly amazing at the same time, but Boone accepted it without question, and his heart and soul were filled with a rare contentment.

Once he looked over and saw Seth sitting on the bench next to his father, gazing at Alton Reynolds with new eyes, eyes filled with respect, and Alton put an arm around his son's shoulders. In their case no words were necessary, either.

As darkness fell, Boone was the first one through the trapdoor. On hands and knees he crawled to the brick pier at one of the building's back corners and peered cautiously out—only to draw back quickly as a sentry walked by slowly. All Boone could see of the dragoon was his boots. There were only four guards now, one at each corner of the meeting hall. This convinced Boone that the captain who had told them they must save themselves was in fact doing everything in his power to facilitate their escape. During the day a dozen guards had been assigned the task of watching the hall. Now there were only four. Could it be a trap? Boone decided that it was an extremely remote possibility. What could be the motive? Why would the Mexicans go to the trouble when all they had to do was march their prisoners out of the meeting hall and shoot them down?

From this corner of the meeting hall a quick dash across about twenty yards of open ground would bring them to the edge of the woods. The meeting hall was located on the edge of town, and since most of the dragoons were billeted in the houses of the Texans now incarcerated in the hall, there were no Mexican encampments to avoid. All they had to do was reach those woods. With the night as their ally they had a fair chance of making good their escape.

Boone went back up through the trapdoor. Hardin and Alton and the rest were anxiously waiting for his report. He nodded and said, "We can do it."

"Let's go," growled Hardin. He and six men headed for the front door. Boone watched them go, ashamed that he wasn't going with them. They were brave men, volunteers all—in fact, every man from fifteen years to seventy had volunteered. Hardin had taken upon himself the dreadful responsibility of selecting those who would give their lives so that the rest could survive.

Alton had been among the chosen, but he hesitated a moment to give Jessy and Seth one last hug. Jessy was crying silently; to her credit she did not make a scene or plead hysterically with her father, for she knew it would be futile to try to talk him out of sacrificing himself.

"Take good care of her," Alton told Boone, his voice thick with emotion.

"I will, sir. Good luck, and God bless you."

Boone put an arm around Jessy as her father moved away to join Hardin and the other volunteers.

"Put out the lamps," said Hardin, and the two lanterns that had illuminated the interior of the meeting hall were extinguished, plunging them all into darkness.

When Boone heard the front door of the hall being thrown open, he hurried Jessy down through the trapdoor. "Run for the woods, Jessy, and wait for me there." He turned to help a woman clutching her two-year-old daughter through the trapdoor. By his count there were thirty-five of them, and no time to waste.

As Hardin, Alton, and their six companions burst out the door, the two guards stationed at the front of the meeting hall shouted the alarm and raised their *escopetas* to fire into the Texans. The cut-down Brown Bess muskets roared, spitting flame.

Hardin was hit, but he bulled forward with a growl and closed with one of the dragoons and wrenched the musket from his grasp and used it like a club to fell the Mexican. Then he was hit again, this time by one of the guards rushing around the hall from his station at the rear of the building, and the Brazorian blacksmith slumped, dying, to the ground.

Alton and two others rushed another guard, who managed to shoot down one of his assailants before Alton slammed into him. They fell to the ground, grappling for the soldier's horse pistol. Wedged between their bodies, the pistol discharged. Alton felt flecks of gunpowder burn through his shirt and singe his flesh. The dragoon's body went rigid, then limp, and Alton rolled away from the dead man, gasping for air—and looked up to see another dragoon advancing on him, empty musket in his left hand, the pistol in his right aimed at Alton's face.

Before the dragoon could fire, Seth was on him, leaping on his back like a catamount, clawing at the man's face. The dragoon heaved the boy off his shoulders and fired at point-blank range. Alton's shout, incoherent with fear and rage and denial, came in unison with the pistol's report. He lunged at the soldier, struck him down with his bare hands, grabbed the empty pistol, and clubbed the Mexican with it again and again and again until the man's face was a bloody pulp.

His rage suddenly spent, Alton crawled on hands and knees to the body of his son. Alton was sitting there with Seth cradled in his arms, when Galan, flanked by a dozen dragoons, approached.

Other Mexicans came running from town—the area around the meeting hall was swarming with dragoons, and some carried lanterns and torches.

Galan was standing there, staring at Alton Reynolds, when a junior officer ran up to inform him that the meeting hall was empty.

"All the prisoners have escaped into the woods, Captain."

Galan glanced numbly at the bodies of Hardin and the other Texans who had charged out of the meeting hall only moments ago; they lay mingled with the corpses of three of the sentries. The fourth guard had come through without a scratch. Galan was ambivalent about the deaths of his own soldiers. At least they had died honorably, fighting the enemy. Better that than the ignominy of killing unarmed civilians. And besides, Santa Anna would be the death of them all before this campaign was over . . .

"Shall we go after them, sir?"

"What?" Galan shook his head. "No. I will not lose any more good men tonight."

"What about this one?" The officer gestured at Alton.

Galan drew a long breath. "I suppose we must execute him. See to it, Lieutenant. Immediately. And when it is done, bury him alongside his son."

Alton looked up then, and Galan, before he turned away, saw the gratitude in the man's eyes.

Boone was the last one out of the meeting hall, the last to reach the safety of the woods. The escape had gone as planned. The two guards posted at the rear of the meeting hall had rushed to the front, and all of the Brazorians had gone down through the trapdoor, crawled out from under the building, and fled into the brush. All of them save one.

"Seth," whispered Jessy. She had been waiting for Boone and her brother at the edge of the timber. The others had gone on, some bound for nearby towns or friends or relatives; a group had decided to stay together and make for Galveston, nearly a hundred miles away.

Boone shook his head. "I made sure there was no one left in there, Jessy. He must have gone out the front way to help your father. I'm truly sorry."

"Yes," she said in a small voice, and he marveled at her courage and composure. He held her close. She was trembling slightly, but she did not weep. She'd lost her father and both brothers. Now all she had was Boone. "We'd better be going," she said at last, and they plunged deeper into the woods, Boone leading the way, her hand gripped tightly in his own.

An hour later they stopped. There was no sound or sign of pursuit. Boone decided it was safe to wait for morning. They lay close together on the ground, and Jessy slept with her arm thrown across his chest and her head on his shoulder. Boone didn't sleep. At sunrise he gently woke her.

"It's time to move on."

"Where are we going, Boone? What are we going to do?"

"I've got to find Sam Houston and the army. There's bound to be one more fight. This one will be winner take all. I've got to be there, Jessy. I owe it to your father and your brothers and Hardin and my friend, Gabe, and all the others. We've got to win, so that they won't have died for nothing."

"Your friend might still be alive."

"I doubt it. I'm pretty certain Santa Anna's killed him by now."

She stood up and brushed dirt and leaves off her dress and looked at him with bright, clear green eyes, firm resolve stamped on her face.

"I'm ready," she said.

"You can't go into battle, Jessy. I can't let you go in harm's way."

"You're all I have left. If you think you're going to leave me behind, then you had better just think again, Boone Tasker."

He couldn't help but smile. "God knows I love you."

"And I love you. We're going to be married, and we'll have lots of children, and we'll live happily ever after. But first we've got to whip Santa Anna. So why are you just standing there? Let's get going."

He stepped up to her and kissed her on the lips, and she responded with a passion that startled him—but then she pushed away, her hands resting on his chest, so that she could feel the beat of his galloping heart.

"I think you had better marry me before we go any further, Mr. Tasker," she said coyly.

"Yes, I think I'd better," he agreed, laughing, and took her hand.

They headed east, into the morning sun.

CHAPTER TWENTY-FIVE

The Crossing

On the way to Gonzales, Sam Houston had seen dozens of Texan families fleeing eastward, their wagons and horses laden with the belongings they had not been willing to leave behind. They were calling it the "Runaway Scrape," and Houston sympathized with the plight of these people, chased out of their homes by the Mexican invaders, never knowing when the ubiquitous Mexican cavalry might plunge out of the woods and descend on them with lance and saber. He felt ashamed, too, that he was as yet unable to defend these citizens and their homes from the menace of Santa Anna.

Now he and his tiny ragtag army had joined the Runaway Scrape. Sam Houston was retreating, and it galled him mightily. But he had no choice.

He had arrived in Gonzales to find the four hundred volunteers collected there distraught and discouraged. The widow of Almeron Dickenson, Travis's lieutenant, had appeared with the tragic news of the Alamo's fall. She was one of a handful of noncombatant survivors Santa Anna had allowed to leave that mission turned fortress alive. Her husband had fallen in defense of his country.

More than twenty of the Gonzales volunteers deserted after hearing her firsthand accounts of the siege and battle. Houston didn't hold the widow accountable; she was a staunch patriot and only sought to inspire her fellow Texans with details of the Alamo's gallant defense. Privately, Houston was surprised that more did not desert, especially when one considered that over thirty men from Gonzales had perished with Travis. The unnerving lamentations of the mothers, wives, and children of those brave men would ring in Houston's memory forever.

Houston had taken one good look at Gonzales and the volunteers and ordered a withdrawal. The volunteers had not been taught even the bare rudiments of soldiering, and the fate of Travis confirmed Houston in his opinion that this force must not be caught within fortifications. If Santa Anna laid siege to Gonzales, they were doomed. There would be no relief column marching to the rescue.

The order to retreat was not well received by the volunteers. They hankered for a fight. There was scarcely a man in the ranks who didn't have a blood grievance against the *santanistas,* and most of them were absolutely convinced they could whip those "carrion-eating convicts" who marched under Santa Anna's bloodred banners, even if the odds *were* ten to one against them. But Houston coldly, firmly held his ground. Grumbling, the men turned their angry faces east.

Houston knew he would have his hands full keeping this little army together. These men would not follow a leader whom they did not respect.

And they despised military discipline. Houston understood this egalitarian frontier attitude. His mentor, Andrew Jackson, had demonstrated the best way—indeed, probably the only way—to command frontiersmen. Old Hickory had been a general in the Tennessee Militia; he had led volunteers very much like these Texans against the Red Stick Creeks and the Seminoles and the British. On one occasion he had faced down an entire company of volunteers whose enlistments had run out and who were dead-set on going home right in the middle of a campaign. But Jackson had stopped them, all by himself, threatening the whole lot with a musket, which, as it turned out, would not have fired. He had vowed to shoot the first man who took another step in the direction of Tennessee home and hearth. And the volunteers had backed down, more out of respect for Jackson's courage and iron will rather than fear, even though no one who knew Old Hickory could doubt for an instant that he was capable of carrying out that threat. Houston hoped he would not be confronted with a similar situation. The key was respect. The problem was that every day they retreated he lost a little more respect in the eyes of his volunteers.

He had every intention of turning to fight once he crossed the Colorado River. Behind that river he could organize a defense, and he had reason to hope that Fannin at Goliad would obey his most recent order and meet him at Burnham's Ferry with his force of four hundred bravos.

The spring rains continued to fall, transforming the roads into quagmires and dampening the spirits of the men even further. The days dawned bright enough, but by late morning the clouds appeared without fail, and by early afternoon the deluge had come. But the rains weren't all bad. They made the Colorado swell its banks, presenting an impassable barrier for the Mexican Army if only Houston could defend three river crossings. He posted strong guards at these points and proceeded to drill his men, wondering whether Fannin or the enemy would be the first to appear.

The enemy appeared first. Houston had several first-class scouts at his beck and call, among them Henry Karnes, a hero of the first battle at Bexar, Deaf Smith, and Nathaniel Jones, a graying Kentuckian who had forgotten more woodlore than most men ever knew. Thanks to their efforts, Houston was forewarned that Santa Anna's cavalry under General Ramirez y Sesma, some eight hundred strong, were making for Beason's Crossing. The prospect of battle excited Houston's men. In high spirits, they marched to the crossing. Once there, however, Houston refused to agree to his lieutenants' suggestions that he cross the river and attack Sesma, who was encamped on the other side. He would not surrender the tactical advantage and attack across a flooded river under the enemy's guns.

For six days the two sides glowered at one another across the Colorado. Then the shocking news of Fannin's defeat and capture arrived. These were Houston's darkest hours. Now he realized that his small army was the last hope for Texas. If only Fannin and Travis had obeyed his orders in a timely manner! Houston ordered a withdrawal to San Felipe.

Hundreds of men had joined his ranks in the past few days, secure in the knowledge that the big scrape would at last be fought at the Colorado. Now, thoroughly disgusted, hundreds simply walked away. The whispers began. The army was being led by a coward! They would do better with a new commander! Houston's subordinates openly challenged him. Hotspurs like Sidney Sherman and Robert Coleman made their displeasure known. Against Sesma's eight hundred men they had mustered over a thousand. For the first time the numbers had been in their favor. The retreat would be an ineradicable stain on the honor of Texas.

"We might have won," conceded Houston. "But it would have been a Pyrrhic victory. Our losses in an attack would have been high. Santa Anna's cavalry are the best trained units at his disposal. But Sesma is not the main threat. That remains Santa Anna. We would have been in no condition to fight a second battle. In short, Sesma's defeat would have meant nothing in the long term."

And then there was Urrea, commander of the southernmost enemy column. Scouts reported that Urrea had crossed the Colorado at Wharton with fifteen hundred men, and was now in a position to outflank the Texans and perhaps cut off their retreat. Urrea's cavalry detachments were said to be striking at towns along the Brazos. Houston knew he had to get his army across the Brazos before the Mexican dragoons seized all the crossings.

After dallying for a fortnight at San Antonio, and

bleeding his army in an attack on the Alamo fortress, a strategically worthless position, Santa Anna suddenly decided to press on with all haste. He got his columns across the Colorado and marched them swiftly toward the Brazos, in spite of the rain and the deplorable road conditions. But when he got to San Felipe, he found the town in ashes and his quarry safely across the river. Houston had eluded him.

But it had been a very close run thing . . .

At a time when no one could be sure where Sam Houston and the Texas Army was—or even if an army existed—Pierce Hammond put it down to blind luck that he arrived in San Felipe on the day that Houston was trying to get his men across the Brazos River.

Confusion reigned in San Felipe. There were about a thousand armed men who needed to get to the east bank of the rain-swollen river in a hurry, along with dozens of civilians who had fled their homes—and there was only one ferry to accomplish the task. When Pierce arrived with what was left of the Alabama Red Rovers, the town was packed with volunteers, and the vast majority had yet to be transported across the Brazos.

The men who rode with Pierce were a grim lot. In the course of their three-day journey westward, they had received word of the disaster that had befallen Colonel Fannin and his command. There could be no question that Captain Jack Shackelford and the ninety-odd Alabamians who followed him were with Fannin at Coleto Creek. But it was not until they reached the Brazos that they learned the fate of their comrades. Houston's men had only recently heard of the massacre, and those who waited on the east bank shared the news when they found out that Pierce and his companions were Red Rovers. The ferryman confirmed it. Martin, Gregg, and the others said nothing. Pierce thought about Gabe Cochran and Boone Tasker. They hadn't actually been friends. It occurred to Pierce that he didn't have a single real friend to his name. But he felt bad, all the same.

As soon as he got into San Felipe, Pierce asked where General Houston could be found, and was directed to a dogtrot cabin not far from the river crossing.

"My name is Pierce Hammond," he informed a man named Hardin, who was acting as Houston's aide-de-camp. "These men and I are all that's left of the Alabama Red Rovers, I fear."

Hardin told him to wait and went inside. A moment later, Sam Houston emerged. Pierce had never met the man, or even seen a rendering of him, but he knew in a glance that this had to be the fellow the Cherokees called Raven, and whose detractors dubbed "Old Drunk." He was a big man, six foot six, with a craggy face full of character and piercing blue-gray eyes. He wore a leopard-skin vest under his travel-worn frock coat, a pair of pistols stuck in his belt, and he looked to Pierce like a man who carried the weight of the world on his shoulders.

"You've heard, I suppose," said Houston gravely, "of the fate of your comrades. I was acquainted with Jack Shackelford. A fine and gallant gentleman. You must have been proud to follow him. But tell me, how is it that you came to be separated from the rest of the command?"

Pierce told him of their convalescence on Galveston Island, and of their mission against the fugitive slaves.

"Yes, I've heard there's been some trouble with runaways down along the Trinity."

"Won't be no more trouble, General," said Gregg. He gestured at Mingo and Marriah. Both had their hands bound behind their backs and sat astride a stray horse the Red Rovers had found along the way. "These two are the last of 'em. We'd have hanged 'em along with the rest but for Hammond here."

"I know the man," explained Pierce. "His name is Mingo Green. He came to Texas with me. He's a runaway, it's true. He had the misfortune to fall in with the rebel slaves. He took no part in the murders they committed."

"Or so he says," rasped Gregg.

"He was trying to get away from the others when we showed up," continued Pierce. "He and the woman, both. That in itself is proof enough they wanted no part of an insurrection."

"We don't know why they was runnin'," said Gregg.

Annoyed, Pierce grimaced. "All I'm saying is that they ought to have a fair trial, at least."

"You'll find no court in session these days," said Houston.

"Then I will gladly submit this matter to you, General, and trust in your good judgment."

Houston glanced at Mingo and Marriah. Perturbed, he shook his leonine head.

"I have a republic to defend, an army to save, and Santa Anna hot on my heels. I don't have time for this sort of thing."

Pierce feared Houston would solve this minor annoyance by the simplest expedient—a curt order to hang Mingo and Marriah and be done with it.

"You have my word of honor, sir, that these two were not involved in any murders."

Houston waved an impatient hand. "Your word, sir? You are in no position to give your word on that subject, for you have no way of knowing whether you are correct in your assumption. However, your loyalty is admirable."

At that moment a man rode up, leaped from his saddle, and approached them, angry resolve stamped on his haggard, bearded features. He wore a buckskin jacket, a serape over one shoulder, ragged stroud trousers, and old brogans on his feet. He fairly bristled with weapons—two pistols, a cane knife, a hunting knife, and an Indian Pattern Brown Bess riding on his back, compliments of a rope sling. In short, there was little to distinguish him from the hundreds of other volunteers in Houston's army.

"Captain Baker," said Houston with a nod.

"I'm here to tell you that my company and I refuse to retreat one more inch," snapped Moseley Baker. "We're gonna stand right here and fight.

Wiley Martin and his boys aren't crossing the damned Brazos, either."

Pierce saw Houston's eyes flash with anger, and he stepped back, expecting an explosion.

"Time and time again you told us we were gonna turn and fight," continued Baker. "Instead, you keep runnin'. Well, runnin' don't fit my nature, and it don't suit the men who ride with me, either."

"You're a damn insolent fool, Baker," said Hardin. "General Houston knows what he's doing. He's our only hope—"

"That's enough, Lieutenant," said Houston. "Captain Baker, you go right ahead and defend San Felipe and this crossing. I will proceed eastward with the army, and I will fight Santa Anna at the right place and time. And, furthermore, I will endeavor to ensure that your sacrifice will not have been in vain."

Moseley Baker wasn't sure what to say to that. Pierce sensed that the man had not expected such swift acquiescence from Houston. Or was it capitulation? Pierce had had his taste of commanding volunteers; he supposed it had to be twice as difficult as commanding regular troops. Army discipline took the independence out of a soldier. Not so with men like Baker, though; this particular volunteer had decided that Sam Houston was no longer worth following.

With no adequate retort to Houston's comments, a surly Baker got back on his horse and rode away. Houston watched him go with a shake of the head. The confrontation had left him both irritated and philosophical.

"Another Travis. Such men are infuriating in the extreme. But you can't help admiring them." He turned back to Pierce. "I have reason to believe that you will find a riverboat, the *Athena,* twenty miles downriver, somewhere in the vicinity of Fort Bend Crossing. That is generally as far as she comes up the Brazos. But with the river running high, I believe she can make her way here. Go find that boat, Lieutenant Hammond, and bring her to me."

"I'm no lieutenant, sir. Just a—"

"You are now. As commander in chief I have the authority to issue commissions in the field. I will have it in writing for you—by the time you return."

"Forgive me, General, but what on earth do you want with a riverboat?"

"At the present rate, with only the ferry to serve me, it will take today and all of tomorrow to transport this army—or, rather, what's left of it—to the other side of the Brazos. I don't have that much time. My scouts inform me that Santa Anna is moving quickly in hopes of catching us on this side of the river. If he does, I fear all will be lost."

"But how does a riverboat alleviate those circumstances?"

"I will turn her crossways and anchor her, bow and stern, to both banks with makeshift bridges. In a matter of hours I can have these men across."

"I see."

"Should the *Athena*'s captain object too strenuously to the confiscation of his vessel, you have my permission to toss him over the side."

"Thank you, sir," said Pierce dubiously.

"But be warned, Lieutenant," said Houston with

a gravity that alarmed Pierce, "if the *Athena* is there, and the enemy discovers her, I am sure some of Santa Anna's bright young officers or engineers will think to use her in a manner similar to that which I have just described to you. Under no circumstances must she be allowed to fall into their hands. We cannot let them cross the river first and outflank us. If that happens, this retreat becomes a rout."

Pierce was taken aback. Why, if the riverboat was so crucial to the success of the revolution, was Sam Houston entrusting him with this responsibility? *I should tell him that in some circles back in Alabama they think me a coward—and I'm not so sure they aren't correct.* Because suddenly Pierce was afraid—more afraid than he had ever been in his life. Upon further reflection, though, he realized he wasn't fearful of dying, but rather of failure. He did not want to fail Sam Houston, to disappoint this man, who apparently saw something in him that Pierce had never known existed. Something his father had never seen.

Or maybe Sam Houston was just desperate.

"You can rely on us, General," said Pierce—and saluted.

Houston suppressed a smile. "I sincerely appreciate that salute, Lieutenant. I don't even get that kind of respect from Hardin here. Volunteers, you know . . ."

"Sorry, General," said Hardin.

"I don't really care if you know how to salute," replied Houston, "so long as you can fight like ten devils when the time comes. And the time *will* come."

"I know it will, sir."

"Well," said Houston ruefully, "you're probably the only man left in the army who believes that."

"Sir, every Texan fights like ten devils. We'll make those damned Mexicans remember the Alamo. And Goliad, too."

"Yes," murmured Houston. "Remember the Alamo and Goliad. A fine fighting motto."

"General?"

"Lieutenant Hammond, what are you doing still here?"

"What about Mingo and the woman?"

Houston looked at the pair of prisoners on the stray mare.

"Take your boy with you. If he fights for Texas, I'll let him live. If he tries to run away again, kill him. That's a direct order. As for the woman, you may leave her here for the time being. She can help with the sick. We'll decide what to do about her later. Now get going, Hammond, and bring me that riverboat by dawn tomorrow, or there will be hell to pay."

CHAPTER TWENTY-SIX

The Riverboat

They made good time that day, so that before dark they were within a mile of Fort Bend Crossing. Houston had wisely provided Pierce with a guide named Dunlop, a man who had lived for some years in the vicinity. Pierce was mortified that he hadn't even thought to ask for a guide; it hadn't occurred to him that he and his Red Rovers knew absolutely nothing about this country. If this oversight gave Houston cause to wonder that he wasn't making a huge mistake in giving Pierce such an important mission, the general gave no indication he had second thoughts. And as it turned out, it was thanks to Dunlop that they didn't blunder right into disaster.

Dunlop suggested they wait in a grove of trees a mile from the crossing while he slipped in closer to see if the riverboat was there—and to make sure the enemy wasn't. It was Dunlop who had mentioned to Houston that the *Athena* had been employed for the past fortnight in a gallant effort to transport as many Texas refugees as possible down the river to the coast. The little riverboat's doughty skipper, a Dutch emigrant named Vanderhook, was doing his part for the cause. Pierce wondered if the man would mind sacrificing his vessel so that Houston's army could escape the jaws of Santa Anna's trap.

So while Dunlop, who was just as doughty as Captain Vanderhook, reconnoitered, Pierce, Mingo, and the Red Rovers waited for day's end in the cover of the woods. As night fell, like smoke from a darkening sky, Mingo sat down beside Pierce and asked for his freedom papers.

"You gots to give 'em to me," he said. "I'll get down on my hands and knees and beg if that's what you want."

"I'd have thought you'd be too proud."

"I ain't. Please, Marse Pierce. Please set me free."

"What's gotten into you, Mingo? Are you afraid to die?"

"Ain't you?"

Pierce peered into the darkness. "There are some things worse than dying."

"No there ain't."

"Yes, there are. Take you, for instance. You've been willing to die just for the chance to get back to Alabama and that woman of yours. Not to mention your unborn child. Being without them is worse than dying, isn't it?"

"If you know that, then you gots to let me go."

"As for me," continued Pierce, as though he hadn't even heard Mingo's last remark, "I'd rather die than fail Sam Houston—and Texas."

Mingo decided Pierce Hammond was touched by a fever on the brain. "What do you care 'bout Texas? You got no stake in all this. You just after provin' to your pa you ain't no coward, like they all say you is."

Pierce smiled tolerantly. "That isn't the case, Mingo. I'm doing this for me. For once in my life I'm going to stand up and be counted. I'm going to make a difference. And if my father or anybody else ever knows about it is a matter of complete indifference to me."

"You ain't gonna make no difference," said Mingo bitterly. "You just gonna get kilt. And me along with you."

"We're going back together," said Pierce flatly. "Because that's the only way you'll get back."

"With freedom papers I'd get back just fine on my own."

Pierce shook his head. "Use your head for once, Mingo. Papers signed by me won't do you any good in Alabama, not with Slade and my father around. See, that's the point of what I'm trying to say. My signature carries no weight because I haven't stood for anything. A man makes his own destiny. We'll go back together, and we'll get Sadie, and we'll bring her back to Texas, and then I'll see to it that you are both freed. And you know what? Then my signature on your freedom papers will mean something."

Mingo was silent a moment. He understood Pierce. Not that understanding was any consolation. If they were both dead, what good was Pierce Hammond's signature? What good were freedom papers?

"This ain't my fight," muttered Mingo. "I'd fight and die if it was *my* freedom they was talkin' about.

But when they talk freedom, they don't mean for slaves like me."

"You're as thickheaded as they come," said Pierce. "You *will* be fighting for your own freedom. I just explained how. We fight to live, both of us. If you don't fight, you'll die. And if I don't fight, I might as well be dead. I'm just taking up space." He paused, watching Mingo, hoping for some sign that he was getting through. There was no indication. Mingo just looked surly and unconvinced. Exasperated, Pierce said, "You might as well decide now. Stay and fight, or go ahead and make a run for it again."

With a smirk, Mingo nodded in the direction of Gregg and the other Red Rovers. They were barely discernible shapes in the suddenly dense darkness, but he knew they were there, watching him, waiting like a pack of wolves for him to make a break for freedom.

"That's what they want," he said.

"It's what they expect," countered Pierce. "And I couldn't stop them if I wanted to." He laughed softly. "You don't believe I'm sincere when I tell you I want to get Sadie and the child, do you?"

"I cain't see no reason why you would. 'Less it's on account of you think I saved your life back in Mobile, and you owe me."

"I'm not that big of a fool. I've got a pretty good idea what happened back there, and why."

"Then how come you care if I ever see my Sadie again?"

"Perhaps because my father caused the two of you to be apart."

"And you'll be the one to put us back together?" Mingo gave him a long, skeptical look. "No, that ain't why."

"No," said Pierce. "I guess because it's right. What my father did was wrong. I feel responsible for what he does, in a way. That's rather odd, isn't it? I thought it was supposed to be the other way around. The father feeling responsible for the action of his son."

Mingo took in a deep breath and let it out slowly. "Okay. We'll go back together. I guess I ain't got no choice."

Pierce nodded, smiling. "You realize that now you've got to keep me alive."

"You reckon that's funny, don't you?"

"Ironic, maybe. Not funny at all."

"Well, I gots to keep you alive, right enough. Leastways till we get back to Alabama. But it ain't 'cause I like you. I'd make a deal with the Devil hisself to get Sadie."

"Fair enough."

A faint rustling noise in the bush made everybody reach for their weapons. But it was just Dunlop. He had been gone less than two hours. He sat on his heels in front of Pierce. The Red Rovers gathered around. Dunlop bit off a chew from a twist of tobacco before giving his report.

"Got some good news and some bad news," he drawled. "The boat, she's right where I thought she'd be. Bad news is the Mexicans got her."

"Damn the luck!" muttered one of the Red Rovers.

"They come sashaying down to the crossin' just as I got in close enough to see. Vanderhook, he was loadin' some folks to take 'em on down the river. He didn't have a chance to get away."

"How many?"

"I counted twenty. They sent one man back, I reckon to report."

"Leaving nineteen," said Gregg. "And thirteen of us."

"Fourteen if you count Mingo," said Pierce.

"I ain't countin' him," replied Gregg. "Not countin' *on* him, neither. But nineteen to thirteen's pretty good odds, you ask me."

"Were they cavalry?" Martin asked Dunlop.

Dunlop nodded. "Dragoons, by the looks of 'em. Tough as they come."

"We came to get that boat and take it back to Sam Houston," said Gregg. "I aim to do just that."

"As much as it pains me to do so," said Pierce dryly, "I must agree with Mr. Gregg in this instance. We must do it, and do it now, before that man they sent off returns with the whole Mexican Army."

"I'm with you," said Martin. The others murmured agreement.

"I got only one question," said Dunlop. "Just how you aim to get on that boat? There ain't no cover to speak of, so's you can't just sneak up on them devils, even at night, without them seein' you."

"They're watching the banks, not the river," replied Pierce. "Isn't that right?"

Dunlop scratched his stubbled chin, where some tobacco juice had leaked from the corner of his mouth. "Reckon it is."

"Then we get into the river and let it carry us down to the *Athena*."

"No," said Gregg. "That won't work."

"You have a better idea?"

Gregg just glowered, thin-lipped.

"It's on account of he cain't swim," remarked Martin.

"You got a mighty big mouth for such a small feller," snapped Gregg, "and I might have to teach you to mind your own business one of these days."

"Don't worry," said Pierce casually. "I won't let you drown. Personally, it wouldn't bother me if you did, but we're all Red Rovers, and so we stick together through thick and thin. What do you boys say?"

"I say we do it," replied Martin, looking about him at the others. "I say we show those Mexicans that Captain Jack Shackelford's Alabama Red Rovers aren't finished yet. Let's do this for our comrades who fell at Goliad."

The others wholeheartedly agreed.

It did not go exactly as Pierce had planned.

He led his men down to the riverbank, where they found several logs in the flotsam the high-running river had deposited along its course. Pierce wanted them to keep together as much as possible, with three or four men to a log. They would float the logs downriver, clinging to them until they drew near the *Athena*. While still upriver from the boat, they would leave the logs and strike out for their goal, letting the current do most of the work for them.

Pierce hoped the noise of the high-running river would mask the sounds he and the others made as they approached the boat. He was also counting on the attention of the dragoons being focused on the land approach to the *Athena*. They would certainly not expect an attack from the river, concluding that no one would be crazy enough to attempt swimming the Brazos in its present condition.

Pierce was a good swimmer. He and Jubal's son had spent many a warm afternoon in the swimming hole of the creek that marked the northern boundary of Magnolia plantation. As for the others, he doubted that many of them could say the same. To their credit, though, only Gregg protested. These were brave men, indeed, and Pierce felt honored to be among them. He knew they wouldn't let him down. And it was incumbent upon him not to let them down, either. At the same time he was concerned about how he would perform if they actually did get aboard the riverboat and confronted the enemy. He had never been in a shooting scrape before, and he was scared.

Mingo, Martin, and Dunlop were teamed up with Pierce on one log, and they set out first. Pierce thought it was only right that he be the first man aboard the *Athena*, since he was, unfortunately, in command. He had never wished more fervently that Jack Shackelford hadn't picked on him. But it was done, and he had to live with it. Or die with it, as the case might be.

The water wasn't too cold—the recent spring rains had been the product of storms coming in from the Gulf of Mexico—but it was cold enough to set Pierce's teeth to chattering. The current caught them and the log to which they clung, and they were catapulted downriver at a nerve-racking speed. Pierce and the others kept their pistols and muskets on the top of the log, hoping to prevent the powder from getting wet; but in this regard they did not meet with complete success, which gave Pierce further cause for concern.

He looked back once, trying to see whether the rest of the Red Rovers were coming down the river as planned, but he could see no sign of them. The night was pitch black; the moon had not yet risen, and the sky was partially obscured by low clouds scudding swiftly northward. He took some consolation in knowing that if he could not see under these conditions, then the dragoons aboard the *Athena* would not be able to, either.

In a matter of minutes they were nearing the crossing. Dunlop tapped Pierce's arm and pointed at the *Athena*, but Pierce had already spotted the riverboat. Several lamps were lit aboard—one in the pilot house atop the upper deck. Though he couldn't see every detail of the craft, Pierce could tell it was nothing at all like the "floating palaces" that he'd had occasion to see on the Mobile River—and, in one instance, had actually booked passage on down the Mississippi all the way from Memphis to New Orleans. The *Athena* consisted of only two decks rather than the three found on larger boats. She was a stern-wheeler, about one hundred and sixty feet in length and about forty feet wide. Long and narrow, with a sharp keel, she had been designed with Texas rivers in mind. Her bulwarks were low amidships—so low that Pierce was confident they would have no trouble climbing aboard.

The current was cooperating. It was bringing them quite near the western bank, where the *Athena* was moored to a rather ramshackle wharf. No town had grown up around this crossing, only several structures that Dunlop had told Pierce were occupied by the ferryman and a merchant who operated a trading post. There were a number of wagons visible near the wharf, but Pierce could spot no movement on the landing.

It was time to leave the log that had conveyed them this far down the river. Pierce fought an urge to just hold on for dear life and be swept on down the Brazos, past the *Athena* and the Mexicans and on to safety. But then he remembered Sam Houston. The general was relying on him. So was his little army. And so was the Republic of Texas, for that matter, because if Houston didn't get this boat, the army might be lost tomorrow, and then Texas would be lost, too.

He cast off from the log, counting on the others to follow his lead. Holding rifle and pistol aloft in one hand—the latter dangling from a finger hooked through the trigger guard—he let the current sweep him forward. A bit of swimming was required to bring him near the hull of the low-slung steamboat. Clutching at the sill of the main deck with his free hand, he arrested his progress. The current, formerly his ally, now became his enemy, trying to drag him away. He strained to get aboard, kicking a leg up and over, then rolling onto the deck, under the low railing. A sodden and shivering mess, he lay there a moment, then saw a hand clutch the sill, and he laid his weapons aside and gave Mingo a helping hand aboard. Dunlop and Martin followed. Pierce looked around. Forward was the long cabin, and behind it the boiler room. He could hear voices issuing through the open door of the latter and saw light as well. Aft was the open cargo area. Above him was the hurricane deck, where the pilothouse was located.

But where were the dragoons?

That question was answered a few seconds later. Pierce heard a thump from somewhere near the bow, and then a shout from the hurricane deck. He saw shapes, then men coming out of the river forward—the rest of his command. They had been seen. A rifle spoke. Then another. Pierce watched in horror as one of the Red Rovers—in the darkness he couldn't identify the man—let out a cry of pain and pitched over into the river. The dragoons were on the deck above, firing down into the interlopers now bunched up at the bow of the *Athena*.

Pierce reached for his weapons. Glancing at Mingo, he handed the pistol to the slave.

"Time to fight," said Pierce.

Mingo nodded.

CHAPTER TWENTY-SEVEN

The Crucible

Access to the riverboat's hurricane deck could be accomplished by means of open staircases fore and aft. Pierce had the presence of mind to realize, if the dragoons were preoccupied with Gregg and the other Red Rovers at the bow of the *Athena*, it would make sense that he, Mingo, Dunlop, and Martin try the aft staircase.

But before they could put this plan into action, a dragoon emerged from the boiler room and fired his pistol into their midst without hesitation. The muzzle flash was a bright explosion in the deep shadows of the main deck. Martin was crouched right beside Pierce, and Pierce heard him make an odd noise and crumple to the deck. Without thinking, Pierce swung his rifle around and pulled the trigger. Even as he did, he wondered if the powder would be dry enough to ignite. To his amazement, the rifle discharged, and the dragoon jackknifed and sprawled facedown on the deck. Dunlop rushed to the body, ready to finish the Mexican off with his Bowie knife. He rolled the man over, then looked up at Pierce and nodded. "Good shootin'."

Another man emerged from the boiler room, and

Dunlop almost eviscerated him, but the man threw up his hands and declared himself an American, though it was hard to tell what he was with the dark smudges of ash and grease that covered his face and neck. "Name's Grogan," he said. "Rest of them bastards are up above. They left that one down here to keep an eye on us. Reckon they was afraid we might try to blow up the boilers. Probably would have, too."

"Don't do that," said Dunlop, "or you'll answer to Sam Houston."

Pierce had turned to kneel beside Martin, who lay on his side, clutching at his belly. "I'm done for," gasped Martin. "Gut shot. Forget about me and go on with your business."

"Lie still," said Pierce, and rose to gesture curtly at Mingo and Dunlop to follow him. Grogan went to Martin, but Pierce doubted that there was much the riverboat's engineer could do for the wounded Red Rover.

Ascending the aft staircase, Pierce reloaded his rifle from shot pouch and powder horn. They took the starboard passageway past the crew cabin and captain's quarters and stormed the pilothouse, which was occupied by a stout fellow in a blue peacoat and mariner's cap who sported a prodigious set of muttonchop whiskers on a jowly face. Pierce assumed him to be Vanderhook, the *Athena*'s skipper. But he didn't have time to introduce himself because Vanderhook had two visitors—a pair of dragoons, one of them an officer.

About a dozen dragoons were forward on the hurricane deck, engaged in repelling the Red

Rovers, who were valiantly storming the forward staircase. The attention of the two Mexicans in the pilothouse were likewise turned on the melee forward, so that when Pierce and his companions burst in, they had the element of surprise on their side. Dunlop shot the dragoon at point-blank range. The officer whirled, turning his pistol on Pierce, but before he could fire, Mingo had pounced on him, driving the pistol downward so that when it discharged the bullet splintered the decking. At the same time Mingo drove the Mexican backward, and the officer lost his footing and fell at Vanderhook's feet. Mingo aimed his own pistol, but Pierce grabbed his arm.

"Wait," he said. "He might be of more use to us alive." He turned to the officer. "I hope for your sake you speak English."

The officer answered with a belligerent glower.

"Well, then, forget it," said Pierce, and in an offhand manner added, "go ahead and finish him, Mingo."

"I speak English," admitted the officer.

"Order your men to lay down their arms."

"Never."

"You are hopelessly outnumbered. We've got thirty men on board at this moment, and fifty more waiting ashore. I can give you my word as a gentleman—and an officer in the Army of the Republic of Texas—that you and your men will be treated as is the due of prisoners of war."

The officer glanced fearfully at Mingo, and at the pistol in the slave's hand—then nodded.

In a matter of minutes Pierce Hammond found

himself in undisputed possession of the *Athena*, with twelve prisoners. Five dragoons had been killed. The two who had been posted on the landing had slipped away on the premise that discretion was the better part of valor. But the price of victory had been high. By the time Pierce got back down to the main deck, where Martin had fallen, he found that the Alabamian had breathed his last. Gregg and two others had also been killed. It was Gregg who had fallen into the river, shot in the neck. Two other Red Rovers had sustained slight wounds.

There were more than a dozen Texas refugees locked in the crew cabins—they had been boarding the *Athena* with all the belongings they could carry, leaving their wagons behind, when the dragoons first appeared. Pierce gave them a choice, disembark and find some other means to reach safety, or come with him upriver to San Felipe.

"You may or may not be safe with the army," he told them. "That depends on where Santa Anna is at this moment."

All but one family decided to stay aboard. Pierce told Vanderhook to get under way immediately. He explained to the riverboat captain what Houston intended for his vessel.

"And vat vill happen to my boat when Sam Houston ist done vit it?"

"That's up to General Houston, sir. But I should warn you that if it appears that the enemy will again seize this vessel, you may be sure the general will order her destroyed."

Vanderhook's crimson jowls quivered with rage.

"I vill destroy her myself before dat happens a second time."

Pierce smiled. "I can safely say that you and General Houston will get along just fine, Captain."

Pierce made arrangements to drop Dunlop and two others off to retrieve the horses and return with them to San Felipe. Then, as soon as Grogan reported that the steam was up in the boilers, they cast off from the wharf and headed north. Vanderhook told Pierce they could make two or three knots an hour against the current. By Vanderhook's keywinder, that would put them in San Felipe around daybreak. Pierce had to take the man's word for it. His own timepiece had stopped. It was ruined. He assumed its submersion in the Brazos had done the damage. Even though his father had given it to him, Pierce tossed the watch overboard without a twinge of regret.

Now that he had time to think about it, sitting in the pilothouse, sipping some brandy compliments of Vanderhook, Pierce thought about the man he had killed. He managed to be philosophical about it. The dragoon had been a soldier, willing to die for his country. And so he had died. It might have gone the other way. But it made more sense to Pierce to die for a reason than to die on the "field of honor" over some trifle involving the payment of a gambling debt. That wasn't worth dying for. Self-respect was. And self-respect, along with the right to determine one's own fate, was the issue in this war. Pierce could see that quite clearly. Vanderhook saw it, too, as did the refugees huddled in the crew's quarters. Martin and Gregg had understood it before they died. Self-respect and the freedom to live their own lives the way they saw fit. Not the way Santa Anna dictated that they live. That was all Texans wanted—and Pierce realized it was exactly what he wanted, as well. He would live that way, too, and not according to his father's preconceived notions of how a true Southern cavalier must live.

That kind of freedom was definitely worth dying for.

Vanderhook's calculations were amazingly precise—they arrived at San Felipe at dawn, and thanks in large measure to the Dutch skipper's expertise, the *Athena* soon lay athwart the current, made fast to either bank with stout lines, her bow nudging the western bank, and her stern wheel about thirty feet from the eastern. Houston had made preparations on the assumption that Pierce and the Red Rovers would accomplish their mission; a house standing near the crossing was cannibalized for lumber, which was used to make a pair of gangplanks fastened to the flanks of the sternwheel box, and stretching from the riverboat to the bank. In this way the *Athena* was made into a makeshift bridge, over which two columns of men walking single file could cross at once, one column down the starboard side of the *Athena* and over one gangplank, the other along the port side and over the other. In a matter of hours the entire army would be across the Brazos.

These were tense hours for Sam Houston. He had no solid intelligence pertaining to the whereabouts of Santa Anna and his army, and he awaited reports from his scouts. But he was not so preoccupied that he forgot to commend Pierce Hammond for a job well done. Pierce was pleased. The general's heartfelt thanks and unreserved praise meant a great deal to him.

"I regret the deaths of your comrades," said Houston. "But by giving their lives they have saved Texas. As for you, Lieutenant, I think you and your men and Lieutenant Hardin and his brave Brazoria boys should be combined. Small as it is, your combined forces will act as my reserve. My version of Napoleon's Imperial Guard, if you will. You will be under my direct command." Houston's smile was wry. "It will be the only unit I'm sure I *am* in command of in this army."

Pierce nodded. He understood Houston's predicament perfectly. Two groups of volunteers—Moseley Baker's and Wiley Martin's—had already balked at further retreat and were determined to stand and fight at San Felipe. Pierce wondered how much farther the others would follow Sam Houston. If the Old Chief continued to withdraw, he would have no army left.

Of course Houston refused to cross the Brazos until the last of his men was safely over, and that left Pierce and the Red Rovers with little to do except stick close to the cabin where the general had established his headquarters. Pierce took the measure of his men, as well as Hardin's Brazorians, and came away convinced that in every case loyalty to Sam Houston was steadfast. There wasn't a man in the lot who wouldn't die in his tracks, fighting for the Old Chief. And die they surely would, mused Pierce, if Santa Anna struck this morning, with part of the army west of the river and part of it east.

But it did not come down to that. The scout Nathan Jones appeared, to assure Houston that Santa Anna's vanguard, slowed by the heavy roads and the exhaustion that came of hard marching for several consecutive days, was still several hours away. The grizzled frontiersman was confident that the enemy would not arrive in San Felipe until midafternoon. Everyone breathed a sigh of relief.

A short time later, as Pierce sat near a fire, drinking coffee and eating hoecakes, compliments of a San Felipe civilian, he looked up to see Boone Tasker and a tall, auburn-haired young woman walking toward him.

"My God!" exclaimed Pierce, leaping up to grasp Boone's hand. "I thought for sure you were dead."

"Not by a long shot," replied Boone, marveling that he was genuinely pleased to see Pierce alive and well. "Could that be coffee I smell?"

Hardin came up. "Jessy? Jessy Reynolds, is that you? What are you doing here?"

Jessy clutched Hardin's arm. "The Mexicans came to Brazoria, Tom. I'm afraid I have some bad news for you."

"My father did something very foolish, didn't he?" asked Hardin, his voice hollow, his face a carefully impassive mask.

"No. He did something very heroic."

As the Red Rovers and Brazorians gathered round the fire while Boone and Jessy warmed themselves and drank coffee, Boone related what had happened in Brazoria. The Brazoria men were relieved to know that their friends and, in some cases, families had escaped execution. They were angry, too—angry that their homes had been invaded, that the Mexicans had been prepared to murder innocent civilians in cold blood. And finally, they were proud as well as saddened by the noble sacrifice of Alton and Seth Reynolds, Hardin's father, and the others.

Standing there in this group of men—dirty, hungry, tired men, beset at every turn by tragedy and trial, the odds stacked steeply against them, their futures bleak—Pierce felt a strange contentment. This was where he belonged. There was no place he'd rather be than right here, with these men, at this moment, as they stood, joined by a bond forged in the crucible of adversity, on the brink of their rendezvous with fate. Looking at their grim, haggard faces, Pierce actually felt sorry for the Mexican Army. Because, win or lose, these men and all the other brave souls in Sam Houston's ragtag army would exact a terrible toll upon the enemy before this business was concluded.

CHAPTER TWENTY-EIGHT

The Retreat

Moseley Baker's defense of San Felipe was valiant—but brief. After shelling the Texan defenses with his artillery, Santa Anna decided not to sacrifice his men in a frontal assault, and made plans to swing south with the balance of his army while Sesma's cavalry watched Baker, and find a crossing of the Brazos that was undefended.

Juan Galan was surprised by Santa Anna's apparent concern for the welfare of his troops. Since the Tampico Regiment had rejoined the main column after its foray in search of much needed provisions, Galan had tried to prepare himself for another bloody clash with the Texan rebels. He had struggled for days with the letter to Natalia, the death letter he hoped would never be sent. But he couldn't shake that premonition of disaster, which had been dogging him for weeks. He felt as though he were descending, like Dante, deeper and deeper into Hell.

The campaign had become a nightmare. And he was certain that God had abandoned their cause. God could not possibly be on the side of an army that operated under orders to murder innocent women and children. If only he had seen the truth before, during the campaigns against the insurrectionists of the southern provinces. But in those days, though the massacres, the raping, and pillaging had all disturbed him, he had been willing to accept Santa Anna's argument that such extreme measures were justified in waging war against the rebel forces of a popular uprising. Only with the support of the people could guerrillas maintain their struggle, so it was only logical that one made war on the people until their will was destroyed.

Now Galan knew how wrong he had been. The scales had been completely plucked from eyes. In those days he had naively believed Santa Anna to be the savior of Mexico. In reality, Santa Anna would lead Mexico into ruination. And the beginning of the long descent into chaos and ruin would begin here, in Texas.

He learned that Santa Anna had completely altered his strategy. Sam Houston's continued retreat had finally convinced His Excellency that the Texan Army—if such it could be called—was no longer a serious threat. If he could have trapped it at the Brazos, fine. But he would waste no more effort on trying to bring cowards to bay.

Santa Anna's new target was the provisional government of the ill-conceived and soon to be defunct Republic of Texas. Once he had captured the ringleaders of the revolt and hanged them, Houston's army would disintegrate. They would have nothing left to fight for. Santa Anna especially wanted to get his hands on Lorenzo de Zavala. His old nemesis was now vice president of the Texas

Republic. Zavala had caused Santa Anna numerous problems in Mexico, obstructing His Excellency's seizure of power at every turn before retiring to Texas in semi-exile. Because of Zavala's popularity, Santa Anna had not been free to deal with him as summarily as he might have wished. But now Zavala had committed high treason.

Many of his officers privately disagreed with Santa Anna's change in strategy. They worried that if the pressure was removed from Houston's army, the Texan volunteers would have time to recuperate and train. This was the moment to press on, to come to grips with the last large force of rebels still in the field and bring the issue to final resolution. Houston's defeat would surely end the revolt. But, of course, no one dared challenge openly the decisions of the Napoleon of the West.

All of Galan's military training and experience might have led him to side with the other officers. But he no longer really cared about winning the campaign. He knew they weren't going to win. All he cared about was getting home alive, returning to Natalia so he could live the remainder of his life with her. He would never go to war again.

So Galan was relieved that Santa Anna had decided to leave Sam Houston and his rebel army alone—because that army was as dangerous as a wounded wolf. *If we get too close, it will turn on us.* And it would turn with a righteous fury that would not be denied, demanding recompense in blood for the murder of Crockett, and the massacre of Fannin and his defenseless men, and the war

Santa Anna had so brutally and mercilessly waged on innocent people.

Moseley Baker had to burn San Felipe and retreat when he discovered that Santa Anna had found a way across the Brazos some miles downstream. Apparently, the Mexicans had ambushed a ferryman and used his conveyance to reach the eastern bank. Baker also learned that Vanderhook had blown the boilers of his riverboat and sent the *Athena* to the bottom when confronted by the likelihood that the vessel would be captured by the enemy. Baker and his men rejoined Houston, who had moved on to Groce's plantation.

The Old Chief was surprised when his scouts informed him that Santa Anna had turned southeast after crossing the river. It didn't take Houston long to figure out what his foe was up to. The Napoleon of the West was after the provisional government of Texas. President David Burnet and company had fled Washington-on-the-Brazos and by all accounts were moving toward Harrisburg, near Galveston Island. And Houston soon had cause for indifference when it came to Burnet's fate.

The president had dispatched Houston's friend Thomas J. Rusk, the secretary of war, to Groce's to deliver a letter.

Sir,
The enemy are laughing you to scorn, You must fight them. You must retreat no further. The coun-

try expects you to fight. The salvation of the country depends on you doing so.

Rusk, a reserved and urbane man, a lawyer by trade, and so by training as well as nature quite capable of inscrutable detachment, waited with perfect equanimity while Houston cursed a long and livid blue streak. Only when Houston had exhausted his copious supply of epithets did Rusk speak.

"Do you have a reply for the president, Sam?"

"Yes," said Houston with a smile that Rusk thought bore an uncanny resemblance to a wolf's snarl. "Tell him to watch out for Santa Anna's dragoons."

Rusk chuckled good-naturedly. "It really wouldn't do, you know, to let the government fall into the hands of the enemy. How would that look?"

"You and Lorenzo de Zavala are the only two members of the government I care spit about."

"I am sure I can speak for Lorenzo when I say we deeply appreciate your solicitude. But I really need to tell the president something with regard to your plans."

"I need some time to rest and resupply my army," sighed Houston. "Then I will seek out Santa Anna and do battle with him. But I will do so only at the time and place of my own choosing. Now, Thomas, how about a drink? Mr. Groce was kind enough to present me with this bottle of cognac."

"There is an offer no sane man could refuse." When he had his drink in hand—expensive cognac in a battered tin cup—Rusk continued. "I am told Andrew Jackson has the United States Army on the Louisiana side of the Sabine River. No one is certain what Old Hickory has in mind. But I have heard rumors that you've made arrangements with him to lure Santa Anna all the way to the Sabine, at which time the federal troops will join forces with your men to deal decisively with the Mexican Army."

Houston had a good hearty laugh. "That is so ludicrous it's amusing. I've no idea what General Jackson has in mind. He and I have not corresponded in six months. I can assure you I have no secret arrangements with him. And I wouldn't count on his sending the United States Army into Texas. Sentiment against involvement in our difficulties is entirely too strong in the Northern states. The Whigs would win the White House for certain. It would be a political catastrophe for the Democratic Party, and General Jackson will not risk it."

"So I can safely say to President Burnet that you have no intention of withdrawing as far as the Sabine."

Houston peered at Rusk with eyes like blue ice. "Are you one of the many who think me a coward, Thomas?"

"I know better, Sam."

"Well, I thank you for that. As for Burnet, tell him anything you like."

Rusk set out for Harrisburg, and Houston went about preparing his army for the task that lay ahead.

Jared Groce was one of the most successful

planters in Texas. A Virginian by birth, he had previously owned property in Georgia and Alabama. In 1822 he and his oldest son had led a caravan of fifty wagons to Texas, accompanied by ninety slaves and a large herd of livestock—mules, horses, cows, sheep, and hogs.

He selected a site on a high bluff near the Brazos River. A log cabin was constructed and the ground cleared for planting corn and cotton. The severe drought of that year resulted in the failure of the first crop, but Groce doggedly hung on; he, his family, and the slaves subsisted on the plentiful wild game. From that point on the situation improved. The rich Texas soil produced abundant cotton. Groce built a landing and floated his cotton bales on homemade flatboats down the Brazos to Velasco, where it was loaded on schooners and transported to New Orleans. In 1825 Groce's oldest son brought the first cotton gin to Texas.

As time and finances permitted, Groce built his plantation house, a rambling log home named Bernardo. The cottonwood logs, a foot thick, were hewn and counterhewn until they were perfectly square. A broad porch supported by posts of polished walnut extended the full width of the house. Roof shingles were post oak; the floor planks were planed and polished ash. A broad staircase in the fifteen-foot-wide downstairs hallway provided access to the bedrooms upstairs. Every room boasted its own fireplace. A kitchen, dairy, and bachelor's hall stood behind the house.

Groce made his home available to Houston. He's sent his family off to safety, remaining behind to protect Bernardo, alone if need be, from the Mexican invaders. So he was delighted to play host to the Old Chief and his army. He fed the men from his herds and gardens. Muskets, wagons, and accouterments were mended in the plantation's blacksmith shop.

Houston thanked Groce for the offer of Bernardo for use as his headquarters, but indicated that the dwelling would better serve as a hospital. The army was ailing. An outbreak of measles had incapacitated nearly a hundred men. Others suffered from influenza, whooping cough, pink eye, and dysentery. Groce was glad to oblige. He gave the handful of doctors who marched with the army every assistance.

Houston spent nearly a fortnight at Groce's, and he put this respite to good use. While the sick recuperated, the general put the able-bodied through long hours of drill. Some grumbling accompanied this military training. Why learn to be soldiers, asked the malcontents, if they weren't going to get the chance to fight Santa Anna? But at least they weren't retreating anymore. Morale was on the rise. on April 11 a pair of cannon arrived, donated by the citizens of Cincinnati, Ohio. The men christened them the Twin Sisters. Volunteers began to come in, far outnumbering those who had deserted the ranks. Before long, Houston had nine hundred men under his command.

One of the newcomers was a thirty-eight-year-old Georgian named Mirabeau Buonaparte Lamar, a dashing Southerner, a bold talker, and a natural leader of men. He'd met briefly with President Burnet at Harrisburg before joining the army, and apparently had taken to heart Burnet's uncomplimentary assessment of Houston—among them that the commander in chief was a "drunken old Cherokee blackguard." Lamar devised a scheme—highly popular among men longing for action—that called for acquiring boats for the purpose of engaging in riverine raids on the enemy. When informed of Lamar's activities, Houston just shook his head. That was all he and Texas needed—another hotspur like Travis and Fannin. The Georgian with the fancy name would bear close scrutiny.

On April 12 Houston's scouts reported that Santa Anna had divided his forces. Sesma's cavalry was still in the vicinity of San Felipe. Another contingent of infantry had been left behind to guard the wagons and the burgeoning ranks of the sick and wounded, while Santa Anna pressed on toward Harrisburg with six or seven hundred combined infantry and cavalry. The Napoleon of the West was in a hurry again. He wanted to capture the provisional government of Texas and occupy Galveston, thereby severing the rebel lifeline to the United States.

"Obviously Santa Anna no longer considers this army a threat," Houston told his subordinates in a hastily summoned council of war. "Now is our chance, gentlemen. We will march at noon today. Our object is to reach Santa Anna and bring him to battle before he can reunite his forces."

When he got the news from Pierce, Mingo went immediately in search of Marriah, who had been assisting the doctors in the care of the sick. Houston was leaving behind those men who were unfit to travel, and Mingo urged her to stay behind, as well.

"No," said Marriah. "I'm coming with you."

"You cain't. It ain't safe."

"So you do care what happens to me."

Mingo grimaced. "Marriah, if my heart didn't already have an owner, I'd let you have it."

"I could make you forget her," she said, moving closer, and Mingo felt the desire rising up within him, and he was ashamed. He took her by the shoulders and held her away at arm's length, shaking his head.

"You couldn't, girl. Not with all your spells and potions. It's time we go our separate ways."

"You're not shed of me, Mingo Green."

"Stay here," he said firmly, and walked away from temptation.

CHAPTER TWENTY-NINE

The Wedding

When Santa Anna reached Harrisburg, he was very disappointed to learn that President Burnet, Lorenzo de Zavala, and the rest of the rebel government had fled to New Washington on the coast. The Napoleon of the West sent fifty dragoons in hot pursuit, then lingered in Harrisburg for three days to allow his weary troops the recreation of looting the town. While there, he learned that Houston was on the move. Santa Anna was unconcerned by this intelligence. He was confident that Houston would continue to retreat, probably in the direction of Nacogdoches, and that the withdrawal would be slowed by a great number of refugees that had attached themselves to the rebel army. "Houston and his men are cowards," he told his staff officers. "They would not dare seek battle. I will destroy them at my leisure." The staff officers being little more than fawning sycophants in gaudy uniforms, there was no one to argue the point with His Excellency.

Given the chance, Juan Galan would have done so. He had by now concluded that Santa Anna was either drunk with power or deranged. El Presidente had squandered thirteen days at Bexar, then pushed his troops to the brink of exhaustion to trap Sam Houston at the Brazos. Now that Houston had eluded him, Santa Anna had changed his mind about bringing the rebel army to battle and had pressed on to Harrisburg in an attempt to bag the Texas government—only to dawdle away precious days while his men pillaged to their hearts' content. This was not the same Santa Anna who had so vigorously prosecuted the campaigns against the insurrectionists of the southern provinces.

Finally, Santa Anna moved. Ordering Harrisburg put to the torch, he headed for New Washington. There he learned that the dragoons had just missed their prey. Burnet and the others had shoved off in small boats, bound for a schooner lying off behind the reed, as the dragoons galloped into town. The officer in charge of the detachment had ordered his men not to open fire on the boats, since there were women aboard. When he heard this, Santa Anna was furious. But Galan and other field officers hailed the dragoon officer's gallantry. At least someone in the army had some honor and integrity.

As Burnet and the provisional government set sail for Galveston Island, Santa Anna's scouts reported that Houston was not bound for Nacogdoches after all, but rather the town of Lynchburg on the Trinity River. From there the rebel army might board ship and join the government at Galveston. For some reason that Galan could not fully comprehend, Santa Anna was determined to prevent this from happening. His Excellency set his troops on the road to Lynchburg, dispatching what was left of the Tampico Regiment on ahead with orders to reach Lynchburg before the rebels and, if necessary, hold them there until the rest of the column could arrive. Galan's company had been reduced to thirty-five men. Many had fallen in battle with Fannin's rebels; many more were too ill to ride. The regiment could muster only about one-third of the men with whom it had crossed the Rio Grande. Those that were left were exhausted, as were their mounts. Rain had been a daily occurrence, the roads heavy, provisions in chronic short supply. Galan doubted that the regiment could hold Houston's army at Lynchburg; he did not share Santa Anna's low opinion of the rebels' fighting ability. The many atrocities committed at Santa Anna's behest would harden Texas resolve, while the morale of the Mexican Army was at an all-time low. Of course, His Excellency refused to believe any of this.

To Galan's relief, there was no sign of the rebels at Lynchburg. And then the news came that Houston had appeared at Harrisburg, instead! Galan reacted to this news as he might have to his own death sentence. Now the rebel army lay between Santa Anna's column and Cos and Urrea and the rest of the Mexican Army. *We are cut off from our reinforcements, and for the first time we are outnumbered by the rebels.*

With those very words Juan Galan began a letter to his mother. Elena Galan was a strong person, accustomed to personal tragedy, and Galan could be candid with her. He wanted her to be there for Natalia, to share her strength with his bride should the worst come to pass. He had his death letter, the one he would keep on his person in the event he was killed in action. The letter to his mother he would bribe a dispatch rider to carry to Urrea's headquarters, in the hopes that from there it would find its way back to Mexico. He had followed Santa Anna down the road to hell, and he was fairly certain he would never see Tampico and his loved ones again. But he assured his mother that he would do his duty. That would give her comfort, even though it gave him none.

While Sam Houston was at Harrisburg, one of his scouts, Deaf Smith, brought in a Mexican courier. The man carried his dispatches in deerskin saddlebags that bore William Barret Travis's name. Obviously the soldier had been present at the Alamo, and more than a few of Houston's volunteers wanted to skin him alive. The dispatches revealed that Santa Anna and seven hundred men were in the vicinity of Lynchburg, completely cut off from the rest of the Mexican army. Houston realized his one opportunity to save Texas had finally come. Forming his men in a hollow square, he addressed them.

"Men, we will cross Buffalo Bayou and meet the enemy. Some of us may be killed. But I know you will not falter. You will prevail. Because you will remember the Alamo. You will remember Goliad. You will guarantee that the supreme sacrifice of your brothers-in-arms will not have been in vain."

"Remember the Alamo!" shouted the men. "Remember Goliad!" The refrain was taken up by every volunteer in the ranks, ringing out long after Sam Houston had walked away.

Standing beside Pierce Hammond, Boone heard something in the timbre of those shouts that made his blood run cold. It was a howl of vengeance. "I don't think we'll be taking too many prisoners, Pierce," he remarked.

With only a log raft and a leaky skiff, the army took most of the day to cross the bayou. They marched along the eastern bank until midnight. Like all the other volunteers, Boone collapsed on the soggy ground, exhausted. But he wasn't too exhausted to stay awake for a while, thinking about Jessy. The wagons and the refugees and more sick men had been left behind at Harrisburg—or what was left of that community after Santa Anna's visit. Boone had prevailed on Jessy to stay behind and assist the ailing, since most of the Texas doctors were still at Bernardo.

"We'll have our big scrape in the next day or two," he told her. "That's why you can't come with me. It's too dangerous."

A lesser woman might have wept and caused a scene. Not Jessy. She wanted to be with him, of course, but she loved him too much to burden him with her presence. It was hard to let him go—the hardest thing she had ever done—but she knew it would be easier for him if he went into battle without having to worry about her well-being.

So she agreed—on one condition.

They were married in Harrisburg by a local preacher. The town's church was one of the few structures spared by the Mexicans. Pierce Hammond and the Red Rovers were present, as were Hardin and his Brazorians, all of whom knew Jessy Reynolds. Boone had no ring to give her, but Jessy didn't mind. In her plain, travel-worn gingham dress, standing barefoot in front of the pulpit, she looked more radiantly beautiful than any woman Boone had ever seen. The ceremony was brief. An odd thing happened to Boone when the minister proclaimed them man and wife. He didn't have anything except a few books and the clothes on his back, but at that moment he felt like the richest man in the world. Jessy was his bride, and she was all he needed to make life complete.

In a derelict barn on the outskirts of town, the Brazorians and the Red Rovers built a fire and passed around a few jugs of bald-faced corn liquor. The frolic commenced. One of Hardin's men broke out a fiddle and played some tunes. Boone was a deplorable dancer, but he gave it his best. Pierce asked Jessy for the honor of a dance, and she granted it. Later, when the liquor had been consumed and the fiddler was all fiddled out, Pierce gave a silent, prearranged signal, and all the men trooped out of the old barn, congratulating Boone one by one, and a few giving him a sly wink in parting. Pierce shook his hand. "You're an extremely fortunate fellow," he declared, a little wistful.

"He's lucky to have friends like you and the others," said Jessy, and Boone nodded, smiling gratefully at his wife, for she had put his inexpressible feelings into words.

And then they were alone, and by the light of a

dying fire Jessy took off her dress and took him in her arms and made it known that there was something else she wanted from her husband before he left her to go and fight.

Now, lying on the muddy ground, wrapped in a thin, tattered blanket, on the banks of the Buffalo Bayou, Boone Tasker suffered the anguish of thinking about Jessy's warm, lithe body pressed against his, of the taste of her kisses and the soft, passionate touch of her hands, and the pure ecstasy as they became one. He knew what had been in the back of her mind all along. She had wanted his seed, his child, in the event that they would never see each other again, and he realized the torment she must be suffering at this very moment, not knowing whether she would ever see her husband alive again. Boone promised himself that, if he survived, they would never again be apart.

He was eager for the fight, wanting to get it over with, wanting to drive Santa Anna and his soldiers out of Texas once and for all, because he was impatient to get started on his future with Jessy. Texas would be a land full of promise, especially for those who had put their lives on the line to win her independence. So in Texas they would stay. Boone wasn't sure what he would do for a living—something that had to do with words. He liked schoolteaching well enough, but precious few schoolteachers flourished. Before meeting Jessy, he had been perfectly content with a little money in his pocket and some books stacked under his bed. Not any more. He would succeed, because Jessy deserved the best. They had very little at the moment—his bride had stood before the minister and recited her vows in her bare feet, for heaven's sake! One day soon, though, she would be well provided for. She would want for nothing. He would see to it.

He missed her terribly, but he was glad she was in Harrisburg, as safe as anyone could be while Santa Anna was on the loose. Now Boone had something to fight for—to keep Jessy safe and make Texas free. They were, essentially, one and the same. Funny how things worked out. He'd come to Texas to escape heartbreak, and found the woman of his dreams. He'd found his reason for living. And to live he had to risk death. There was the irony. But he wasn't afraid. He knew he would fight bravely when the time came. Could he do any less? Any less than Alton and Seth Reynolds had done, and the other men who had sacrificed themselves so that the other Brazorians could escape their death sentence? No, he could certainly do no less then they. Every man in Sam Houston's ragtag rebel army felt the same. They *would* fight. They *would* prevail. Because they were in the right, and God was on their side. Boone was sure of it.

Reveille came at daybreak. Boone had gotten very little sleep, and he was starving. But Houston said there was no time to eat—they had to march. Scouts had brought word that Santa Anna had quit New Washington—leaving that town a smoking rubble, of course—and was making for Lynch's Ferry. Houston wanted to get to the ferry first. It meant success or failure. Nobody really knew what the Old Chief was thinking, and there was, naturally, some grumbling in the ranks. But not too much. The army could smell a fight brewing, and every volunteer had a score to settle.

So they marched hard and won the race to the ferry. Houston had them occupy a grove of oaks along the banks of Buffalo Bayou. Here at last, late in the morning of April 20th, the men built their cookfires, brewed up some coffee, and slaughtered several beeves so that everyone could have a little half-cooked meat in their bellies.

Houston called his subordinates to council. Pierce Hammond was present to hear the general explain his plans.

"I have always been willing to give up land to gain precious time," he said. "Texas had plenty of land, and never enough time. Now, though, Santa Anna has divided his force once too often. Finally, the terrain is in our favor. The country to the west was too open. There, Santa Anna had the advantage over us with his superior numbers and well-trained cavalry. Take a look around you, gentlemen. What do you see? Woodlands and swamps. We have the San Jacinto River on our left flank, and the bayou behind us. Santa Anna can come at us from only one direction—the south."

Sidney Sherman, the young leader of fifty Kentucky mounted riflemen, spoke up. "But, General, if our lines should break, we are destroyed. We have only the ferry with which to transport our men across the river to safety."

Houston's blue-gray eyes were like daggers. "Our lines will not break, sir. Santa Anna will not attack us. We will attack him."

Sherman's smile was like a wolf's. "General, I confess that perhaps I misjudged you."

"Tomorrow," said Houston gravely, "history will judge us all."

CHAPTER THIRTY

The Vigil

At ten o'clock in the morning of April 21st, Sam Houston rode out of camp on his horse, Saracen, accompanied by his aides, Lieutenants Hammond and Hardin. He wanted to observe the enemy's position. Santa Anna had arrived on the scene yesterday, establishing his camp on high ground about three-quarters of a mile from the Texans. Behind him lay a marsh and a lake, and on his right flank was the San Jacinto River. The Napoleon of the West placed his infantry on the right, his cavalry on the left, and his artillery in the center. A breastworks composed of saddles, baggage, casks, and other paraphernalia was erected, with embrasures in the center to accommodate the cannon.

During their reconnoiter, Houston and his companions saw three or four hundred Mexican infantry marching across open ground from the road to New Washington. These were reinforcements for Santa Anna, and Houston grimly eyed their progress.

"We may be outnumbered now, General," remarked Pierce.

"No matter," Houston replied curtly. "Santa

Anna will wait for more reinforcements before he dares attack. That is his way. The only battle he is willing to fight is the one in which he has two or three times the number of his foe. No, he will wait. But we cannot."

"The men are ready," said Hardin.

Pierce was thinking of Shakespeare. "Cry havoc, and let slip the dogs of war." *Julius Caesar*, wasn't it? The Texans were itching for a fight. Late yesterday, Sidney Sherman had requested permission to attack an outpost of Mexican infantry that had ventured out in front of Santa Anna's right flank. Houston gave permission, and Sherman's Kentucky Mounted Rifles had driven the Mexicans back to their lines.

But Sherman wasn't satisfied. He insisted that Houston allow him to charge the enemy artillery. Santa Anna's cannon could be taken, argued the hotheaded Kentuckian, and with the center of their line breached the enemy would be thrown into confusion. Houston didn't think so. He approved a reconnaissance, but forbade Sherman from engaging the Mexicans. Yet when dragoons sallied forth to drive Sherman's detachment away, the impetuous Sherman ordered a charge. The dragoons wavered, then regrouped, and counterattacked with lance and saber. From his own lines Houston watched with apprehension; his friend Thomas J. Rusk, the Texan secretary of war, had recently returned to take part in the big scrape, and he was riding with Sherman. Now Rusk was surrounded by enemy lancers, and he would have lost his life but for Mirabeau Lamar, who charged to the rescue, his big stallion bowling over one dragoon's mount, giving Rusk the opening he needed to escape unscathed.

All of Houston's subordinates begged the Old Chief to let them lead their volunteers out to aid Sherman's beleaguered Kentuckians. Houston adamantly refused to expose his infantry to the Mexican lancers. But Colonel Burleson's Texans marched out anyway, ignoring Houston's angry orders to return to the timber along Buffalo Bayou. Fortunately for all concerned, Sherman had already called for a withdrawal. The Kentucky cavalry and Texan infantry pulled back into the trees—to watch Mirabeau Lamar perform one more act of heroism.

One of the Kentuckians, struck by a Mexican lance and hurled from his horse, had been left for dead on the field. But suddenly he was up and stumbling after his compatriots. Seeing this, several dragoons set out after him. Lamar spurred his stallion forward, blocked the path of the Mexicans, and shot one with his pistol. Henry Karnes, one of Houston's scouts, arrived to haul the wounded Kentuckian up behind him and, covered by Lamar, returned to the Texan lines. From across the field came the cheers of the Mexican cavalry, applauding Lamar's bravery—which the Georgian hotspur acknowledged with a bow from the saddle.

That night the conversation around the Texan campfires centered on whether Sam Houston was fit to command. Did he have the guts to fight? Why hadn't he allowed the infantry to attack? Sherman was convinced that if a full assault had been carried out, victory would have been assured. Even Pierce was beginning to wonder about the Old

Chief's fortitude. On the 20th the Texans had outnumbered their foe. Now, one day later, Santa Anna again enjoyed superior numbers.

Returning from his reconnoiter, Houston dispatched scout Deaf Smith and six volunteers to destroy a bridge spanning the bayou eight miles to the west. This was designed to delay a column of Mexican troops under the command of General Vicente Filisola, which was marching on the double to join Santa Anna. Houston knew that if Filisola affected a juncture with Santa Anna the war was over, and Texas would once again be a province of Mexico.

The Old Chief settled down to write another dispatch. After that, a letter. Pierce watched in growing disbelief. What was the man waiting for? Now and then Houston would glance up from his labors to check the position of the sun, a heatless white orb behind a cataract of thin cloud cover. Tense silence reigned. All along the lines men cleaned their rifles, sharpened their knives, and grumbled surly discontent. Pierce paced restlessly, and when he grew weary of pacing, he joined Mingo and Boone and a few of the other Alabama Red Rovers around a campfire.

Sitting on his heels beside Mingo, Pierce reached under his mud-splattered and sweat-stained cutaway coat and brandished a folded paper, which he handed to the slave.

"Just in case," he said wryly.

Mingo unfolded the paper and looked at what was written on it, but he couldn't read, and he threw a puzzled glance at Pierce.

"That's what you've been waiting for ever since we left Magnolia," explained Pierce.

"My freedom?" Mingo couldn't believe it. What was Pierce trying to pull?

Pierce simply nodded.

"If you was gonna give this to me, why didn't you do it a long time ago?" asked Mingo angrily.

Pierce looked over at Boone, feigning surprise. "Now that's gratitude for you, eh, Boone?"

"You said this wouldn't do me no good in Alabam'," said Mingo. "That Marse Hammond wouldn't honor it."

"He probably won't, unless he understands that your freedom was my dying request."

Mingo stared at Pierce, then at the paper in his hand. "So what you be sayin' is that this ain't no good to me lessen you be dead."

"Something like that. You can leave now if you want, but I suggest you at least hang around until this battle is over, just to see if I'm dead or alive. If I'm alive, you'd do well to go back home with me. If I'm dead, well, now you've got your papers."

Boone watched Mingo and Pierce and tried to figure out whether the two men hated each other. Their relationship was ambiguous, to say the least. There was animosity there, but something else, too. Grudging admiration, perhaps. Though it made absolutely no sense to Boone that a slave and a slaveholder would admire one another. He imagined that Mingo might suddenly consign his much sought-after freedom papers to the cookfire's flames and declare that he and Pierce would go home to Alabama together or not at all—such melodramatics would not have been altogether out of keeping with the peculiar dynamics of the relationship that had developed between these two men. But Mingo stuffed the document under his shirt, instead. Boone decided that maybe the only reason Mingo cared whether Pierce Hammond survived was because alive Pierce would be of more use to him in his endeavor to free Sadie.

"Guess I'll just wait and see," said Mingo gruffly. "Makes me no never mind, you livin' or dyin'. Don't reckon I'll ever see Sadie free, anyway."

Pierce was genuinely surprised. "That's a hell of a thing to say! If you felt that way, why the blazes have you been trying to run off ever since we left Magnolia?"

"'Cause I'm a father. And a husband. Most of all, 'cause I'm a man."

What could Pierce say to that? His silence was full of profound respect. Boone knew then that Pierce Hammond would never make a good master. Mingo Green had gotten to him. The slave had demonstrated by his actions, and now by his words, the fundamental flaw in slavery. One could not make property of human beings. Property did not have dreams and aspirations. Property did not love. Property did not have courage and conviction. Pierce realized this now. Maybe he had always suspected it. Boone was willing to concede that he had misjudged the man.

Lieutenant Hardin walked over. "The Old Chief wants to see us, Pierce."

Pierce nodded and left the campfire, returning to the place where Sam Houston sat cross-legged on the ground, an Indian blanket beneath him, and above him a wagon tarp tied to three saplings. He stood as they approached, and handed them both some papers.

"Copies of my orders," he told them, "so that there can be no mistake. Find the officers of the respective commands and make certain they fully comprehend my wishes, as expressed in these orders. At three-thirty this afternoon they will parade their men. Precisely one hour later, the Twin Sisters will be fired. That will be the signal for the advance. The entire army must move in unison." Houston fished a keywinder from his pocket and consulted it, then glanced across the open ground in the direction of the Mexican lines. The enemy could not be seen from the trees lining the bayou; a rise covered with high grass extended from one side of the field to the other. They could advance about two-thirds of the way to Santa Anna's breastworks, a distance of about three hundred yards, before the Mexicans could do any real damage to them.

But once we progress beyond that rise, mused Pierce, *it will be like walking into Hell.*

"I request permission to ride with the cavalry, General," he said.

"No. I want you and Mr. Hardin at my side." Reading the chagrin on the faces of his aides, Houston smiled grimly. "Do not despair, gentlemen. I am confident that before the day is out, you and your men will be given ample opportunity to die for Texas."

Climbing into the saddle on his Kentucky mare,

Pierce reached for his own timepiece—only to remember that it lay at the bottom of the Brazos River. Hardin, also mounting up, said, "In a couple of hours we'll know if there's going to be a Republic of Texas or not."

Pierce could only nod, and rode off along the Texan lines to deliver Sam Houston's orders.

Squinting into the afternoon sun, Juan Galan peered anxiously at the low rise that concealed the enemy lines from his view.

Like the rest of Santa Anna's cavalry, he and the remnants of the Tampico Regiment held the left flank of the line. His Excellency had expected the rebels to attack yesterday. But this morning General Cos had arrived with reinforcements, and now Santa Anna had changed his mind and was convinced that Sam Houston would not dare attack a superior force. As a result, His Excellency had given the order for his troops to stand down.

The colonel had sent Galan to Santa Anna's headquarters to protest the order, knowing that Galan would be an enthusiastic advocate for continued vigilance. But a staff officer blithely informed Galan that El Presidente could not be disturbed for any reason. He was very tired, having spent an anxious night—supervising the strengthening of the breastworks and awaiting the arrival of Cos. Furthermore, a very attractive mulatto girl, a former slave who had become a camp follower after fleeing from her Texan master, had caught Santa Anna's eyes, and he was presently engaged in entertaining her in the privacy of his tent, having given instructions that under no circumstances was he to be disturbed.

Galan was furious. He insisted that the order to stand down was incredibly foolish. Scowling, the staff officer, a devoted *santanista*, explained that His Excellency, as always, knew exactly what he was doing. Sam Houston would do one of two things—maintain his position and wait for an attack, or try to slip away during the night. Either way, the rebel army was doomed. By tomorrow morning Filisola and his troops would arrive. Then the rebels would be outnumbered by two to one. If they were still here, His Excellency would attack, and the enemy would be destroyed. If the rebels tried to run, they would be pursued and crushed. And Galan, advised the staff officer haughtily, would be well advised to keep his opinions concerning His Excellency's decisions to himself.

So Galan returned to his command and told the colonel that he and his company would *not* stand down. The colonel decided that half the regiment would remain at the ready for four hours, at which time the other half would stand to while the first half rested.

Galan realized how important it was for the cavalry to hold the line on the left. For it was to the left, down the road to New Washington, which afforded the only means of retreat for the army if Santa Anna was wrong and Houston did attack. If the Texans charged, the army would be unprepared, thanks to El Presidente's overconfidence. And if the left flank folded, the army would have no place to go, with a river on the right and a swamp to the rear.

Gazing at the low grassy rise, Galan was apprehensive. He had a premonition of disaster. The rebels weren't going to run anymore. This was where they would make their last stand. This was where the issue would finally be resolved.

He tried not to think about Natalia. It distressed him too much to contemplate his lovely young bride and the future they might have had together . . .

CHAPTER THIRTY-ONE

The Judgment

The Twin Sisters—the two cannon donated to the cause of Texas independence by the citizens of Cincinnati, Ohio—opened fire at 4:30 in the afternoon of April 21, 1836. And thus what would become known as the Battle of San Jacinto commenced.

Pierce Hammond had been concerned that he would see no action in his role as aide to General Houston. He quickly realized that his fears were unfounded. Sam Houston was in the front lines when the battle started. With him went Hardin's Brazorians and what was left of the Alabama Red Rovers, twenty men all told.

As the volunteers advanced across the open prairie toward the low rise, Houston galloped along the line at full speed astride his stallion, Saracen, exhorting his men to hold their fire and attempting to dress the line when it began to disintegrate. From across the rise came the sound of Mexican pickets crying out, *"Centinela alerta!"* the bleating of trumpets and the rat-tat-tat of drums. Then the enemy artillery opened up, and cannonballs came screaming over the rise, only to fall behind the advancing Texan line.

Houston expected the Mexican cavalry to strike before the Texans reached the rise; the dragoons would attempt to disrupt the advance, and Houston had stationed Mirabeau Lamar and the cavalry on the right flank. Houston had promoted Lamar to commander of the cavalry in reward for yesterday's heroics, and in consideration of his immense popularity with the men. Concealed in a grove of trees, Lamar's task was to engage the Mexican dragoons before they could reach Houston's infantry. But Santa Anna's sabers were slow to react. Houston was perplexed. He did not know that his adversary had ordered his troops to stand down.

As a consequence, only half of the Tampico Regiment, fewer than a hundred men, were prepared to leap into action when the battle began. Juan Galan wanted to take his dragoons into action immediately, but his colonel ordered him to wait until the entire regiment could advance together. Galan chafed at the delay. There was not a moment to lose. All his doubts and fears were gone now; the professional soldier took over. The sooner the cavalry engaged the rebel infantry, the better. They could ride in with lance and saber and blunt the Texan advance, perhaps even repel it. But Galan had to wait and speculate as to whether the colonel's sudden caution would prove fatal.

The Texans reached the rise in good order. Sporadic firing issued from the Mexican lines. Santa Anna's army had been caught unprepared. Many of the troops had just settled down to supper around their campfires, confident that the rebels would not attack. Hadn't Santa Anna, the Napoleon of the

West, the military genius who had defeated all of Mexico's enemies, given them his assurances on that score? And now, as those who rushed to man the breastworks began shooting soon realized, the late afternoon sun was in their eyes. Thin cloud cover muted the sun somewhat, but it was bright enough to affect their aim.

As soon as his men reached the rise, Houston ordered them to halt, dress ranks, and fire a volley. The line erupted in smoke and barrel flash. Some of the volunteers rushed impetuously forward. Houston tried to stop them, wanting a second volley. Suddenly, Thomas Rusk rode out onto the field. "If we stop now, we are cut to pieces!" he shouted at Houston. "Don't stop! Go ahead, and give them hell!"

The volunteers heard. They didn't wait for Houston to decide. They could wait no longer. This was the big fight, the moment they had all been waiting for. There was no holding them back. "Remember the Alamo!" shouted some. "Remember Goliad!" answered others. The cry was taken up—a roar of bloodthirsty outrage welling up out of hundreds of throats. The line disintegrated completely as the Texans surged forward. Above the din a four-piece drum and fife band played "Will You Come to the Bower?" as they marched bravely into the fray. The saccharine melody of the sentimental ballad was a peculiar counterpoint to the roar of the cannon, the crackle of musketry, the roar of the vengeful Texans, and the screams of dying men and horses.

Pierce and Boone kicked their horses into a gallop, followed by the rest of the Red Rovers. Houston and the Brazorians came along right behind. Then Houston's horse went down, hit five times. At the same instant that Saracen died, a bullet smashed the general's ankle. Pierce checked his Kentucky mare, but a pair of Brazorians reached the Old Chief first. His craggy face twisted in anguish, Houston gestured angrily for Pierce to go on. "Break their damned lines, Lieutenant! Don't stop now!" As Pierce wheeled his horse around and headed once more for the Mexican breastworks, he heard Houston roaring at someone to bring him another mount.

Boone was well ahead of Pierce now. Texans were running full tilt on either side of him. Most didn't bother to stop and shoot, and Boone shouted himself hoarse as he urged them on. Powder smoke stung his eyes and nostrils. His heart raced. His mouth was filled with the taste of copper. Then he felt the horse beneath him shudder and stumble, and he kicked his boots out of the stirrups and tried to jump clear as the mount went down, somersaulting. It occurred to him, fleetingly, that he'd had very bad luck with horses—this one had belonged to one of Sherman's Kentuckians, a man who'd been wounded in yesterday's fracas.

Hitting the ground hard, Boone wheezed for air as he scrambled to his feet and looked about him—only to realize that the Mexican artillery emplacement was but a few yards away. At that instant one of Santa Anna's fieldpieces roared, spurting flame, and Boone thought he could feel the wind of the cannonball's passage on his face. He gave thanks to

Almighty God that they weren't using canister—he'd have been cut to bloody ribbons.

Leaping forward, pistol in one hand, the knife Gabe Cochran had given him in the other, Boone cleared the embrasure and shot a cannoneer at point-blank range. An artillery officer came at him with sword raised, and Boone fell back against a wheel of one of the cannon. A Texan hurtled the breastwork and struck the officer with his musket, shattering the stock. Boone distinctly heard the Mexican's neck snap. The Texan rushed on, yelling at the top of his lungs. Boone picked up the dead officer's sword and pressed on. The crews of Santa Anna's artillery—those who were still alive—had abandoned their posts. The Mexican cannon were silenced.

Santa Anna's troops were fleeing. The Texans fell upon them, clubbing them with their rifles, slashing with their Bowie knives. Some of the Mexican soldiers threw down their weapons and raised their hands, or fell to their knees, begging for mercy. *"Mi no Alamo! Mi no La Buhia!"* they cried. But the Texans could not be reasoned with. They showed no mercy. They embarked on a killing spree.

Boone found himself in the midst of Juan Seguin's detachment of *tejanos*. Houston had offered to exclude these men from combat, fearing that his troops would not bother trying to distinguish friendly Mexican from foe. But Seguin had angrily reminded the Old Chief that he and his men hated the *santanistas* just as much as the Anglo Texans did. Houston was won over. Seguin agreed to one precaution. The *tejanos* would put pieces of cardboard in their hatbands to identify themselves. They fought with the ferocity of tigers, giving no quarter and expecting none, shouting *"Recuerden el Alamo!"* Boone saw one of Seguin's men fall, impaled on a *santanista* bayonet. Rushing forward, Boone thrust the sword he carried into the Mexican soldier, driving it in to the hilt, so that the blade came out the back. "Remember Gabe Cochran," he muttered, and gave the dying man a hard shove, letting him fall with the sword still in him.

Picking up a discarded Brown Bess, bayonet fixed, he moved resolutely on. A Mexican soldier was sitting on the ground, one leg shattered by a bullet. He saw Boone coming and babbled incoherently, fearing for his life. Boone let him be and walked on, turning back when he heard the thunder of horse's hooves, in time to see Hardin, mounted on a wild-eyed pony, blow the wounded Mexican's brains out with a pistol shot. "Great sport, eh, Tasker?" snarled Hardin, and rode on, as wild-eyed as his horse. Looking at the man Hardin had killed, Boone remembered Hardin's father, the blacksmith who had so gallantly given his life at Brazoria. Suddenly nauseated, Boone came to his senses at that moment. He was released from the madness that had seized him, the madness that seemed to possess every volunteer in the Texan army. Victory had been achieved, and Boone decided he was done with killing. He held back as his comrades-in-arms charged onward in pursuit of the routed Mexican troops. Numb with physical and emotional exhaustion, he moved along the breastworks, applying a tourniquet to the bullet-shattered arm of a Mexican soldier, giving water to another, and saving several from execution at the hands of vengeful Texans.

On Santa Anna's left flank, the Tampico Regiment and other elements of the Mexican cavalry belatedly got into action. Galan and his company were in the lead as a slashing counterattack was launched against the Texans.

Pierce Hammond saw the banners of Santa Anna's cavalry, heard the crescendo of gunfire, and surmised what was happening. He steered his thoroughbred in that direction. By the time he'd reached the Texan right flank, Mirabeau Lamar had led Houston's horsemen out of the grove and broken up the Mexican charge. Mounted hand-to-hand combat ensued, with sabers flashing in the dull afternoon sun, pistols and sawed-off muskets going off, men and horses falling.

Suddenly, the Mexican cavalry—or what was left of it—turned and ran. Only a handful held their ground. Among these were Juan Galan. His horse shot out from under, Galan fought on afoot. The men of his company begged him to withdraw. Galan refused. "I have been in ten battles and never shown my back!" he yelled. A dozen dragoons rallied to his side. The remnant of the Tampico Regiment was swept away by the tide of battle. Galan saw his colonel die. But he continued to fight, his slashing saber claiming several rebel lives. He and his men were out of ammunition for their pistols and *escopetas*. Their horses were killed. But they stood, holding the Texans at bay with lance and sword.

Pierce Hammond rode into the fray. "Don't shoot them!" he shouted. The courage of this handful of dragoons, surrounded by Lamar's horsemen, moved him. But the Texans would not heed him. One by one the dragoons died. Seeing that one of Sherman's Kentuckians was drawing a bead on the Mexican officer who now stood defiantly alone, the bodies of his loyal men heaped at his feet, Pierce knocked the Kentuckian's rifle up just as it discharged. "Don't shoot, damn you!" yelled Pierce. His words were drowned out by several guns fired simultaneously.

His body riddled with bullets, Galan fell. With the last of his strength he reached under his crimson jacket and withdrew the death letter to Natalia. The bloodstained envelope slipped from numb fingers, and he watched the wind of battle carry it beyond his reach. He did not pity himself. He was dying as a soldier should, in battle with his men, and in the end nothing else mattered.

By the time Pierce had reached Galan's side, the gallant officer was dead.

Back aboard the Kentucky mare, Pierce rode forward, past the abandoned breastworks and Mexican encampment. Santa Anna's soldiers had fled into the marsh behind their lines. Many plunged into a small lake, where they were killed by Texan riflemen—so many killed, in fact, that the waters of the lake turned red with blood. Pierce tried to stop the slaughter. "If Jesus Christ came down from Heaven and ordered me to stop shootin', I wouldn't do it," one volunteer informed him; then, rifle reloaded, the man took aim and picked off another Mexican who was floundering in the boggy shallows of the lake. Pierce saw wounded men clubbed to death, and the dead scalped. The volunteers were oblivious to the threats and pleas of officers who tried to stem the carnage.

Sickened, Pierce headed back to the Texan camp in the woods along Buffalo Bayou. The sun seemed not to have moved since the onset of battle, and for an instant he wondered, absurdly, if time had stood still. Less than twenty minutes had elapsed since the opening salvo, but it felt like an eternity to him.

He was almost to the low rise when a bullet hit him, and he didn't even hear the gunshot.

When the dead were counted, more than six hundred Mexican soldiers—half of Santa Anna's total number—had perished. Three hundred more were captured by nightfall. That this many had been spared astonished Sam Houston. Only a dozen Texans had lost their lives.

But the one prisoner Houston most desired—Santa Anna himself—remained at large. The Old Chief, lying on a blanket beneath an oak tree, his bullet-smashed ankle causing him tremendous pain, knew that victory meant nothing if the Napoleon of the West escaped. Between them, Generals Filisola and Urrea had several thousand effectives, and Houston didn't like his chances in another battle. His men were exhausted and disorganized. Many had already headed for home, convinced the war was over. No, he had to have Santa

Anna as a bargaining chip. His Excellency would be given a choice: withdraw his soldiers and recognize the Republic of Texas, or die. Houston was confident that Santa Anna would choose to live.

The next day Houston was dozing when a commotion brought him around, and he looked up to see a Mexican in a private's uniform being brought forward under guard.

"I am General Antonio Lopez de Santa Anna, President of the Republic of Mexico, and a prisoner at your disposition."

"We caught him hightailin' it for Vince's Bridge," said one of His Excellency's buckskin-clad captors. "Only the bridge warn't there."

Vastly relieved, Houston nodded. Santa Anna had been trying to reach Filisola's column. Had he succeeded—Houston shuddered to think what might have happened.

"I believe the army would very much like to hang this fellow, Sam" remarked Thomas Rusk.

"He deserves death for the murder of Texan prisoners," replied Houston. "But he is worth more to us alive."

A few hours later, when an armistice had been signed, and Santa Anna had written orders for Filisola and Urrea to withdraw their troops, Sam Houston penned a proclamation.

Tell our friends all the news, that we have beaten the enemy. Generals Santa Anna and Cos are taken. The Republic of Texas is saved. Tell them to come and let the people plant corn.

CHAPTER THIRTY-TWO

The Redeemed

On a sultry August day Pierce Hammond returned to Magnolia plantation. The fields were carpeted with cotton nearly ready for the picking, and he recalled how those very fields, covered with white frost, had looked much the same on that morning nearly six months ago when he had departed for Texas.

Six months! It seemed more like a lifetime. So much had happened. He wasn't at all the same man who had run away last winter. Yes, run away. He could admit as much to himself. He had been running away from his father and everything Daniel Hammond represented. Most of all he'd been running from himself, from the kind of life he led, the kind of man he'd become.

Everything was very clear in Pierce's mind as he guided his Kentucky mare up the lane toward the big house. He could look at his past objectively, with an eye unclouded by emotion, as though he were on the outside of life looking in. Like Texas, he had won his freedom—freedom from the past.

There was a commotion up at the big house when they saw him coming, and as he drew closer, his father emerged onto the veranda. Pierce had wondered how he would feel at this moment of reunion. All he felt was affection mixed with pity. Daniel Hammond looked much older than Pierce remembered. He looked haggard and careworn. Magnolia was a demanding mistress, sucking the life out of its owner.

As Pierce dismounted, a boy scampered up to take the mare's reins; Pierce thanked him and turned to his father. Daniel Hammond couldn't help staring at the empty sleeve of Pierce's new broadcloth coat.

"Dear God," he breathed, then regained his composure, seemed to inflate himself with a deep breath, and put a hand on Pierce's shoulder. "I am proud of you, son. I misjudged you. I don't mind saying so. You're quite the hero, by all accounts."

Pierce was inscrutable. "Hero? Not really. The fight was over when I got shot. No one knows who did the shooting, whether the bullet that took my arm came from a Mexican or a Texan rifle. It was just a fluke. A stray bullet. And I was unlucky."

"Come," said Daniel Hammond. "We will sit on the porch for a spell. Pearl will bring us some refreshment. What will it be? Mint julep? Whiskey sour?"

Pierce opted for a good stiff shot of sour mash. It helped dull the pain. Oddly, the arm was gone, but at times the pain came back—especially after a long day in the saddle. Sitting in a cane chair on the veranda, he gazed across the cotton fields and made the comment that it looked to be a good year.

"We shall have a fine crop this season," concurred his father. "We'll realize eight hundred bales out of a thousand acres in cultivation."

"Not *we*, Father. I'm not staying."

"But this is your home, Pierce. All this will be yours someday."

"No. Magnolia is your dream, not mine. Texas is my home now."

"Texas!" Confusion, resentment, and resignation flashed across Daniel Hammond's features in quick succession. "I see. And what do you propose to do in Texas?"

"I've decided to study the law. Perhaps dabble in politics. I'm not cut out to be a planter. I think I'll be settling down in a town called Youngblood. A friend of mine will be there. Boone Tasker. You may remember him. He used to be the schoolteacher here. Now he's married and starting up a newspaper."

"Texas," muttered Daniel Hammond, staring bleakly off into the heat-shimmered distance.

"We won a battle. Texas is an independent nation. But Mexico refuses to recognize us. And the United States Congress refuses to deal with the issue of annexation."

Hammond nodded. The Northern free states were reluctant to admit a new slave state into the Union. He anticipated that the debate on annexation would rage for years.

"So the fight isn't really over in Texas," continued Pierce. "That's one reason I'm going back. Then, too, I won't deny it's a real advantage to be known as one of the men who fought with Sam Houston at San Jacinto."

"Of course," muttered Hammond.

Pierce leaned forward. "What of Mingo? Was he here?"

"He was. A couple of months ago."

"Did Slade give him any trouble?"

"Slade is gone. He was . . . too insubordinate. A good overseer, yes. Got a lot of work out of the hands. But he was disrespectful. Forgot who was running the show. I could no longer tolerate him."

"What about Mingo? He and I were going to come back together. But you could say I was indisposed after the battle. They brought me to New Orleans. The same surgeons who worked on General Houston's ankle were consulted regarding my arm. They succeeded in saving the general's ankle, but failed in my case. When I reached New Orleans, there was a tidy sum of money and a ceremonial sword waiting for me, compliments of the Bank of Mobile on behalf of the people of Alabama. I don't suppose you had anything to do with that."

"Certainly not," replied Hammond stiffly.

"I thought not. At any rate, I gave Mingo enough money to buy Sadie's freedom, since I wasn't going to be fit for traveling for a while . . ."

"As I said, he showed up two months ago. I felt honor-bound to respect his papers, though you had no legal right to manumit him."

Pierce nodded, smiling. He had written a letter for Mingo to show his father—and any other white man who might confront him—explaining how Mingo had saved his life in Mobile and again aboard the *Athena* at Fort Bend Crossing, and how he had valiantly served the cause of Texas independence. Of course he hadn't mentioned Mingo's escape from Galveston Island, or how he had fallen in with Big Tom's cutthroats, or that the slave had taken no part in the battle at San Jacinto. Pierce didn't hold the latter against Mingo; it hadn't been his fight. The only reason Mingo had been there at all was to find out whether Pierce was going to be alive at the end of the day. Pierce had assumed his father would be obligated to Mingo for saving his son's life, and it didn't matter if Hammond thought his son's life was worth saving or not.

"But he didn't buy Sadie's freedom," continued Hammond, "because Sadie was gone. She'd run away from Ravenmoor a fortnight after you and Mingo left for Mobile. Ambler didn't find her. We assume she made it to Florida. There are lot of runaways these days in the swamps down there."

Pierce was stunned. He felt sorry for Mingo. After everything the man had been through, to come home and find his wife and unborn child gone!

"Where is Mingo now, Father?"

"Oh, he went after her, of course. I doubt we'll ever know what becomes of him. Or Sadie. Not that I care. Troublemakers, the both of them. Have you any word of Jack Shackelford, by any chance?"

"He's alive," said Pierce. "But still a prisoner in Mexico. Since he was a doctor they let him live to treat their own wounded."

"A gallant gentleman. I wish him well. I understand he lost his son at Goliad. Tragic."

Pierce mumbled an accord, reached into his pocket, and withdrew a muslin sack full of twenty-dollar gold pieces, which he held out to his father.

"What is this?" asked Hammond.

"The two hundred and fifty dollars I took from your account at the Bank of Mobile. And a thousand more. For ol' Jube. I want to take him back to Texas with me."

Hammond looked at the money sack, but didn't reach for it.

"You could say no," said Pierce, looking his father straight in the eye. "But I want you to say yes."

Hammond stood up, took the sack of gold, and turned away quickly. "I will write out a bill of sale," he said curtly, and went inside the big house.

A moment later, Pierce stood in the doorway of the blacksmith shop. Old Jubal was at the forge, hammering a wheel rim back into shape, his deeply lined face glistening with sweat. The interior of the shop was breathlessly hot. Wasps thumped against the rafters. Jubal was humming a tune, an old spiritual, but he stopped when he saw Pierce, his mallet frozen in mid-swing, and rheumy eyes lit up with joy.

"Praise de Lord!" he cried. "You come back safe, after all, Marse Pierce! You come back safe!"

"I couldn't find Jobe."

"No matter. No matter, s'long as you be safe."

"I want you to come to Texas with me, Jubal. We'll keep looking for your son until we find him."

"Marse Hammond, he won't never let—"

"I've already settled things with him. I bought you. But you'll go to Texas a free man."

"Free?"

Pierce nodded. "Yes, free. That's what going to Texas is all about."